THE LADY OF LYON HOUSE

Someone had been following Julia Meredith night after night—someone whose footsteps rang on the fog-wet cobblestones when she walked, and stopped when she stopped. And so her guardians sent her to the country to stay with an old friend, Corinne Lyon, Mistress of Lyon House. But even there, protected by fever-scarred Corinne and Edward, her handsome, erratic nephew, Julia still felt that unseen eyes were watching...waiting...

THE LADY OF LYON HOUSE

THE
LADY OF
LYON HOUSE

by
Jennifer Wilde

Magna Large Print Books
Long Preston, North Yorkshire,
England.

British Library Cataloguing in Publication Data.

Wilde, Jennifer
 The lady of Lyon House.

 A catalogue record for this book is
 available from the British Library

 ISBN 0-7505-0138-3

First published in Great Britain by Severn House Publishers
Ltd., 1992

Published in Large Print 1993 by arrangement with Severn
House Publishers Ltd.

Printed and bound in Great Britain by
T.J. Press (Padstow) Ltd., Cornwall, PL28 8RW.

CHAPTER 1

It had been raining during the day and there were flat black puddles in the streets. They gleamed darkly under the lamp light, sometimes reflecting the green and blue and yellow lights from the cafes that lined the street on either side. It was still early, and the cafes were not bursting with noise and activity as they would be later. Only an occasional carriage rumbled over the cobbles, splashing the puddles. The fog was not yet thick. It was a thin, vaporous white mist, swirling around the lamp posts where the gas lamps burned dimly.

I walked slowly, forcing myself to measure my steps and not break into a run. I was not in a hurry to get to the music hall. I had over an hour. It was not because I was late that I wanted to run. I had the same uneasy feeling that I had had for the last week. I felt someone was following me. Even when I stopped and turned around and could see no one, I felt eyes watching me. It caused me to shiver, and it made this walk from the boarding house to the music hall a thing of anxiety. I had always enjoyed sauntering through the streets before, but now I was almost afraid.

I could leave early with Mattie and Bill, but Mattie would think it strange and want an explanation. I could not explain this feeling of uneasiness. It was not something I wanted to talk about. They thought me a dreamer anyway—always lost in thought, always reading a book, always handling the puppets and making up stories for them to enact. If I told Mattie and Bill about this new sensation, they would laugh. Mattie would prescribe some dreadful home remedy to rid me of the vapours, and Bill would talk to me in his jovial manner and before long be off on one of his endless stories about his youth.

I loved both of them. They had looked after me ever since I was a little girl, treating me like their own, and I was as close to them as I would have been if they were truly my parents. My mother and father had been members of Bill's shabby little theatrical troupe, travelling all over England to play short engagements in third-rate theatres. My father died of consumption, and after her handsome husband was gone, my mother seemed to lose any will to live. She died three years later, leaving my sister Maureen and me without a single living relative. Bill and Mattie unofficially adopted us, carrying us along with them from town to town and bringing us up as best they could.

I had been five at the time, my sister Maureen almost fifteen. She disappeared almost five years later, running off with a middle-aged actor who had promised her a life of luxury. The actor soon vanished, leaving her to fend for herself. Maureen had too much pride to come back to Bill and Mattie. I had no idea what had become of her, although frequently there were letters from different parts of England and, recently, small sums of money enclosed in the envelope. I had not seen her for eight years, not since the day she eloped with her actor.

So I had no one but Mattie and Bill. They treated me like a daughter and showed a great deal of concern about my upbringing. In recent years there had been tutors for me, and once I had even attended a private school for a few months, but the financial situation had always been a precarious one and the school had cost too much money. Bill had disbanded the troupe and bought the music hall, running it himself with some small success. A little later he bought the boarding house. Mattie ran it with a firm hand, dividing her time between the house and the music hall. For the first time in years the Jamesons had a bit of security in their lives, although it required titanic labour to keep the two establishments above water.

I did not want to bother them with my problems. They had enough to worry about without me adding to it. I was not sure that there really was a problem. I was not sure that it was not all my imagination, and I walked on down the street, trying to rid myself of the feeling that plagued me.

It had started almost a week ago. I had been walking to the music hall at the regular hour, just after the sun had set and darkness began to cloak the city, and I heard footsteps behind me. I turned around, but there was no one there. I imagined I had seen a man in a checked cloak step quickly into a darkened doorway, but I was not sure of it. As I continued on my way, I heard no more footsteps behind me, but I had the feeling of being followed. I arrived at the music hall and forgot all about it until the next night, when the same thing happened again.

Three nights ago I had met an old woman selling violets. I stopped to purchase a bunch, and as I handed the woman a coin I glanced back at the sidewalk I had just passed over. There was a man standing beneath the lamp post at the corner, half a block away. I could not see him clearly because of the fog, but I noticed the checked cloak. As I stood there with the bunch of violets in my hand, he crossed the street and disappeared into the fog. It had upset me, and I had been on edge ever since.

When I left the music hall late at night, I was always with Bill and Mattie and usually some of the players who boarded with us. Nothing ever happened as I walked back with the noisy group. It was always when I was alone that I had this strange feeling. At first I had wondered if it could have been some stage door Romeo who had seen me on stage and was too bashful to speak to me openly. There had been many of them in recent years, and I had discouraged them all with

11

cool disdain. I was eighteen years old and more than ready to fall in love, but I was not going to have anything to do with actors or the fickle, debonair young men who hung around the theatre. My ideas about romance had been formed from the countless novels I read, and there was nothing romantic to me in the men I had observed courting the other girls who worked at the music hall.

If the man who was following me—if, indeed there was one—was a stage door gallant, surely he would have spoken to me, I reasoned. He would not linger behind me, out of sight, following me down the street and never speaking. I tried to tell myself that it was all my imagination, that there really was no one there, but I still could not shake this feeling.

I walked on down the street, my crinoline underskirts rustling. I was almost two blocks from the music hall now, and the fog was growing thicker, the mists descending rapidly and shrouding everything in white vapour. My heels rapped sharply on the pavement, and the sound echoed behind me. The tapping noise repeated itself, loud, sharp taps coming just after I stepped. I knew it was an echo. I knew there was no one behind me. I paused. I heard the echo of my last step. Then there was a heavier sound, a scrape, immediately following. It was no echo. Someone was there. I was sure of it now.

I looked back the way I had come. The fog swirled gently, curling around the lamp post and stroking the sides of the buildings. The pavement gleamed wetly, casting back reflections of the lights that were almost hidden now by the fog. I saw a dark, shadowy figure just in front of one of the cafes, but I could not be sure it was a man; the fog was too thick. I continued to walk, listening intently to my own light rapping footsteps. Now there was a heavier sound, keeping time with the sound of my own steps.

I felt a cold shiver, and I had to restrain the urge to run. If I arrived at the music hall out of breath and panting, I would be forced to answer questions, and I did not want that. I did not want a group of concerned faces hovering over me. What if there was someone behind me? Anyone had the right to walk down the street. There was probably some reasonable explanation for all this. Still, I wished I could see whoever it was. I wished even harder to see a bobby in his dark, slick rain cape and his buckled hat, swinging his stick as he covered his beat.

I walked quickly now, paying no need to the noise I made. I did not know if I was still being followed or not. I was intent on getting to the music hall. I crossed the wet street and hurried down the block to the alley that led to the stage door of the music hall. I turned into the dark alley, wishing that they had turned on the lamp that hung over the door. I paused, leaning against the damp brick wall, trying to compose myself before I went inside.

I watched the entrance to the alley. The fog swirled in front of it. A carriage rambled down the street. I saw it pass, jostling over the cobblestones. I listened intently. There were footsteps, growing louder and louder. A man sauntered past the alley. He wore a brown and yellow checked cape, the long heavy folds covering his body. There was a tall hat on his head, the brim pulled over his face. He walked past the alley casually. He did not pause. He did not glance into the darkened recess where I was standing. There was nothing at all out of the ordinary about his conduct.

The sound of his footsteps died away, and I could hear nothing but the pounding of my heart.

I stood there in the alley for several moments, composing myself. I decided I would tell Mattie about the man. I would mention it casually and watch her reaction. I would not tell her about my feeling of uneasiness, but perhaps she would be uneasy herself when I told her about the man. She might suggest that I come to the music hall early, or she might send one of the waiters to come and escort me back each night. We were in a fairly respectable part of London and there was seldom any kind of trouble, just the usual drunks and late hour roisterers. Certainly it was not infested with thieves and muggers as were some parts of the city.

I opened the stage door and stepped inside, glad to be out of the fog and shadows. I welcomed all the marvellous odours of backstage as I closed the door behind me. I could smell the grease paint and chalk and shabby velvet and rust. I walked past the stacks of clumsily painted cardboard backdrops, ran my hand along the railing of the iron staircase that led up to the dressing rooms above the stage. The stage was dark, an ugly, dusty expanse that would take on an aspect of glamour when the footlights illuminated it. The shabby, yellow-gold curtains that hung around it, closing off the backstage areas, fell in ponderous folds that hugged the floor. The front curtain of worn red velvet shut off all the sounds of the great hall where waiters served food and beer to the groups of people who crowded the little tables.

Bill would be behind the bar, polishing the flat marble surface, or else he would be dusting the bottles while he chatted with a customer. Mattie would be perched on the stool behind the cash register, or she would be in the office, marking up accounts in the ledger. She had the level head and acute business sense that kept things running on an even keel, while Bill contributed the affable manner and casual charm that kept the customers contented.

Jameson's was a second rate music hall, without the glitter and sparkle of the more expensive places, but it was the best second rate. The food was good, the liquor the best, the beer was unwatered and the entertainment provided was noisy and pleasant, however uninspired it might be. It was a rowdy, lively place, full of noise and activity. For all their merriment, the customers were usually well behaved. If a fight broke out, as frequently happened, Bill and his muscular bouncer soon squelched it. Most of the customers were regulars, men and women who came in two or three times a week to relax and enjoy the congenial atmosphere.

We had one celebrity, and that had been an exciting night for me. It was three years ago, when I was fifteen, and I had already begun to put on a puppet show between intermissions. It had started as a fill-in for some of the acts that couldn't go on for one reason or another, but the audience had enjoyed it so much that the puppet routine became a regular part of the show. There had been a tiny write-up about it in the paper: Julia Meredith and her puppets make debut at Jameson's Music Hall. The article mentioned my age and the nice reception my act had received. It was this article that brought Mr Dickens to the music hall.

He sat at the front table, a large, florid man with thick, dark hair and clear blue eyes that twinkled with merriment. He wore a loud, colourful vest with an impressive gold watch chain draped across it. His hair was a little mussed, and he frequently stroked his 'door-knocker' beard. When I put my puppets through their paces, he laughed loudly, banging the table with his fist. His laughter was rich and melodious, filling the room with its lovely sound. The other customers sat in awe of the great man, laughing when he laughed, silent when he was silent. When the show was over, he asked to see me, and Bill brought him backstage.

I was embarrassed and flustered, not knowing what to say to such a great person. He seemed to be aware of this, and he shook my hand and told me I had given him much pleasure. I stammered that he had been giving me pleasure for years, as I had read every one of his books as they came out. He laughed and said he hoped the next one would please me as much. He promised to send me a copy, and I forgot that promise until one day a package wrapped in brown paper was delivered backstage. I tore away the papers to find *A Tale of Two Cities*. It has always been my favourite of his books.

I stood backstage now, pulling off my gloves. I hung my cloak up on a peg and brushed my skirts. It was a little chilly here, the air crisp and bracing. I stood in front of the long mirror that hung beside the entrance. My hair was slightly damp, and it fell in rich, silvery-blonde curls to my shoulders. I brushed a lock away from my temple and studied my face. I was a little pale, although there was a spot of pink on each cheekbone. My eyes seemed very large and still a little frightened. They were a deep blue, almost violet, surrounded by long, dark lashes that brushed my cheeks. There were soft grey shadows about the lids, delicate shadowing that most people thought was artificial. Below each cheekbone there was a slight hollow, softly moulded, giving me a rather pensive look, even when I smiled. My lips were firm, a pale coral colour that owed nothing to rouge. If I was not beautiful like my sister Maureen had been, at least my face was interesting, with unusual colouring.

As I stood studying myself in the mirror, Laverne Maddux came down the staircase, her heels clattering on the iron steps. She was a large, buxom redhead with enormous brown eyes and a pixie smile that delighted the customers. Laverne sang brassy, slightly risque songs with

19

the audience joining in for all the choruses. She had a salty tongue, a carefree manner and a warm, generous nature. She roomed with the Jamesons, her room right down the hall from my own, and I considered her my best friend, even if she was in her late thirties. Now Laverne was wearing a pink dress glittering with spangles. Her red hair was piled on top of her head and tied with a large pink bow. She was perspiring, despite the chill.

'Blast!' Laverne cried, seeing me. 'To think I spend hours over this face of mine and can't achieve half the effect you do just by opening your eyes. You're a little early, aren't you?'

'There was nothing left to do at the boarding house. I finished sewing the sitting room curtains and folded up all the laundry.'

'You work yourself to a frazzle,' Laverne said. 'Always doing something, never just sitting and resting your feet.'

'It's the least I can do,' I replied. 'Mattie and Bill are so good to me—'

'You've got a point there,' Laverne agreed. A frown crossed her brow. 'You're going to have to go on early tonight, kiddo. Bert's been hitting the bottle again and Sarah has him up in the dressing room, trying to sober him up in time for the last spot. If that man doesn't lay off the stuff, Bill's goin' to throw him out.'

Bert and Sarah Clemmons did a song and dance routine that had been pleasing the audiences for almost twenty years. They had been members of Bill's original troupe, and I knew that he would never fire them, no matter how Bert drank. They had lost a child a few years back, and he had started drinking then, consuming more and more as the years passed. He and Sarah were both quiet, both quietly charming, and in their black costumes sewn with large silver buckles they did slow paced numbers that caused the audience to sigh with nostalgia. They also lived with us at the boarding house, and sometimes, if I happened to be sitting alone in the parlour when Bert came in, he would sit down and talk to me about my parents, who had been his best friends.

'Do you think you'll have my blue thing done by Saturday?' Laverne asked.

'I'm sewing on the sequins and feathers

now,' I replied. 'I should have it done by then.'

'I want to wear it Saturday night,' she said. 'I'm getting tired of this rag—' She swept her hands over the pink dress. 'I'm sure the fellows are, too.'

In addition to doing a routine with my puppets, I was the official wardrobe mistress for the music hall. I did most of the sewing up in my dressing room, making all the bright, spangled costumes for the troupe. Besides Laverne and the Clemmons, there were eight chorus girls working for Bill. They shared a large, barn-like dressing room near the attic that always sounded like an aviary full of exotic birds. Most of the girls were in their middle or late twenties, loud, brassy creatures who treated me like a favoured child. They were always running into my dressing room to have me sew a feather on or take up a hem. All of them brought their dresses to me for repairs, and twice a year I made a new set of costumes for them. I loved the work, and it was one of the ways I could pay Bill and Mattie for their kindness.

'Is there a crowd tonight?' I asked Laverne.

'About the same as usual. Pretty good for a Thursday night. They will come packing in later on—always do. By the way, your boy friend is out there again tonight.'

'My boy friend?' I said, startled.

'Sure. Don't tell me you haven't noticed him.'

'No, I haven't.'

'He's always at the same table, right up in front. He sits there with a glass of beer until you come on, and when your bit's over, he pays for the beer and leaves. Same thing every night for a week now.'

'Are you certain, Laverne?'

'Sure. He's there tonight, same table. A good looking fellow, too. Classy. All the girls have commented on him. They say he comes just to see you.'

Laverne smiled, her hands on her hips. 'You sure he hasn't come round to see you? You don't have a secret romance, do you, kid?'

'Nothing of the sort,' I protested. 'I want to have a look at this remarkable creature.' I tried to speak lightly, but my voice trembled just a little.

I followed Laverne onto the darkened

stage, moving around all the ropes and pulleys and props. We went over to the curtain and opened the little peep hole through which the performers could survey the house. Laverne looked for a moment and then motioned for me to look. She told me where the man was sitting and described him to me.

I saw the large, crowded hall. Waiters with trays of beer balanced on the palms of their hands circulated among the tables. Men in suits and shirt sleeves and women in colourful dresses and feather boas sat at the tables, eating, drinking, laughing, waiting for the show to begin. I saw Bill behind the bar, polishing the silver handle of one of the great wooden kegs, and Mattie was perched by the cash register, looking about her with slight disapproval.

'There he is, second table to your right,' Laverne said.

The man was sitting there casually, his fingers wrapped around a stein of beer which he did not drink. He was alone, and he seemed to be separate and apart from the other customers, not belonging for some reason. Draped over the back of the chair next to him was a brown and yellow checked cloak.

CHAPTER 2

He was relatively young, not more than thirty, and he had an air of distinction about him that set him apart from the other people in the hall. He wore elegant clothes, a dark brown suit, a vest of yellow satin embroidered with brown fleurs-de-lis which proclaimed his good taste and good tailor. His hair was rich chestnut brown, one smooth wave fallen over his forehead, and his eyes were dark brown. His brows were black, finely arched over the slightly drooping lids. A thin pink scar made a line from one cheekbone to his chin, and this defect gave him a strange attractiveness. His face was tanned, and his body was the strong, muscular body of one who spends much time outdoors in active pursuits.

'Nice, isn't he?' Laverne whispered.

'I wonder who he is?'

'I have no idea. I know he doesn't belong here, though. He's the white tie and tails sort, not the shirt sleeve and derby kind who hang around here. Probably slumming.

He's always alone, though. That sort usually comes with a crowd to laugh at and mock the other half.'

'He's been coming in for a week?' I asked.

'Regular as clockwork,' she said.

The man seemed entirely at his ease at the table, sitting back in his chair, one ankle propped casually over his knee, his hand resting on the back of the chair beside him. I had an impression of strength and agility, as though the man had great power which he kept closely in check, holding it back. There was a half-humorous smile on his firm pink lips. They were a little too large, the mouth mobile and expressive. He was a man who would laugh easily and just as easily draw back in anger.

I turned away, trying to keep my face expressionless. I was almost certain he was the man who had been following me. I was frightened of him, even more so now that he had become a reality, not just a shadowy form moving through the fog. A tremor of fear went through me and my throat felt a little dry. What did he want? Why did he follow me? Why did he come here every night just to see me?'

'Some beau,' Laverne remarked as we

walked away from the stage.

'I'm sure you must be mistaken,' I said. 'I've never seen the man before in my life. Why in the world should he be interested in me?'

'Take another look in that mirror, kid,' she replied.

'I don't like it a bit,' I said. 'I'm going to tell Bill.'

'And what would Bill do?'

'Have him thrown out of the place,' I answered crisply.

'Wait till you have reason for it, kid. He isn't doing any harm.'

'Isn't he?'

'Why are you so upset?' she asked, her voice concerned. 'You're pale. Your hand is trembling. Say—tell me the truth now. Has this fellow been bothering you?'

'I—no. I told you I had never seen him before.'

'Well, if he does, you just let me know. You're just a kid, not one of those chorus dolls who encourage that sort of thing. You tell Laverne if that guy tries anything.'

'I will,' I replied. 'I'd better go on up to the dressing room and get everything ready, Laverne.'

'Yeah, the band's tuning up. It's almost

time for me to go out and do my turn. See you later, kid.'

I climbed up the winding iron staircase to the area above where my dressing room was located. Three of the chorus girls came hurrying out of their room as I passed, large, blonde women with painted faces and shrill voices. They wore green dresses spangled with blue sequins, and green and blue feathers in their hair. They waved at me, talking loudly as they clambered down the staircase I had just come up.

My dressing room was very small, one tiny window looking down on the street below. It was cluttered with costumes in the process of being repaired, bright dresses hanging on the wall, a pile of feathers and beads on one chair. A stack of books was on the floor beside a cot, and a tiny stove perched in one corner, affording little heat. All the walls were damp, the plaster chipped, concentric brown moisture stains on the ceiling. This was my retreat, the one place where I felt secure and at ease. Tonight it gave me little comfort. I was on edge, and my head was throbbing.

I sat down on the cot and took the puppets out of their long, flat red box. Many years ago Bill had given me a puppet to play with, and I had been so intrigued that I soon learned to make it walk and dance and move like a real person. That puppet was long since gone, but the four I had now I had made myself, carefully constructing them of soft wood and painting them. I made all their clothes, and over the years they had become almost like people to me: Gretchen with her wide blue eyes, Hans with his moppish shock of blond hair, Dil the Dragon with green scales and humorous pink tongue, Miranda with her bright red mouth and flashing brown eyes.

Bill had built a miniature theatre, complete with revolving stage and velvet curtain and moveable backdrops, and my puppets enacted their playlets with scenery and props, just as in a real theatre. I stood behind the stage, manipulating the wires, and it was only when the act was over and the house lights came on that the audience could see me. I was hidden from view most of the time, just exposed for a few seconds as I took my bow.

I thought it odd that the man should come night after night just for those few seconds. I wanted to believe that there was some other explanation for his presence, but I couldn't. He had some secret interest in me, an interest strong enough to make him follow me to the music hall every night and sit through the show until I made my brief appearance. It terrified me. I felt vulnerable and defenceless against this strange behaviour.

Down the hall I could hear Sarah Clemmons talking to Bert, trying to sober him up. In a few minutes Bert himself came staggering down the hall and into my dressing room. He was wearing a blue suit with a vivid blue and green ascot, and his large grey eyes were sad. His fading blond hair was rumpled. He carried a folded newspaper, and he tilted a little as he stood in the doorway.

'Hello, Julia baby,' he said warmly. 'You don't mind goin' on a little early? Sorry about this, real sorry. Sarah's throwin' fits. I hate to ask you to do this.'

I smiled. 'I won't mind a bit, Bert. Dil looks rather upset, I must say, but Hans will keep him in line.'

'Adorable little girl,' he said. 'Little girl with her dolls. Do hate to ask you to do this. Really do.'

'Will you be all right?' I inquired.

'Sure—sure. Sarah's makin' some more

coffee right now. Gave her the slip so's I could come 'pologize to you. Hey—by the way, have you heard from your sister recently?'

'No. There was a letter three months ago from Bristol.'

'She send any money?'

'Why—a few pounds,' I replied, surprised by the question.

'Didn't mean to be pryin',' Bert said, supporting himself against the door frame. 'Guy was askin' me all about her this evening. Asked if you ever saw her, asked if you knew where she was. Seemed to be real interested. Asked if she ever sent you money and if so, how much. Told him none of his damn business. Didn't like th' guy at all.'

'What—what did he look like?' I asked, trying to sound normal.

'Big bruiser of a guy—enormous shoulders. Looked like his nose was broken. Ugly lout, really ugly, wearin' a heavy black coat and grey silk muffler. Talked in a hoarse, gruff voice. Didn't like the looks of him at all.'

'Where were you when he asked these questions?'

'Finnigan's Bar, down the street. The

guy bought me a couple of drinks, insisted on it. He 'n another guy were standin' at the bar when I came in, like they were waitin' for me.'

'What did his companion look like?'

'Tall, thin, mean lookin'. Had blond hair and grey eyes and thin lips. Looked like a couple of crooks to me, they did. Wonder why they were so interested in little Maureen?'

'I have no idea.'

'Sad thing, that. Maureen, I mean. Shame. Runnin' off like that and no tellin' what happenin'. No tellin' what kind of crowd she got in with—'ticularly if these guys were any example of 'em. Told 'em they needn't be botherin' you with any questions 'cause you didn't know any more about her than I did.'

Bert sighed and shook his head. In a moment he left. I noticed he had dropped his newspaper, and I picked it up and threw it on the cot. For a moment I had thought that the man asking questions might have been the same one who followed me, but Bert's description did not fit at all. I wondered who the men were and why they were so curious about my sister. They had sounded perfectly dreadful, and

I hated to think she would be involved in any way with that sort.

I had few illusions about Maureen. I remembered her as a beautiful, rather surly young woman who had been discontented with everything around her. She was vivacious, with dark brown eyes, glossy black hair and a pouting red mouth, completely unlike me in every way. She took after my father, whereas I was like my mother in colouring. We had been very close, Maureen and I, and when she ran away with the actor it had broken my heart. Over the years there had been letters, of course, but none of them told me anything about her. She mentioned small jobs in the theatre and she kept saying she would send for me when she had enough money to keep us in style. I knew that she never would. Maureen was only a memory to me now, and the letters were the letters of a stranger.

I glanced at the tiny porcelain clock on my work table. I had half an hour before I had to go on. I sat down on the cot and opened up the paper, hoping to distract myself until it was time to go down. It was a yellow tabloid, one of the many scandal sheets that delighted people with dull, uneventful lives. There was a story about a Duke who found his wife with the stable groom, and a descriptive account of an axe murder. The front page was filled with news of the Mann case, as Scotland Yard called it. Two weeks ago Clinton Mann, a wealthy dealer, had given a private showing of a collection of uncut precious jewels in the Mann Galleries. That night thieves had broken into the place and stolen the stones, brutally beating Mann, who had his apartment over the galleries. Mann had died of injuries, and Scotland Yard had no clues about the case. It was the kind of story the public loved: precious jewels, a wealthy, influential art dealer, robbery and murder. I tossed the paper on the floor, feeling more depressed than ever.

I sat back on the cot, Hans and Miranda beside me, Dill at my feet, Gretchen in my lap. I looked at the brightly painted creatures. Their world was so simple, so innocent, so full of fun and humorous misadventures. Every night they danced and jiggled before a painted backdrop and caused the audience to howl with laughter. After it was over, they went back into their box, knowing only laughter, only joy. I wished the real world was as easy to live in as that of my painted puppets.

For fifteen minutes I stood in the dark behind the brightly lit box, my fingers nimbly manipulating the strings. I heard the roars of laughter and, finally, the round of applause. The lights came on and I took my bow, smiling demurely. The puppets lay in a lifeless heap on the floor of their theatre as the curtain came down. I stepped quickly across the stage and peered through the peep hole. The man was paying the waiter. He left a tip on the table and walked out, moving slowly, that slight smile still on his lips.

A stage hand moved away the puppet theatre and the chorus girls began to line up. I was in the darkened recesses backstage when the curtain rolled up ponderously and footlights bathed the girls, glittering on sequins and spangles, making their rather coarse, painted features soft and attractive. The music swelled and the girls sang, slightly out of harmony, slightly shrill, delighting the men in the audience. I went down the short flight of stairs that led from backstage to the hall and moved through the crowded room to the bar where Bill was standing.

'It was great tonight, Julia,' he said, smiling at me. 'They all loved it, as usual.'

Bill was a tall man, slightly stooped. He had a hooked nose and a large, ugly mouth, but there were laugh lines about his clear blue eyes and the mouth was always turned up in a smile. His hair had once been a glossy brown, but now it was thin and streaked with silver. His ears stuck out like handles on either side of his head. Bill was so homely that he commanded affection wherever he went. He was easy going, relaxed, completely at ease with himself and the world around him.

'Anything I can do for you, baby?' he asked.

'Bill—that man who just left, the one in the checked coat, do you know who he is?'

'Handsome fellow with a scar?'

'Yes, that's him.'

'No, can't say as I know who he is. He's been coming in every night for a week now, doesn't drink anything but beer, but he leaves a large tip. Polite fellow, well bred, not the usual sort who comes in here.'

'He leaves the same time every night,' I remarked.

'Come to think of it, he does, right after your show. I think you have a fan, baby.

Maybe he's one of these newspaper fellows who's going to write an article about you. Hope so. We could use the publicity.'

'Is Mattie in the office?' I asked.

'Yes, and in a foul temper, too. She's been going over the books and you know what that always means. See if you can put her in a good mood, will you, baby?'

'I'll try, Bill,' I replied.

Bill grinned and winked at me. He drew a stein of beer for one of the customers, then picked up the chamois cloth and began to polish the grey marble bar. Bill's world was a pleasant one, a foul tempered wife his greatest handicap, and that wasn't a real one, as everyone knew that Mattie's foul temper was mostly legendary.

I went through the green velvet portieres, crossed the foyer and opened the door to the office. Mattie was sitting behind an immense mahogany desk, a ledger opened in front of her. Her sharp grey eyes were squinting with concentration, and she was nibbling on the end of a pencil. Mattie had beautiful iron-grey hair, worn in a tight braid on top of her head. Her features were severe, almost hard, but she had lovely bone structure. She presented a hard, gruff, formidable exterior to the world, speaking sharply, moving decisively, but those who really knew her knew that this was just a pose.

Mattie was kind hearted to a fault, but she concealed her kindness behind a brusque bark and a stiff front. No one was taken in. She would do anything for anyone, although she liked to think of herself as having a granite heart. This was her defence against Bill's natural, affable nature.

She looked up now, unhappy at being disturbed. She wore a light green dress with a cameo brooch. There were stiff white cuffs on her sleeves, and her fingers were stained with ink.

'Good evening, Julia,' she said. 'How did the act go?'

'Oh, the same as usual.'

'That's fine. I could hear them laughing all the way in here.'

'They always laugh,' I said, rather disheartedly.

'Is something wrong?' she asked. 'Where is that sparkle? You seem to be disturbed about something.'

'I am, Mattie.'

Mattie closed the ledger and looked at me. She was frowning. I had the strange sensation that she knew what I was going to tell her before I even began. Her frown grew deeper as I talked, growing into a harsh line between her brows. Her grey eyes grew dark, and the corner of her mouth twitched a little. I told her all about the man following me, about him coming in every night and leaving just after I finished. I even told her about the man Bert had seen at the bar and how I had thought at first that it was the same man asking him questions. Mattie was silent for a while after I finished. Her hands were folded in front of her, and she stared down at them intently.

'What do you think?' I asked.

'Why—I don't know, Julia. Men have shown interest in you before, you know. You're not a little girl any more. It's only natural that they should notice you.'

'This is different,' I protested.

'Is it?' She looked up, her grey eyes challenging me. It was a good bluff, but it didn't fool me. She was brisk, getting up from the desk and arranging some papers in a neat stack. She seemed to have dismissed my problem from her mind, but I knew that she hadn't. I could tell how upset she was. Her hands trembled a little as she fooled with the papers. There was more to this than even I knew, far more. Mattie knew something, and she did not want me to see it or grow alarmed. What I had told her was merely part of something much larger, and she was afraid. I had never seen her afraid before.

She put the papers in a drawer and looked up at me. There was a smile on her lips, but it rang as false as her abrupt dismissal had. I could tell that she was acting, and Mattie was not a good actress. She began to talk about some sewing I was doing for her, and she talked too rapidly, too cheerfully. Mattie knew something, something important, and she was afraid to tell me about it. I wondered what it could be. I wondered why she was trying so hard to conceal her alarm.

CHAPTER 3

The boarding house was a large, rambling building, grey frame, with dark green shutters and a shabby green roof. Three crumbling red brick chimneys leaned precariously at odd angles. It towered out of the fog like a rather tired monster whose claws had been clipped. A stone wall shut the narrow yard away from the street, concealing the scabby patches of grass and an unhealthy flower bed. Three tall oak trees grew around it, and the back of the house opened onto a dark alley that ran the length of the street. Once a grand residence, now it was a desolate place out of step with the thriving businesses that surrounded it.

The inhabitants kept odd hours, sleeping late in the mornings and staying up until all hours of the night. We all generally got back from the music hall between midnight and one, and there was a late supper in the dining room: cold sausages, beer, sliced roast, pickled beets. We sat up until after three. Two or three of the chorus girls usually had late dates after the show was over and they would come in very late, all full of chatter about the grand times they had had. Bill and Bert Clemmons would play cards in the front parlour with old Greenley, the stage manager, and Sarah would sit before a lamp, writing letters to distant relatives and old friends. Sometimes Laverne played the piano, banging it noisily into the night, singing raffish songs. Mattie would circulate briskly from room to room, attending to various duties, and I would help her, or else I would sit in the parlour and sew or read a novel.

It was an eccentric establishment, buzzing with noise and activity during the night while all around was dark and silent, closed up tight and silent itself from morning till noon while all the surrounding businesses were opening their doors and clamouring with noise. We were all accustomed to it, and we all loved the old place, haggard and threadbare though it might be. To me it was home. I loved the noise. I loved the unusual hours. I loved my little room under the eaves on the top floor, and I loved the odours of boiled cabbage and ancient grease that permeated the wallpaper.

I could not sleep that first night when we got home from the music hall. I kept thinking about Mattie's bewildering attitude, and it worried me. It was after three, and the house had been shut up for a long time. The last chorus girl had come in over an hour ago, and everyone had gone to bed early. The men did not play cards. Laverne didn't play the piano. Mattie went into her room immediately after supper and had not come out. Everyone seemed to be dispirited and listless, the usual vitality dampened. Now I was the only one awake, sitting up in bed and staring at the frosty starlight that came through the window and illuminated the opposite wall with dancing silvery spangles.

I thought about the man who had been following me in the fog. There seemed to be no rhyme or reason for it. If he had intended to do me harm he would surely have done it already, and if that had been the case, he would not have been so brazen as to come to the music hall every night and leave so obviously after I had finished my act. The girls had commented on him; Laverne had noticed him, called him my boy friend. If he had sinister motives, he would have been stealthy in all of his movements. Yet I was certain that the man sitting openly in the music hall and the man moving stealthily through the fog were one and the same man. What did he want?

He was watching me. Why? It was almost as though he were a detective from Scotland Yard, keeping me under surveillance. Why should he be interested in what I did? I thought about this, and then my mind wandered to the men Bert had seen at Finnigan's Bar and the questions they had asked him. Could there possibly be some connection? They had sounded like such awful people. I was glad Bert had told them to go on about their business.

I do not know how long I sat there, nestled on the pillows, watching the starlight dancing on the shabby old wallpaper, I was wide awake and I knew that sleep would not come for a long time. I listened to all the noises of the old house. They were familiar to me, unfrightening. The limbs of the oak tree scratched against the windowpane, and when I had been smaller I had thought it sounded like someone trying to break into the house. Now it was merely a steady, monotonous noise that I usually didn't even notice. The old house settled, and the floorboards groaned. There was a creaking noise, like someone creeping up the staircase, and that, I knew, was the wind blowing the back gate on its rusty hinges.

The wind whistled softly, moaning. It caused the loose shutters to flap and bang lightly against the house. There was a whole symphony of sound, once frightening, now reassuring. This was my home. Here I was safe from the fog and the cold night air and the shadows that lurked in darkened doorways. Here there was warmth and all the old ordinary things that I saw everyday and touched and loved.

The shutters flapped, the tree limbs scratched, the wind moaned and the noise was comforting. I do not know at what point I noticed something out of tune. The rhythm was broken. There was a noise that did not belong. There was a clatter in the alley behind the house, but that was not unusual. Cats frequently prowled among the cans and boxes, and they sometimes knocked off a lid or pushed over a box. Then I heard a slow, creaking sound, as though someone was opening the back gate cautiously. I paid no particular attention to the sound.

There was a long silence, almost as though the house was holding its breath, then the noises began again. They were soft, muted, not at all loud, steady. There was something wrong. I sat up, all my senses alerted. Something did not fit. I could not identify the noise that was out of place, but I knew instinctively that something did not belong. I strained my ears. There was a loud creak, a pause, a shuffle, another creak. It sounded like someone coming up the backstairs. It was not the wind. It was not the shutters.

The noise was not repeated. It ceased altogether. I sat on the edge of the bed, alarmed. Several minutes passed. I could hear nothing unusual, and I was beginning to think I had imagined it all, yet I was unnerved, and I sensed something wrong. I knew this house thoroughly. I was attuned to it. I knew its moods, its atmosphere, all its smells and sounds. It was a living thing to me, like an old friend, and now there was something that did not fit into the pattern. It was in the air. It was almost tangible.

I heard a floorboard creak in the hall outside. There was a soft sliding sound, as though someone were moving along the wall. I felt my wrists grow limp, and my throat was dry. I tried to remain calm, but I couldn't. I was paralyzed with fear. I wanted to scream, but no sound would come. I listened, straining every nerve. There was silence; the silence was more frightening than the noise had been. I felt something hovering outside, something dark and sinister.

The starlight danced on the wall opposite my bed, making spots of moving silver on the old blue wallpaper, but the rest of the room was in shadow. The furniture made dark forms. The window was open a little and the curtains rustled, blowing inwards. I could see the door to my room and the tarnished old brass doorknob. It was not locked.

The doorknob turned slowly. I watched with horrified fascination as it revolved, so slowly, so cautiously. It stopped. The door began to open. It opened several inches, and I could see the dark of the hall. My heart was pounding so loudly that I was sure someone must hear it. I watched as the door opened almost halfway, making a soft, swishing noise that was barely audible. I could see a tall, shadowy form standing just inside the doorway, a darker shape against the darkness. I shook my head, trying to tell myself that this wasn't happening. It was like a nightmare, not real at all. The only thing real was my pounding heart and my hands gripping the edge of the bed.

'Julia—little Julia—'

It was no more than a whisper, hoarse, the words shaped softly and thrown into the darkness.

I had the presence of mind to light the lamp. My hands flew to the matches on my bedside table, the fingers trembling as I struck one of them. The sudden flare of yellow-orange blinded me, and I groped for the oil lamp, almost dropping it. I held the flame to the wick, and in a moment a bright glow began to spread into the room, driving away shadows and restoring everything to proper dimensions. The wallpaper was faded blue, unadorned with starlight. The furniture was oak, painted white. The curtains were white, with green braid borders. The door was closed, a flat wooden surface, painted green, the tarnished brass doorknob still and innocent.

The fear was gone. It had fled with the coming of light. So had the feeling of disharmony. The room was as it had always been, and it was incredible to believe that but moments ago something dark and sinister had been standing in the doorway, threatening the sanctity of it. I was alarmed at myself, trembling now with irritation, not fear. The nightmare had been so vivid, so real. I had been wide awake, or so I thought. I supposed the experience was the culmination of a week of nervous tension.

I got up, pulling on a ruffled blue robe over my white nightgown. I stepped over to the mirror and examined my face. The violet blue eyes looked enormous, surrounded by shadows, and the cheeks were pale. I had evidently been asleep, drifting off without knowing it, the nightmare curiously merging with the reality. I rubbed my cheek, staring at the face that looked back at me in the cloudy glass. I wore my hair in two long blonde braids, and they rested one on each shoulder, tied with blue bows.

I could feel the old house all around me, large and silent. I had that curious feeling that always comes over one when everyone else is asleep. I felt like the only survivor in a house of death, and it was a comfortable feeling that I could break at any moment if I chose to make enough noise and awaken everyone. I picked up the lamp and left the room determined to satisfy myself that I had had a nightmare. I knew that I could never sleep until I had proven that.

I walked down the long hall, my slippers

making soft noises on the worn carpet. The light of the lamp cast flickering shadows on the wall. The house was rather cold, tomblike, the air chill. I turned a corner and stood at the top of the back staircase. It was steep and narrow, making a sharp turn halfway down. I hesitated for a moment, looking into the pit of darkness. I was afraid, but it was only the ordinary fear everyone feels when confronted with darkness, a fear easily put aside. I held the lamp high and started down.

The heels of my slippers clattered on the bare wooden steps. I had to hold onto the bannister, and my hand slid over the cool wooden surface. There was a window high up over the staircase. It was opened and the wind blew in, fluttering the curtains over my head. I could smell the odours of the kitchen which was immediately beneath the stairs. Mattie had been baking bread that afternoon, and the smells lingered, mixed with the smells of wax and copper and coal.

I stood at the bottom of the stairs. The lamp cast moving waves of light over the kitchen, dancing over the old oak table, burnishing the copper pans that hung along the wall, stoking the surface of the gigantic black iron stove that hovered in one corner with a yawning mouth. An old straw broom leaned in one corner, and the house cat slept curled on a pallet in front of the pantry door. I moved silently across the newly waxed tile floor over to the back door. It was securely locked, and no one had tampered with it. The bolt was pushed firmly into its socket. I tested the doorknob. It did not yield at all. The window over the drain board was locked, too.

I peered through the window at the alley behind the house. I could see the crumbling brick backs of the buildings that opened out from the other side of the alley. There was a darkened doorway, and a pile of rubbish beside it. Long black shadows slid over the walls like huge, stroking fingers. Scraps of white paper and bits of rubbish blown by the wind drifted along the alley like weird nocturnal butterflies. A black cat prowled silently among the heap of rubbish.

I was satisfied. The back door and window were locked, and no one lurked in the alley behind the house. I felt rather foolish, standing there in the deserted kitchen with a lamp in my hand while everyone else was sound asleep. I decided to go through the hall and check the front door, just to be certain. I might as well be completely reassured before I went back up to my room.

I pushed open the kitchen door, trying to keep the hinges silent. They creaked loudly, and the noise was a little unnerving in the dark. The door swung shut behind me. I moved slowly down the long narrow hall. I passed the old grandfather clock that stood across from the front parlour and saw that it was after four o'clock in the morning. I passed into the front foyer and touched the doorknob of the front door. Thin blue curtains were stretched in tight pleats over the glass, and fragile rays of moonlight streamed through. The doorknob turned in my hand and the door opened. Moonlight spilled over my feet. The screen was unlatched, the wind banging it a little against the door frame. I stood there for a moment, looking out over the small yard enclosed by the stone wall. The heavy iron gate that opened onto the sidewalk was closed. I wondered if it was latched.

I stepped across the narrow front porch and went down the flat steps into the yard. The night air was cold and the limbs of the oak trees groaned. A cat curled on the stone wall, his body flat against the stones. I went to the gate and touched the rusty latch. It hung loosely, unfastened. I fastened it, unreasonably angry. The last chorus girl to come in had not only left the gate open, she had also left the front door unlocked. It was probably Addie, I thought, an amiable, scatterbrained creature who never remembered anything.

I went back into the house, fastening the screen door and shoving home the bolt of the main door. I went through the front parlour, and as I turned towards the front staircase, I paused, startled. I could hear voices, low, muffled voices coming from one of the rooms on the other side of the house. I crossed through the parlour and saw a small sliver of light beneath the door of the little sitting room which Mattie used as her study. I wondered who could be up at this hour.

I blew out the lamp, not wanting to be seen. That would entail explanations which I wasn't ready to give. I did not want to discuss my nightmare and the exploration that followed it. I paused in front of the sitting room door, not meaning to eavesdrop. I merely wanted to listen to the voices and determine who was in the room. I stood there, leaning against the door, hidden by the darkness. I could hear Mattie's voice. It was loud and distinct. Bill's was muffled, as though he was sleepy. There was no other voice, but I had the strange impression that there were three people in the room.

'Of course it is a dreadful mess,' Mattie was saying, 'but exactly what do you propose to do about it?'

'I don't know,' Bill replied, his voice very low.

'Nothing. Nothing at all. You never have any ideas of your own. I have to do all the thinking.'

'All right, Mattie. Calm down—'

'Calm down! The girl is in danger.'

'What would you have me do? We can't go to Scotland Yard.'

'Think of a better idea if you don't like this one. You don't want to send her away. Neither do I. I want her near me, where I can keep an eye on her, but that's not reasonable. You know it's not. It isn't safe. We can't afford to think about what we want. We must think about Julia and her safety—' Her voice broke.

'I'm as concerned as you are,' Bill replied, trying to soothe her. 'I realize how serious this is.'

'That poor child—' Mattie said, her voice almost a whisper. 'She has no idea. We mustn't let her know.'

My shoulders were trembling, and I tried to get hold of myself. I tried to push aside the waves of terror that threatened to envelop me. I wanted to fling open the door and rush into the room. I wanted to be in Mattie's arms. I wanted her to reassure me that this was just a continuation of the nightmare that had begun in my room. I leaned against the doorframe, my forehead pressed against the cold wood, my eyes closed tightly.

'Lyon House is the only answer,' Mattie said flatly.

'I suppose it is.'

'She will be safe there for the time being.'

'That's all that matters,' Bill replied.

There was a short silence. I heard someone shuffling in a chair and a rustle of some stiff material. Bill coughed. I don't know why I had the impression that there was a third person in the room, but it was a very strong one. Mattie and Bill were not alone in the sitting room. I was sure of that. I wished I had the courage to open the door and see for myself, but all the courage had been drained out of me. I doubted if I had enough strength left to go back up to my room.

'I'll tell her tomorrow,' Mattie continued. 'We must be very jolly about it. We mustn't let her suspect.'

'It's going to be hard,' Bill said, 'damned hard.'

'I know,' Mattie replied. 'She's like our own. I hate to send her away, but it's the only solution. We have to do it.'

A chair scraped against the floor as someone got up. I moved quickly away from the door and fled into the darkness. I hurried down the hall and up the back staircase. The house seemed to spin around me, black walls pressing in on every side. I do not know how I managed to get up to my room. I threw myself on the bed, burying my face in the pillows. I tried to cry, but I couldn't. I lay on the bed, staring up at the ceiling as the darkness slowly dissolved. I could hear the clock ticking on top of the bureau. I don't know how much time passed, ticking slowly on that clock. The room turned grey, misty. Everything took proper shape, emerging out of the darkness, and a bird began to sing on the branch of the oak tree outside. The first apricot coloured fingers of dawn were reaching into the room before sleep finally came.

CHAPTER 4

The bright blue curtains of the dining room were pulled back, and sunlight poured into the room in dazzling rays, making silvery bursts of light on the polished surface of the long table. Outside, the leaves of the oak tree were dappled with yellow, and the ground was a network of alternate sunshine and shadow. A bird sang lustily, hopping from branch to branch. All the active, cheerful noises of a business day in London surrounded the boarding house: the clattering of wheels on the cobbles, the shouts of the news vendor, the constant tinkling of the bell hanging over the door of the bakery across the street.

Inside, there was an aura of lethargy.

It was after noon, but the inhabitants of the boarding house had just gotten out of bed. We sat in the dining room, sleepily eyeing the food Mattie brought in from the kitchen. Bill and Bert were reading newspapers, rattling the sheets as they turned them. Old Greenley, the stage manager, dozed in his chair. Sarah sat in a corner with her knitting, having eaten earlier in the kitchen with Mattie. Addie and Stella and Janet, the chorus girls, sat with their hair up in curlers, their faces shiny with face cream, all their natural vitality subdued by the process of waking up. Laverne sat with her elbows on the table, a circulating library novel propped up in front of her. Her red curls spilled over her face as she read. I sat at the window, watching the bird as it hopped among the branches.

I had asked Addie earlier if she had left the gate and door open. She protested her innocence, blinking her enormous blue eyes and swearing that she had shut the gate firmly and latched it behind her. She seemed quite positive about it, and I did not press the issue. In the sun spangled brilliance of day, last night's episode seemed a dream, an ugly thing that had no reality. The only reality was the gleaming surface of the table, the silver bowl of blue and purple larkspurs, the sleepy faces of the people I knew so well and loved. Everything was normal. Everything was ordinary. It seemed impossible that a dark shadow of fear had passed over this house.

Although I had had so little sleep, I was wide awake now. My head felt quite clear and I was alert and receptive to all the things around me. I seemed to be viewing them for the first time: the chipped blue cups and saucers, the faded pearl-grey wallpaper with its blue border, the shabby grey carpet, worn almost threadbare in places. This was real to me. This I knew. Last night, and all that had preceded it, was a bad dream. I could not believe in the figure in the fog, the voice in the darkened doorway of my room, the tense, mysterious conversation I had overheard as I stood in the darkness.

'Cockney lad won a fortune at the races,' Bert remarked, turning a page of his newspaper noisily. 'Poor lad. He'll probably marry a duchess and live a life of misery.'

'I could stand a little luck,' Stella replied.

'Lost ten pounds last week. Fellow told me about a sure thing. The only sure thing was half a month's pay gone down the drain.'

'I never play the horses,' Addie told her.

'I shouldn't think so, Dearie,' Stella said. 'It takes brains. A person has to be able to add two and two.'

'Really?' Addie said, fluttering her long lashes. 'I had no idea. How do you manage?'

'No new developments in the Mann case,' Bert said. 'Scotland Yard thinks it was done by a gang. Seems to be a woman involved. Mann was involved with some mysterious, dark haired creature shortly before the robbery and murder. Police are looking for her, as well as her accomplices.'

'There's always a woman involved,' Janet remarked.

'That poor man,' Sarah said, looking up from her knitting. 'Such a brutal way to die, and all for a handful of stones.'

'Those stones are worth almost a million pounds,' Bert informed her. 'Uncut, too, and easy to dispose of. They'll probably never be found.'

'Such dreadful things happening,' Sarah

muttered. 'It makes you wonder—'

'I wonder if I dare have another roll,' Addie remarked, looking at the pot of orange marmalade. 'Three already. I must think about my figure.'

'I can't imagine why,' Stella said acidly. 'No one else does.'

'You girls don't squabble,' Mattie said, coming into the room with a plate of steaming sausages and fluffy yellow scrambled eggs. 'If you must release hostilities, you might practice the line dance routine. It seems both of you were out of step last night.'

Conversation subsided, and we ate the food in silence. Later, when everyone had gone about their business, I cleared the table and went into the kitchen to help Mattie with the dishes. She seemed to be nervous. It was quite clear that she didn't want me around, but I insisted on staying. I took the dish rag out of her hand and began to dry plates and saucers, stacking them neatly on the drain board. Mattie dug her arms into a sinkful of suds, wiping the dishes with a soapy rag.

I could tell that she was on edge. Several times she seemed on the verge of saying something to me, but her lips always clamped shut at the last moment. She wore a pink cotton house dress and a stiff white apron. Her iron-grey hair was coiled on top of her head, and a pencil was stuck into one of the coils. Her fingers were stained with ink, as always, and her face was a little drawn from lack of sleep. I wondered when she would tell me whatever it was that had seemed to be so important last night.

The dishes were done and the kitchen gleaming before she summoned enough courage to speak. The kitchen was full of light, the yellow tile floor glistening, the white walls gilded with sunshine. Several pots of ivy set around, the green leaves shiny and bright. Mattie spread a yellow oil cloth over the table and took out a bowl of peas she wanted to snap. She sat down at the table and began to work with the peas. I stood by the stove, waiting. The house cat yawned and pranced across the floor, arching his back. Mattie pressed her lips tightly together. I could see her forcing herself to speak.

'Julia,' she asked, 'are you happy?'

'Of course I am,' I replied.

'I wondered. This isn't much of a life for you. It isn't healthy. We keep such strange hours. The atmosphere of the music hall isn't the proper kind for a young girl growing up. The noise, the people—no, I don't think it's the right place for you.'

'You've never worried about it before, Mattie,' I said. 'I love the music hall. I love the people. They're wonderful all of them. I am gloriously happy.'

'Are you—really?'

'You know I am.'

'Julia—I've been thinking—' She hesitated.

'Yes?'

'A change of pace would do you good. You've been looking pale and drawn recently. You need some fresh air, something to put some colour back into your cheeks. How would you like to spend a month or two in Devonshire?'

'Devonshire?'

'Yes. It's lovely this time of year. Not at all like London. No fog, no uproar, no polluted air, just lovely countryside. There are flowers and trees and little streams, and the sea is nearby. You can smell the salty tang in the air—'

'How would you know, Mattie?'

'I was born there. I lived there until I married.'

'You want to send me away,' I said

quietly. There was sadness in my voice.

'No, darling. It isn't that—'

Mattie looked up at me. Her grey eyes were troubled, and there was a crease in her brow. I knew this was hard for her. She was not good at dissembling. It was not easy for her to appear off hand and casual when all the time she was sick with worry. She could tell from the look in my eyes that she had not succeeded in her little pretence, and she turned back to the bowl of peas, snapping them briskly and throwing the broken ends into a paper sack at her feet. I loved her so much. I wanted to make this easier for her.

'You want me to go?' I asked.

'Yes, Julia. For a little while.'

'Will you tell me why?'

'I can't, darling.'

'It—it has something to do with that man who was following me, doesn't it?'

'I—yes, yes it does. Bill and I are both worried about that. We think you should get away for a while.'

I could see that she was evading something. There was something more she was not telling me. I did not doubt that the man who had been following me to the music hall was partly responsible for this decision to send me away, but I knew there was another reason, too. This Mattie did not intend to tell me about.

'You can be honest with me, Mattie,' I said. 'I'm not afraid. I want to know why you want to send me to Devonshire.'

Mattie pushed, the bowl of peas away from her. She looked down at her ink-stained fingers for a moment, her head bowed. She seemed to be making some decision in her mind. She looked up at me, and her face was calm. The clear grey eyes stared into mine with a level gaze.

'Julia,' she said quietly, 'do you trust me?'

'You know I do,' I replied.

'And do you believe that I would only do what was best for you?'

'Of course, Mattie.'

'Very well. You must trust me now. You must believe that this is the best thing for you at the moment. I wouldn't send you away if there was not a good reason. Please don't ask me any more questions. I should only have to evade them, and I haven't much art at evasion.'

'All right, Mattie,' I replied humbly.

'I have a very good friend in Devonshire, Corinne Lyon. She's a bit eccentric, but she's a lively old thing. You'll like her. She has a lovely country place, Lyon House, just outside a charming little village. It's surrounded by woods and fields and there is a stream that runs through the estate. She lives there with Agatha Crandall, her paid companion, and her young nephew, Edward Lyon, who's just finished his studies at Oxford. I've written to Corinne, about you and she is wild about having you at Lyon House.'

'All the arrangements have been made?' I asked.

'Yes. There's a train leaving Sunday morning. You'll go then. We shall spend today and tomorrow shopping. You'll need ever so many things. It will be great fun.'

Mattie continued to talk. She told me about her childhood in Devonshire and gave glorious descriptions of the countryside. She told me all about Corinne Lyon who, in her late fifties, was still the terror of the county. I listened passively, asking no questions, merely replying when it was necessary. Mattie snapped the peas and talked. She seemed relieved now, and when she looked up at me her eyes were full of tenderness that she did not try to hide. I knew that she loved me. I knew that she was doing what she thought best. She would not send me away without a good reason. I accepted that. It was enough for now.

The music hall closed early Saturday night. We had a private party. There was an enormous cake and several bottles of cheap champagne. Old Greenley had strung crepepaper banners over the stage, and the chorus girls had helped with the other decorations. There was a pile of gaily wrapped presents for me on a table. Now, well after midnight, glasses of champagne circulated freely and everyone was trying to force an air of merriment into an occasion that was sad. The girls were wearing their spangled costumes, and Laverne was in the new dress I had just finished. She sat at the piano, banging out tune after tune, and a few of the girls sang. Bert and Sarah had done a soft-shoe number, and Bert was already a bit drunk, sitting in a chair with a wide grin on his face.

I opened the presents. There were new hair ribbons, a purse, a pair of scarlet slippers, a brush and comb set of plated silver, silken undergarments hidden under layers of pink tissue paper. I tried to laugh, to seem grateful, to act happy over my 'holiday,' but I couldn't manage it properly. I had to force back the tears, and it took much effort. Mattie seemed aware of this. She roamed all over the stage like a brooding hen with a flock of disconsolate chicks, refilling glasses, trying to inject a little spirit. Finally she sat down, letting the sadness she felt take over.

Bill kept coming over to me and putting his arm about my shoulders. He seemed to be on the verge of tears, and I noticed that he had drunk far too many glasses of champagne. I cut the cake and made a wish. Addie passed the cake around, scattering chocolate crumbs all over the stage. An hour passed, everyone determined to keep up a good front. One of the girls got drunk and burst into tears. Laverne tried to calm her down. I managed to slip away during the confusion.

The music hall was in total darkness, only the stage illuminated by a string of lights. The backstage areas were shadowy, although a little moonlight poured in through the high set windows. I climbed up the iron staircase, moving slowly and trying to make no noise. Upstairs, it was cold and damp. Everything was bathed with moonlight, serene. It was a world of velvety shadows and black floors and silvery-blue mist. I opened the door of my dressing room. Far below, I could hear the noises of the party, muffled now, distant. I sat down on the cot and took out the long red box.

I took out Hans and Gretchen and Miranda and Dil. I held them in my arms, and tears filled my eyes. The puppets were silly things made from wood, their features painted, and it was foolish to cry now as I cradled them in my arms. But I was not crying because of the puppets. I was crying because I had to leave everything I knew and loved, and the puppets were representative of all that. Nothing would ever be the same again; I felt that strongly. I would go to Devonshire, and I would come back, but it would never be the same.

These last two days had been frantic, full of preparations for the journey. Mattie had tried to make our shopping trips festive, and we had spent far too much money, but it had been a chore for me. For all her forced cheerfulness, Mattie had been nervous. I had noticed her glancing over her shoulder as we walked from shop to shop, and once she had taken me by the arm and guided me around a corner rapidly and into the first door we came to. I thought it odd, but Mattie laughed it off. As we stood in the shop examining bonnets, Mattie kept glancing out through the plate glass window, as though she were expecting to see someone walk past.

At night we did not go to the music hall. We stayed at the boarding house and sewed and packed. Tonight was the first time I had been back, and Mattie and I had come late, just in time for the party. I had not done my act. I put the puppets back in their box now, wondering if I would ever use them again. I smoothed Gretchen's curls and straightened Hans' collar. It seemed to me that the painted wooden faces were sad as I shut the lid.

I had not lighted a lamp. The dressing room was illuminated by moonlight that floated in softly through the window. Everything was blue and black and misty silver, and a light would create a harsh effect. I sat there on the cot, watching the millions of tiny motes that whirled slowly in a bar of moonlight. I thought of all the years I had spent here in this dressing room, how I had loved it, how it made me a part of this world. Now I was being shoved out. I did not belong in Devonshire; I would not belong anywhere. My comfortable nest must be evacuated, and I felt lost and lonely.

I heard somebody moving down the hall to one of the dressing rooms. That was strange, I thought, because I had not heard anyone come up the stairs. It did not alarm me. I had been lost in thought, and one of the girls had probably gone to the dressing room without my hearing her. It was a little strange that she had not lighted a lamp, but then I had not lighted one myself. Someone else had wanted to get away from the depressing atmosphere of the party and be alone for a little while.

I stepped into the hall. I could hear the noise of the party drifting upstairs in muffled bursts of sound. Someone was singing. I could hear the piano. I stood by the doorway of my dressing room, hesitating. I did not want to go back down, but I supposed I must. They would miss me. I braced my shoulders and wiped a tear away from my cheek. I did not want them to know I had been crying.

I walked down the hall towards the

staircase. Some old cardboard backdrops leaned against the wall, draped with a canvas cover. There was a coil of rope and a broken pulley on the floor. I heard someone come out of one of the dressing rooms at the other end of the hall. I presumed it was one of the girls, deciding to go back down just as I had. The sound of footsteps echoed down the hall. I turned around. The hall was long and dark, dusted with moonlight. The floor gleamed darkly, and there were nests of shadow along each wall. I saw someone move stealthily into the shadows, as though afraid of being seen.

'Are you coming down?' I called. 'I'll wait for you.'

There was no answer. I could barely see the dark form sliding along the wall, moving slowly. A cold chill swept over me. I gripped the handrail of the staircase, my fingers trembling. I was paralyzed, unable to move. My heart seemed to leap into my throat. I clutched the railing to keep from falling. I could sense the evil in the air. It was real, waves of evil flooding the hall like something tangible. It was as real as the smell of damp plaster and old face powder. A shaft of moonlight fell over the top of the staircase, flooding it with silver. Whoever was at the other end of the hall could see me plainly, while I could barely distinguish the dark form. The noise of the party seemed very far away.

'Who is it?' I said. The words rang in the still air. They echoed and faded away, as though they had been thrown into a void.

There was a clatter of footsteps on the staircase. Laverne was coming up. She stopped halfway, seeing me standing there. A look of alarm was on her face. She heaved a sigh of relief and then shook her head, as though in disgust. 'So there you are! We've been looking all over for you. Running out on your own party—bad form, kid, very bad form. Come on down now. The girls are going to do their dance routine, then we're going to have some sandwiches. I'll swear! You're exasperating—'

I looked back down the hall. It was a long, dark alley, and there was no one lurking against the wall. The hall was empty. The dark form was gone. Waves of silver blue mist illuminated everything now, revealing yawning doorways and shadowy corners. A tiny black rat scurried over the floor. I shuddered as Laverne came on up the staircase and took my hand in hers. We went back down and I moved as though in a trance.

The party did not seem real. Nothing seemed real. I smiled and spoke and nodded and moved around with a forced smile on my lips, but I had the sensation of moving under water. I saw the coloured lights and the shabby crepe paper banners and the remains of the cake. None of them were real. I seemed to have no more substance than one of my puppets. I seemed to jerk and move as they did, some invisible master pulling the strings. The party seemed to go on forever like some awful charade.

I sat down in a corner, watching all the forced activity. I wanted to laugh and tell them that this was not real. The only thing real was the danger. It was there, upstairs, waiting for me. I did not know why. There was no reason I could explain for it, but it had been stalking me for over a week. Mattie was sending me away to Devonshire in the morning, away from danger. I wondered if it would follow me there.

CHAPTER 5

I stood on the little station platform, my baggage piled in a neat stack behind me. The train had pulled out long ago, sending pale white plumes of smoke into the air. There had been no one here to meet me, and I felt like an orphan who has been deserted by the world. I tried to look pleasant, smiling at all the various people who passed me by, hoping one of them would come up to me and ask my name. No one did. Mattie had said Corinne Lyon's nephew would be waiting at the station. He had not shown up. I was beginning to get a queasy feeling in the pit of my stomach. I tried not to think it was all some horrible joke.

The train ride had been pleasant. I had never been on a train before. At first I was a little frightened, but gradually the monotonous movement and the sound of the wheels screeching on the metal track had lulled me into a pleasant lethargy. As London faded away and I began to see the countryside through the window, my excitement grew. I forgot all that had happened: rolling green hills with tall trees growing on their crests, yellow buttercups scattered over a field, a ribbon of sparkling blue river that wound through a violet-grey valley. Sometimes there were ugly industrial towns with many smokestacks and soot-covered houses, but more often the villages were neat and clean, like pretty toys flung out on the landscape.

Devonshire was lovely. Against a pale blue sky tall trees raised their stately limbs, throwing light purple shadows on the ground. Wild flowers grew in profusion in the meadows and valleys we passed, and in all the villages there were neat flowerbeds in front of all the houses: this village was no exception. From where I stood I could see the town square, a vivid patch of green, bordered on each side with beds of blue and orange and white crocuses. There was a tarnished old cannon on the square, and two little boys played on it. I could see the tall bronze steeple of the church reaching up to touch the sky and all the oak trees that spread shade over the sidewalks and streets. It was incredibly peaceful and serene. I had never known such beauty.

There was a little tea shop behind me on the platform, pink brick with white door and windows and a white awning rolled out for shade. In the window I could see stacks of tiny glazed cakes and a silver pot. It was late, and I was beginning to grow hungry. Mattie had packed a basket for the train ride, but I had eaten the cold fried chicken and sandwiches long ago. I was almost ready to go into the tea shop when I saw a carriage turn into the street. It was sleek and shiny, with a beautiful dappled grey horse pulling it.

The carriage stopped and a man got out. He looked around, and when he saw me he smiled. He came towards me, pulling off his yellow gloves. I knew it must be Edward Lyon, finally come to fetch me.

He was a handsome young man with thick auburn hair that shone with deep copper highlights. His face was very tanned, and he had large brown eyes beneath darkly arched brows. His nose was Roman, and his lips were large, curled now in a friendly smile. He was very tall, and thin. His shoulders were enormous, and I remembered that Mattie had said he played soccer at Oxford. I could easily believe it. He had a strong, muscular body that rippled with power. He was beautifully groomed, wearing glossy knee-high brown boots and a rust coloured suit with dark brown lapels. His vest was dark green, and he wore a black and white striped ascot. He took my hand and shook it warmly.

'Miss Meredith? I am Edward Lyon. I'm so sorry about being late. I was out riding and completely forgot that I was to pick you up today. Corinne had a small fit when I got in. I hardly had time to change. Will you forgive me?'

'Of course, Mr Lyon.'

'So formal. You could call me Edward, you know, or even Ed. That would be nice.'

'In time perhaps,' I replied.

I spoke rather stiffly, but it was not intentional. This man had an overwhelming presence that almost frightened me. He was virile and vital, charged with life, and he intimidated me. Power and energy and red corpuscles and muscle and strength were bounding, all brought together with a casual, natural charm that made itself felt immediately. He spoke in a smooth, husky voice, and what words did not convey his eyes did. He had what theatrical people called command, a certain magnetism that drew one's attention immediately and riveted it on him. It was a rare quality, and Edward Lyon had it to excess.

He was still holding my hand, and I pulled my fingers away gently. Edward Lyon smiled. He was staring at me in a frank, unabashed manner that made me highly uncomfortable.

'Is there something wrong?' I asked.

'No. Was I being rude?'

'You were staring at me.'

'I'm sorry. I just can't get over my surprise.'

'Surprise?'

'Yes. You see, I had expected someone quite different. When Corinne told me I had to come to the station to pick up the young ward of one of her old friends, I imagined a plain, rather prissy old maid, someone much older.'

'I see.'

'I dreaded it, to be quite frank. I could see myself in weeks to come, playing cards with two women, escorting the old maid to bazaars and church socials and listening to dreary conversation about cats and crochet and tomato plants. I was planning to escape.'

'Escape?'

'Leave Lyon House for the duration.'

'And now?'

'Now I shall anticipate every moment of it.'

'You're being very gallant, Mr Lyon.'

'I hope I sound sincere as well as gallant.'

I smiled, unable to resist his charm. He took my elbow and led me to the carriage, an elegant black surrey with heavy yellow upholstery. He handed me into it, and I spread my skirts out over the seat while he piled my luggage in the back seat. He swung into the seat beside me and took up the reins. He clicked them smartly and the dappled grey horse began to move down the street at a slow trot. We passed under the marvellous oak trees, through the main part of the village, and soon we were on a winding grey road that led out into the countryside.

'Tell me about yourself,' Edward Lyon said.

'There isn't much to tell. I am eighteen years old. I live in London with Mattie and Bill Jameson. I have four puppets. I do an act with them at the music hall. My parents died when I was a little girl.'

'You have no relatives?'

'A sister, Maureen. I haven't see her for eight years.'

I answered the questions rather briskly, not at all pleased that he was being so inquisitive. He seemed to sense this. He smiled, the corners of his lips turning up, and when he turned to me I could see his dark brown eyes dancing with merriment.

'I'm a boorish creature,' he said lightly. 'I don't mean to be rude, but it seems I always am. I can't help it. When I meet people I like, I want to know all about them. The best way to find out is to ask questions.'

He grinned at me. He had the direct appeal of a little boy. While we drove I told him about my life in London. I told him about the music hall and the boarding house and all my friends there. I told him about meeting Charles Dickens and about each of the puppets. Already, as we rode along this lovely country road, it seemed far away, and there was a touch of sadness in my voice as I talked about it.

'It sounds like an enchanting kind of life,' Edward Lyon remarked. 'Why did your guardian want to send you away from it?'

'I—I don't really know. She thought a few weeks in the country would do me good.'

'So it will,' Edward Lyon replied. 'So it will. Still, it seems a little strange.'

'Mattie had her reasons,' I said.

I had no intention of speaking about that other. I wanted to forget about it entirely, and I was not going to think about it if I could help it. It, too, was far away, already a thing of the past, a vague, shadowy nightmare that had no substance here.

'Tell me about Lyon House,' I said, changing the subject.

'It's a lovely place, not too large, but a grand estate just the same. Lyons have lived in it for two hundred years, ever since it was built during the reign of Elizabeth. Rumour has it that the great queen herself once stayed there, but I've never been able to find any verification of the story. It will belong to me one day, when Corinne dies. I'm not sure I want the responsibility.'

'Responsibility?'

'There is so much upkeep on a place like Lyon House, and there are the tenant farms, seven of them, surrounding the place. It takes all one's energies to run such an establishment—doesn't leave much time for fun.'

'Is fun so important?' I asked.

'For me it is. I want to enjoy myself. I want to travel and meet interesting people and ride and hunt and go to parties. I don't want to be tied down by a house, no matter how grand.'

'That's an absurd viewpoint,' I said. 'Life isn't meant for that when you have—well, a tradition to uphold. You should be proud. You should consider yourself fortunate.'

'Nobly spoken,' he replied. He laughed, throwing his head back. I noticed again the rich copper highlights in his auburn hair. The wind ruffled the thick waves and it curled about the nape of his neck. He had long sideburns, beautifully trimmed. Everything about the man was neat and well groomed.

'I'd imagine I'm talking for my own benefit,' he said. 'I love the place, actually. It's just that I have no deep-seated sense of tradition. Since my uncle had no sons, it has always been assumed that I would take over Lyon House, following the illustrious footsteps of my ancestors. There's a whole gallery of family portraits at the house. I used to be frightened of them when I was a little boy—such severe, serious old men with such sober eyes and tight mouths. I don't see myself hanging alongside them in an ornate gold frame.'

'Have you always lived at Lyon House?' I asked.

'Yes. My father was the second son; his misfortune. He went into the Army, and later my mother followed him there. I was born in Calcutta. My mother slowly expired under the climate, and she died three years after my birth. I was sent back to England to live here in Devonshire. When I was seven, my father died of fever in Bengal. I never knew either of my parents.'

'How very sad,' I said.

'So you and I have something in common,' he said lightly, flicking the whip over the horse's back. 'Both orphans, but we've turned out rather nicely, don't you think?'

I asked him about Oxford, wishing to divert the conversation from its rather maudlin course. Edward Lyon launched into a colourful account of his exploits among the halls of ivy. He had been shockingly poor in all his studies and had managed to leave the school only through the grace of a flock of tutors and the strength of the family name. He told me about his drinking and gambling and the mountain of debts, about the frolicsome escapades that had threatened to send him home in disgrace. He told me how he had wanted to throw everything to the winds and run away to Greece with a young companion and write poetry among the ruins.

'Byron's influence, you know. Never came to anything. I stayed to take my exams and, believe it or not, passed them all. Rather a lark, the whole thing.'

'And so now you are back at Lyon House, champing at the bit,' I remarked.

'Not champing exactly. Restless—or at least I was until now. Now Lyon House seems delightfully promising.'

'You're being gallant again,' I said.

'Dreadful of me. You'll have to learn to put up with it, Julia.'

The horse trotted down the curving grey road. We passed fields of grain, waving golden brown in the breeze, and tenant farms, all neat and clean, square white houses with thatched roofs, large red barns, pastures with cows grazing beneath the trees. The pale blue sky was momentarily blotted out as we turned into a long avenue of trees, their branches joining overhead to form a tunnel. Sunlight sifted through them and dappled the road with specks of gold. I looked up at the dark green leaves, seeing occasional patches of sky when they separated. The horse's hooves pounded on the firm packed road.

'Devonshire is lovely,' I said.

'Particularly at this time of year,' Edward Lyon replied. 'There are flowers everywhere, if you care for that sort of thing.'

'You don't?'

'Not madly, no. Corinne does. Her gardens are famous in these parts. They're her great pride.'

We passed over a grey stone bridge that spanned a small river that bubbled over flat white pebbles. Willow trees dripped their jade green branches along the white sand bank and into the blue water. He told me that the stream wound through the Lyon estate, passed through the village and eventually went out into the sea, a few miles away. We passed another farm. A farmer was ploughing in a field, turning over rich black soil with his primitive plough. There was a patch of woods, and then a clearing filled with scarlet-orange poppies growing in wild profusion. Their odour was heady. I closed my eyes to savour it.

'The country has a strange effect on people,' Edward Lyon remarked as we drove over another stone bridge. 'Some people fall in love with it immediately and some immediately grow nervous and long for the pavements of the city. I fall somewhere in between the two categories. Is this your first time in the country?'

'Yes it is,' I replied, 'and it is a revelation.'

Edward Lyon smiled. He flicked the whip again and the horse moved at a brisker trot.

We were passing along a lovely avenue of elm trees, growing tall and graceful behind a white wooden fence on either side of the road. I could see green slopes behind them and, farther off, the crest of a mountain that was merely a purple haze, like a cloud. Edward Lyon told me that we were almost at Lyon House now, and I felt my pulses quicken with nervous excitement.

'I am a little apprehensive about meeting

Mrs Lyon,' I confessed. 'I feel like I am imposing on her, coming like this.'

'Nonsense. Corinne went into fits of excitement when her friend wrote her about you. Lyon House gets pretty lonely sometimes. There is no one but the servants and Agatha and me to keep the old lady occupied during the day. She'll welcome you with enthusiasm. You'll be a diversion for her.'

'What is she like?'

'Corinne? She's a dragon. Terrifying until you get to know her. She always has been. Bossy, temperamental, autocratic, but grand. She is gracious and generous and warm hearted, despite appearances, but she is determined to have her own way about everything. She usually does. There is no one in the county with guts enough to defy her. She loves to shock people and feels she must fly off the handle two of three times a day just to keep in shape.'

'Oh dear, you're making me nervous,' I said.

'Don't be. Stand up to her and snap back, and Corinne will love you. She has spirit, and she loves spirit in others. She's a bit larger than life, a grand old eccentric of the old school. I adore her. She tolerates me.'

'She's a widow, isn't she?'

'Yes, my uncle died five years ago. People of the county expected his death to tone her down some, but Corinne was out riding the morning after his death, charging over the hills and galloping down the roads on her fine white stallion. The people were scandalized, horrified at her lack of respect, but it was the kind of gesture they had grown to expect from Corinne. Anything less spectacular would have disappointed them.'

'Does she still ride?'

'Every morning at seven. She's in her middle fifties, but she's aglow with health. She wears a tan riding habit and a tan derby with a long moss green veil that flies behind her like a banner. It's one of the famous sights of the county.'

'She sounds formidable.'

'She isn't, not after the first shock has worn off. Everyone loves her, in spite of her shrewish temper and scalding tongue. The tenants of Lyon House worship her. There are no finer farms in this part of the country, and that's because the people are happy and work well.'

'Tell me about Agatha Crandall. She's a paid companion, isn't she? I think Mattie told me that.'

Edward Lyon frowned. I saw a dark line crease his brow, and his eyes grew dark. He scowled, and his face was suddenly unpleasant like that of a petulant schoolboy.

'Agatha was a girlhood friend of Corinne's. They went to school together. Agatha's husband died shortly after my uncle, and she came to Lyon House for a visit. She was penniless, had no place else to go, so she just stayed on. Corinne took her in like you would take in a stray cat. Mrs Crandall isn't much companionship. She spends most of her time in her room wearing Corinne's cast off clothes and drinking the cellar dry.'

'You don't like her?'

'Let's just say I don't approve of her. If Corinne wants to have her around, that's her business.'

'How many servants are there?' I asked.

'The cook, the housekeeper, two maids and the gardener. They are all new, haven't been at Lyon House a month. Corinne runs through servants rather quickly. A few of her tantrums and they ask for their pay and leave. I'm hoping this new batch will prove more durable.'

The carriage rolled through the avenue of elms and turned, passing through two grey stone portals. We came upon a large apple orchard, the fruit hanging heavily on the branches of the trees. The apples were still green, though some of them were slowly turning a soft rose shade. The ground below was dark with shade, covered with dead leaves and rotting apples, and I could smell their sharp odour. On the other side of the orchard there was a small cream brick house, tall and narrow with two stories and a dark brown roof. There were brown shutters around each window, and ivy grew up one side of the house, clinging to the brick in dark green strands, dusty. The porch was varnished golden oak, and there was a small portico of the same material. A gigantic oak tree in the front yard spread violet shade over the yard, and there were shabby gardens on either side of the house, a path of grey flagstones winding through them. It was a charming place, and I asked if it was part of Lyon House.

'You might call it the scion of Lyon House,' Edward Lyon remarked. 'It was originally built for young married couples of the family to get away from the parental roof for a while and be alone. In an outburst of democratic feeling fifty years ago, my grandfather gave the house and the seven acres surrounding it to his bailiff, and it passed out of the family. It's owned now by an old woman who lives in London. She frequently rents it out to people who want a place in the country for a few months. It's vacant now.'

It was nearing sunset, and the blue sky had gradually faded to a gleaming silver with only a few soft strokes of blue. The trees along the drive were silhouetted against it, and they spread long violet shadows across the road. We made another turn, and I could see Lyon House for the first time. It was still far away. The horse trotted slowly, bringing the house closer and closer, it seemed, and I watched it with an intense concentration, unable to take my eyes away from the beauty of it.

Lyon House too, was made of cream coloured brick, softly washed now by the dying rays of sunlight, and it, too, was two stories high, rising tall and graceful against the silver sky. Slender white columns across the front supported a portico with a weathered blue roof that had faded to a pale, almost colourless shade. The roof of the house was the same faded blue, and there were three chimneys of light orange brick. Dark blue shutters framed the windows with leaden glass that threw back the sunlight in silvery bursts of light. There was a small lion of black marble on either side of the front steps, and tall evergreen trees grew along the circular drive of crushed shell that led up to the steps. It was the most beautiful house I had ever seen, a thing of form and light and soft colour that graced the place it stood.

Edward Lyon was aware of my awe. He said nothing, but there was a smile on his lips and he glanced at me with satisfaction. Words would have spoiled the magic of the moment. He drove the carriage around the drive and stopped in front of the steps. The shafts moved a little after we had stopped, and then we were still.

I could not move for a moment, and Edward Lyon respected my mood. He held the reins lightly in his lap, enjoying my appreciation of his home. After a while he got out and took my hand, helping me down. We stood on the steps, and I looked at the black marble lions that seemed to guard the place.

I stood under the portico that covered all the long front porch. I saw the immense white door with a brass knocker in its centre shaped as the head of a lion, its mouth holding a brass ring. Soft shadows swept over the porch, and I waited there while Edward Lyon took my luggage out of the surrey. On either side of the house I could see the gardens that spread out in terraced wings under the rapidly thickening twilight. From somewhere I could hear fountains, a melodious, plinking sound that was like music. A bird warbled in a rose bush, and the insects had already begun their nocturnal serenade.

Edward Lyon piled my luggage in a neat stack on the porch and then he stood looking at me, his fists on his hips. A lock of auburn hair had fallen over his forehead, and he had the expression of a little boy who is showing a treasured possession to his friend.

'Like it?' he asked quietly.

'I couldn't possibly say how much.'

'Welcome to Lyon House,' he said.

CHAPTER 6

'Stunning,' Corinne Lyon cried, 'simply stunning. I had no idea! If I had known what a beauty you are, I would never have let you come. Absolutely not! Think what that youth and freshness will do to me if anyone sees us side by side. I shall look like a crocodile!'

I could think of nothing to say in reply. I stood rather timidly, my lashes lowered.

'I shall have to keep you hidden,' she said, nodding her head as if in agreement with herself. 'If company arrives, into the closet you go. Is that understood?'

'Now, Corinne,' Edward Lyon protested.

'Hush, Edward. Run along! What are you doing here anyway? This is women talk. Julia is going to tell me about her love affairs, and I am going to make her blush with a full account of mine.'

'It would take three weeks,' Edward replied, mock serious.

'We have nothing but time,' Corinne snapped. 'You run along now. I don't want to share this delicious creature with anyone just yet!'

She smiled as her nephew left the room, closing the door behind him. We were in the parlour, a vast, light room with white walls and delicate French furniture of white wood and sky-blue satin upholstery. Long draperies of thin blue material swept the floor, covering the French windows that opened out into the gardens. Corinne opened the draperies and threw back the windows, pausing for a moment with her hands on the sill. All the glorious smells of the gardens swept into the room. In the misty blue twilight I could see pink and white rose trees.

'So you like Lyon House?' she asked.

'I adore it,' I replied. 'I think it is the loveliest place I have ever seen.'

'It's nice, quite nice,' she replied, 'a little small, a little simple, but it's the simplicity and smallness that give it its character. I abhor those mammoth greystone monstrosities that mar the countryside with their turrets and towers.'

'It must be wonderful to be the Lady of Lyon House and be surrounded by so much beauty,' I remarked.

'It is, my dear, it is. Of course it was

more exciting in the old days when the place was aswarm with people, when the drive was crowded with carriages and every room rang with laughter and voices. There used to be parties every week, and so many handsome young men—but, alas, I am afraid those days are gone. I seldom see anyone now.'

'You don't go out?'

'Only to ride in the morning and to visit the tenant farms. Haven't been to the village in years, much less anywhere else. And people seldom come to Lyon House. I frighten them away. It's just as well.' There was a touch of sadness in her voice.

She saw that I was watching her closely, and she tapped her lace fan against her palm, folding the lace pleats.

'Can you really blame me for not wanting to see people, to have people see me?'

'I don't understand what you mean,' I replied.

'Come, come, my dear. You're young, but you're no fool, and you are not blind either. I used to be a great beauty, celebrated in twenty counties. Young men used to perish just for a glance of me. Now—' She threw her hands out in a lavish gesture. 'You can see for yourself.'

Corinne Lyon was certainly not beautiful. She was not really old, but her face was a mask of wrinkles, poorly disguised under layers of heavy make up and powder. Her cheeks glowed with rouge, too much and too red, and her thin lids were coated with silver-blue paint, the lashes long and curling and obviously false. Her eyes were a young woman's eyes, dark brown and shining, staring sadly through the mask of age. Her hair was a tumble of auburn curls, frosted with silver, and I suspected that it was false, too, a skilfully designed wig.

'The fever,' she said, 'seven years ago. I wanted to die when I recovered and first saw myself in the mirror. I really wanted to die, but I carried on, though not as before.'

She stalked across the room, moving with a flamboyant grace rather like that of a grand actress who overplays her grandness. She was wearing a dressing robe of tea coloured silk, beautifully tailored. It had frothy brown lace about the throat and wrists, and she wore an enormous topaz ring. She whirled around to face me, opening the fan of yellow lace with one quick slap on her wrist.

'I never go out without a veil,' she said. 'The children of the tenants used to run when they saw me. They thought I was a witch. What do you think of that?'

'I think they must be very rude children,' I replied, 'very poorly trained.'

'Really? And what do you think of me?'

I hesitated. Her brown eyes challenged me, hard and defiant. 'I think you're incredibly vain and incredibly proud. In fact, you strike me as being a very foolish woman.'

'My dear! No one has ever spoken to me like that!'

'I'm sorry. You asked me a question. I've been taught to tell the truth.' The words sounded priggish to my own ears, and I blushed, looking down at the pearl grey carpet. I could feel the colour rushing to my cheeks. Corinne Lyon burst into laughter. It was a rich, raucous sound that filled the room with wicked merriment. I looked up, angry with her now. I had come here as a guest, but I had not come to be mocked.

'You're also rude!' I snapped.

'Rude! My dear, how delightful! You're a treasure. I can see that we are going to get along gloriously. I adore someone with guts! It took a lot of guts to tell me that, didn't it?'

'Yes, it did,' I replied, frowning at the distasteful word.

'You really think I'm vain—and foolish and rude?'

'I do.'

'That's wonderful, almost as nice as being thought wicked. This has stimulated me marvellously. Like a brace of champagne. I think it's wonderful to have you, Julia. Mattie was a dear to think of it. We'll have such a grand time—'

I liked her then, for the first time. Her pose was an outrageous sham, I thought. She was a lonely old woman who had had a great tragedy in her life, and she tried to conceal her unhappiness with flamboyant, highly coloured conduct. Her nephew had told me that she was really generous and kind hearted, and I did not doubt it. I saw that her pose was necessary to her. She had to generate an air of temperament and spirit to draw the attention to herself that had once been summoned by her beauty. Without that attention, she would feel she was living in a void. Sensing this, I felt I could get along with Corinne Lyon quite easily. It would be easy to feed her ego and at the same time appreciate the genuine qualities which the pose couldn't quite hide.

'Now you must want to see your room,' she said, snapping her fan closed again. 'And perhaps you'll want to rest a while before changing for dinner. We're going to be grand tonight—champagne and candlelight. So few people come to Lyon House—this is an occasion!'

She led me out of the parlour and into the large, airy main hall. I had a glimpse of pearl grey wallpaper and gleaming white woodwork before she led me up the gracefully curving white spiral staircase. The stairs were carpeted in sky blue, the nap a little worn, and a great chandelier hung over the stairwell, dripping crystal pendants that sparkled with rainbow colours in their prisms. Corinne moved briskly up the stairs, her tea-yellow skirts rustling noisily. She talked vivaciously as she led me down the hall on the second floor.

'It'll be so nice to have someone new in the house,' she said. 'It does get rather lonely. Agatha isn't much company—poor thing. You'll meet her later on. Edward is always wanting to go gallavanting off to be with people his own age. I can't blame him, really. It looks like you are going to have to put up with me.'

'I think it will be delightful,' I replied.

'Do you play cards?'

'Not very often. I do know how.'

'Marvellous! We can play after dinner. Edward won't play with me anymore. I always win.'

'Do you cheat?'

'He says I do. It's an outrageous lie!'

Corinne took me down the hall to the last room. She opened the door and showed me inside. A maid was hanging my clothes up in the closet. My bags were on the floor opened, half their contents already taken out. Corinne stood in the doorway for a moment, watching me as I looked at the room, and then she left, saying she would see me at dinner.

'And who are you?' I asked the girl who was hanging up my clothes.

'Molly Jenkins, ma'am. I'm to be your personal maid.'

'Goodness, I've never had a maid before.'

'I've never been one before,' she replied frankly.

'Do you think you'll like it?' I asked.

'It's better than getting up at the crack of dawn every morning and milkin' two dozen cows. I hated that. And the chickens—' She shook her head and shuddered, making a grimace.

'You live on a farm?'

'I did till I came here two weeks ago. I was so excited when my Pa told me I was going to work at Lyon House. Bertie wasn't so happy—he's my beau, Bert Martin, works at the dairy and delivers milk at the village. Bertie didn't want me to come here. Said I wouldn't stay.'

'Why didn't he think you would?'

'If you'll pardon me for sayin' so—the old lady. She's a terror. Fired the whole lot of servants just over two weeks ago, had a perfectly smashin' row. Millie Jones, my girl friend, she worked here once, and she said no amount of pay would bring her back. I don't mind, though. My Pa ain't so easy to get on with himself, and the old lady doesn't frighten me none.'

I smiled. Molly was a frank, engaging creature with tousled black curls and bright blue eyes. Her nose was turned up at the end and there was a sprinkle of golden brown freckles over the bridge. Her cheeks

103

were ruddy with health, her mouth saucy and very pink. She told me that she was sixteen years old, almost seventeen, but she seemed more mature. I could easily imagine that life on the farm had taught Molly many things. She was pretty and lively, and I guessed that Bertie Martin had a hard time of it with her. I could imagine a whole sock of strong, rowdy boys, vying for the privilege of being sassed by her.

'Of course she'd been sick,' Molly continued, 'real sick, in fact. They had to order medicine all the way from London, Cook says. She was in bed for the longest time, moanin' and lookin' at death's door. Then she pops up and comes chargin' through the house like her old self, findin' everything all wrong. Screamed and raged, and before the day was over, she'd discharged the whole lot of 'em down to the last maid. Mr Lyon had a hard time gettin' replacements.'

'I can easily imagine that,' I replied.

'Of course, she never goes out. That makes it bad. She just rides every morning, never goes to the village. I like her myself. I just step out of the way when she starts breathin' fire.'

I laughed, thoroughly delighted with the girl.

'She isn't like the other one,' Molly said. 'I don't like her at all.'

'The other one?'

'The one they call Agatha. She nips, you know. Bottles everywhere in her room. She doesn't scream and carry on like the old lady, but she's spooky. Drags around without sayin' a word and lookin' at everyone with that awful smile on her lips like she's just swallowed the canary. No, I don't like her at all. She gives me the creeps.'

Molly finished hanging up the clothes and put the bags on top of the closet shelf. She rubbed her hands together, satisfied with her work. She wore a blue and white striped dress, the skirt turned up a little to reveal the edge of her starched, ruffled petticoat. A white apron was tied around her waist and a ruffled white cap perched precariously on her raven black curls.

'Is there anything else you'll be wantin', Miss Julia?'

'Not just now, Molly.'

Molly made a little curtsey, somewhat awkwardly. It was obvious that she was not accustomed to her role as a ladies' maid.

It would be hard for a girl with such high spirits to conform to the formal, studied attitude of a proper maid, and I liked her better this way.

'You'll forgive me for talkin' so much,' she said at the door. 'My Pa says it's my worst fault—chatter, chatter, chatter all day long, and Bertie Martin just has a fit. He doesn't want to *talk* when he's with me. He just goes out of his mind sometimes, but I know how to handle him. He knows to watch his step, or I'll let Steve Woods take me to the fair.'

'The fair?'

'The county fair. It's two weeks from now. Mr Lyon will probably take you. I wouldn't half mind *that.*'

She gave me a saucy grin and left the room, swishing her skirts. I stood in the middle of the room, studying it for the first time. It was lovely, every detail carefully appointed. The walls were covered with a pale green material, almost white, richly embossed, and the carpet was a dull grey. A pair of French windows opened out onto a little balcony, and the draperies hanging over them were jade green, thin and blowing in to the room. A valance of dark green satin hung over the top, contrasting with the jade material. The bedspread and hangings over the bed were of the same materials. The furniture was sturdy oak, painted glossy white, and the top of the dressing stool was upholstered in vivid yellow satin. A silver-grey vase on the bureau held a bouquet of daffodils of the same colour yellow. For all its beauty, it was comfortable, the kind of room I could relax in.

I pushed aside the draperies and stepped onto the little balcony. It looked out over the gardens on the west side of the house. The last rays of sunlight had gone and the moon was not yet out. The gardens seemed to be suspended in the hazy twilight, not quite visible, not quite dark. I could smell the blossoms from where I stood.

I don't know how long I stood there, watching the shadows darkening and letting the soft zephyrs of breeze stroke my cheeks. I felt a kind of deep contentment, a vague emotion tinged with sadness. I was sorry to be away from Mattie and Bill and all my friends, but I was happy to be here with all this peace and beauty. I liked Corinne Lyon immensely, and I was sure the feeling would deepen into affection. I was charmed by Edward

Lyon and strangely eager to know him better.

It was almost eight o'clock when I stepped back into the room leaving the windows open behind me. The lamps burned brightly now, spreading yellow light to all corners of the room, and I realized that I would have to hurry if I was to be in time for dinner. I was irritated with myself for wasting so much time dreaming, for I wanted to look especially nice tonight.

I chose one of the new dresses Mattie had bought for me, white silk printed with tiny green leaves and pink rose buds. It was simple in cut, with a low neckline and puffed sleeves that dropped off the shoulder. It revealed a little too much bosom for the sake of modesty, but I was sure Edward Lyon would like it. I brushed my hair until it shone with silvery highlights, then fastened it with a grey velvet ribbon. I felt that I had never looked more attractive, and I was eager to see the look in his eye when I came into the dining room.

I left my room and hurried down the hall. Windows were open at both ends of the hall, and soft breezes raced through, stirring the curtains and making everything cool. My silken skirts made a soft, swishing sound. I heard a bird singing outside and wondered if it were a nightingale. The house was peaceful, surrounded with serenity. I could hardly believe the beauty of it.

The dining room was aglow with candlelight when I entered. The mellow light played upon the dark yellow walls above, the richly varnished mahogany wainscotting below. It glimmered over fine plate and silver and softened everything, creating an intimate atmosphere. A silver bowl in the centre of the table held yellow-orange roses, their petals scattered over the fine linen cloth.

Edward Lyon stood up when I came into the room. He came forward to meet me, stopped midway and gave me a long look. I could see by the gleam in his dark brown eyes that he appreciated my dress. He arched one fine dark brow and shook his head a little. Then he smiled. He looked handsome in his formal attire, the black suit with its black satin lapels, the gleaming white shirtfront, but his black tie was a little crooked and his hair was untidy, boyishly ruffled. It gave a casual, relaxed touch to his appearance.

'Is this the child I brought to Lyon House this afternoon?' he asked in a throaty voice, glancing at Corinne for affirmation.

'That dress is wicked!' Corinne cried.

'Mattie chose it,' I said, blushing a little.

'Mattie must want to marry you off! A dress like that is guaranteed to trap a husband. Now don't be tiresome, child. Don't blush! You must wear it with flair—'

'I think the blush is charming,' Edward Lyon said, taking my hand and leading me to my chair. 'It's innocent—a combination of innocence and worldliness. We must remember that Julia comes from the theatre, and you know all those stories about actresses.'

'Bosh!' Corinne said. 'They're tired, boring creatures who have to slave for a living. Besides, Julia is a puppeteer. Now you behave, Edward. Julia is my discovery. Do you like your room, child?'

'It's lovely,' I replied.

'And the maid? Molly, I think her name is.'

'Molly is delightful. She told me you'd been ill.'

Corinne and Edward Lyon exchanged glances. She looked peeved. He looked at her with a curl in his lip, one brow arched, as though waiting to see what she would say. I sensed an air of tension, and I wondered what had caused it. Corinne frowned.

'How very tiresome,' she said finally.

'Did I say something wrong?' I asked, puzzled.

'N—no, it isn't that. Should I?' she asked, looking at her nephew.

'Your show, Corinne. Do as you think best.'

'She's bound to find out anyway—oh, hell! What difference does it make! I'm not ashamed of it. You see, child,' she said, looking at me with those brown eyes surrounded by wrinkles, 'I take laudanum. I have this thing about sleeping—can't sleep without it. I ran out of it. It was quite dreadful, really. We had to send to London for more. I had a wretched time until it arrived—ran a fever and was confined to my bed. Now you know! I suppose you're shocked?'

'Of course not. It's a medicine, isn't it?'

'Yes—' she replied, drawing the word out. Edward Lyon laughed and she shot him an ugly glance. She picked up her feathered blue fan and began to wave it, irritated. She was wearing a dress of silver velvet and a dazzling sapphire necklace around her throat, the dark blue stones flashing.

'I found everything in a terrible state when I recovered,' she continued. 'Those wretched servants had taken advantage while I was ill, and not a thing was done properly. I had to throw them all out!'

'They left of their own accord after she screamed for a while,' Edward said smoothly. 'Can't say that I blamed them.'

'Pour the champagne, Edward!' she snapped. 'You're particularly irritating tonight.'

The bottle of champagne rested in a nest of shaved ice in a silver bucket, the dark green bottle beaded with moisture. Edward Lyon removed the gold foil and pressured the cork out with his thumbs. It popped, and a spray of sparkling foam shot up. The wine sparkled with golden bubbles as he poured it into the glasses. I thought of the last time I had drunk champagne, at the party the night before I left—it seemed so long ago. This was a whole new world, and the other already seemed vague and blurry.

'Isn't Mrs Crandall going to join us?' I asked.

'She seldom does,' Corinne replied.

'I see,' I said, sipping my champagne.

'Agatha doesn't like our company,' Edward Lyon remarked.

'Bosh! Agatha is too busy drinking to like anyone's company,' Corinne said.

The meal was splendid, and after it was over we moved into the parlour. A servant set up a little card table and I agreed to play a game with Corinne. Edward Lyon watched us, standing in front of the fireplace with his arm resting on the mantle. Corinne chattered as she played, but she was a sharp, shrewd player, and I was helpless against her, even when she was not giving all her attention to the game. Edward laughed, accusing her of cheating. She lashed out at him viciously but he merely shook his head and shrugged his shoulders, smiling at her. He was not a man who could be easily provoked into a quarrel, I thought.

We finished the champagne, sitting there in the parlour. Lyon House was silent, closed in by the night, but we could hear the crickets in the garden. The breeze stirred the curtains at the opened French windows. It was very late, and I was tired. Corinnne was too, I could tell.

She looked very old and, suddenly, very sad. She fingered her sapphire necklace, her gloved fingertips touching the dark blue stones. Corinne always wore gloves, and her dresses always covered her throat and shoulders. She did not want to expose more withered flesh than necessary, I thought. It was another sign of her vanity.

'I'm afraid it's going to be rather dull here for you,' she said as we sat on the sofa. Edward Lyon was prowling about the room like a sleek, magnificent animal, caged. 'There isn't much for a young person to do,' she continued. I thought the words could apply to her nephew as well as to me.

'I shall keep her occupied,' Edward Lyon said. 'I'm going to take her for a canoe ride tomorrow.'

'Really?' Corinne said, her tone disapproving.

'The willow trees are beautiful. We'll canoe to the village and back again. She'll like that. And then there's the fair. That's always great fun.'

'Rowdy, disorganized bash,' Corinne said, opening her fan. 'There is always a fight. All those farm boys with their boots and brown hands, all the pigs and cows and poultry and stink. It's a bit too earthy for my taste.'

'Corinne hates the bucolic,' her nephew said, grinning. 'She's been living in the country most of her life and still shies away from the smellier aspects of it.'

'That will be enough, Edward,' she said, her voice shrewish. 'Go see that all the doors and windows are fastened. The servants are so careless about that. I think it's time we went to bed!'

Edward Lyon went through the house, checking to see that everything was locked up. Corinne looked angry. Her hair was a little to one side, which confirmed my suspicion that she wore a wig. She walked upstairs beside me, silent and sulky, and I wondered what could be wrong. I said good night and went to my room. Molly had turned the covers back on the bed and laid out my nightclothes. I undressed wearily and put on the nightgown. The breeze coming in through the opened windows was laden with the scent of roses. I got into bed and blew out the lamp. Moonlight stained everything with silver. The peace and security was euphoric, and I wondered how long it would last.

115

CHAPTER 7

I awoke to the sound of hoofbeats on the drive. Dawn had come and left the sky a stained grey. There were heavy clouds banking up, and the breeze was strong, flapping the curtains in my bedroom. The hoofbeats died away. It was shortly after seven. I supposed Corinne was off on her daily ride. It seemed incredible that a woman her age would submit herself to such rigid discipline. I imagined that anyone seeing her galloping over the roads at this hour would think her eccentric, and perhaps she did it for that very reason. If Corinne Lyon could no longer gain attention with her beauty, she would do it some other way.

I had dressed and was at the dressing table, brushing my hair, when Molly came into the room. She had forgotten to knock, remembering only after she was inside. She smiled, tossing her long black curls. I smiled back at her. Her high spirits were infectious. She was wearing a vivid blue dress with the white apron and ruffled cap, and the rich colour of the material made her eyes all the more blue. The girl was not beautiful, but she had the radiant glow of youth and health that made beauty superfluous.

'Yes, Molly?' I said.

'I'm supposed to see if you require anything. Breakfast will be served in an hour, when the old lady gets back. She's mad, you know, going off like that every morning, spurring the horse on. Mad! Old ladies should sit in front of the fire and knit and look gentle. Not her! She leaps over fences and hedges and raves like a demon!'

'You *do* chatter, Molly,' I said in a way of reprimand, but I couldn't be irritated with her. She was too vivacious and too delightful.

Molly pursed her pink lips and frowned.

'There's no one to talk to,' she said. 'The other servants are all ancient. Cook won't let me near the kitchen anymore after I turned over a pot of coffee, and the other maids—' She made a grimace. 'Village girls, and just too prim for words. They think *I* should be in the stables!'

'You do have a time of it, don't you, Molly?'

117

'Not now that you're here,' she said, grinning. I noticed again the scattering of freckles over her nose. They added just the right touch.

'You've got such lovely hair,' she said, stepping behind me. 'It's silvery, isn't it. Here—' She took the brush from my hand. 'Let me brush it for you, Miss Julia.' She proceeded to do so, smoothly and efficiently. 'Did you enjoy yourself last night?' she asked.

'Yes. The meal was excellent.'

'I didn't mean *that.*'

'What did you mean?' I asked. I already knew the answer.

'He *is* handsome, isn't he?' she said, looking at me in the mirror.

'Very,' I replied. 'I'm sure all the women pursue him.'

'There aren't many suitable young women around here,' she said. 'All the gentry live miles away. Mr Edward doesn't trifle with the village girls, not even Connie Brown. She's the baker's daughter and a ravin' beauty. All the men are crazy for her, and the feelin' is mutual, if you know what I mean. A real hussy, she is. Just let her lay eyes on my Bertie! No, Mr Edward seems to prefer the ladies in London.'

'Does he go to London often?'

'All the time. Maybe he has a special friend there.'

'Perhaps,' I said, not at all surprised at the idea.

'Of course, there *was* that strange woman—'

I looked up. It was evident from the look on her face that Molly had a particularly juicy bit of gossip and was bursting to tell it. I knew I should scold her and forbid this gossip about her superiors, but I was very curious about Edward Lyon.

'What woman?' I asked, trying to sound casual.

'No one knows. She always came at night, in the dark. Millie said she saw her slippin' around in the garden when she worked here. She said Mr Edward went out to meet her and they talked for a long time then walked down to the gazebo. She came more than once, Millie said, always at night and he always met her. Of course, Millie is a terrible liar, and I didn't believe a word of it at first.'

'Something happened to make you believe it?'

'I saw her,' Molly said simply.

'Really?'

'About a week ago. It was late. Bertie Martin had come to see me, and we were out in the garden, sittin' on one of the benches under a tree and watchin' the fireflies. Bertie was gettin' awfully fresh, and we had an argument and I was gettin' ready to go back in when I saw the woman. She was walkin' along the drive, stayin' in the shadows of the trees, and she had a suitcase or something that looked like one. She went onto the porch, and I didn't see her again. Bertie said it was my imagination.'

'Perhaps it was,' I replied.

'No, Miss Julia. I saw her. Mr Edward has a secret friend. Maybe she won't come back now that you're here.'

I flushed, feeling the colour coming to my cheeks. Molly saw it and grinned. She had a devilish twinkle in her dark blue eyes. She finished brushing, and I fastened a yellow ribbon in my hair. I stood up, trying to master the irritation I felt. I was not irritated at the girl. I was irritated at myself. Why should it matter to me if Edward Lyon had a girl friend? He was a handsome young man, full of energy and drive, and I supposed it was only natural for him to have a woman. Despite the vaguely amoral atmosphere backstage at the music hall, where all the girls chattered about lovers and frequently displayed expensive gifts, I knew little about such things. Mattie and Bill had always been very strict with me, and the girls treated me like a little sister, protective in their attitude—everyone had always been protective towards me. I did not feel capable of coping with all the new emotions I was beginning to experience.

Molly was an earthy little thing, bright and observant. Living on the farm as she did, associating with the rowdy country folk, she had probably known at the age of ten more than I knew even now. I frowned. She had immediately sensed my attraction to Edward Lyon, and she seemed to think it delightful.

'I don't think you need to worry about the other woman,' she said, an impish grin on her lips.

'Why should I worry about her in the first place?'

'*I* wouldn't know.'

'I've only just met Mr Lyon,' I said irritably. 'Besides he's ten years older than I am.'

'Really? Twenty-eight. That's so old?'

'You're being impudent,' I snapped.

'I know. It's awful, isn't it. Pa says I should have been born a mute. That's a pretty dress, Miss Julia,' she said, changing the subject. 'The colour goes so well with your hair. You look like an angel.'

The dress was bright yellow printed with tiny brown flowers. It had a very full skirt, a tight waist and puffed sleeves that dropped slightly off the shoulder. It was a younger girl's dress. I stood before the mirror and turned around slowly, observing myself. I was no longer a young girl. I was a woman. The child with the puppets had vanished. Everything was different. I felt a pang of sadness, thinking of all that was lost. I wanted to run away from this new role, to hold my puppets and smile at the painted faces and feel secure in the world of innocence they represented. But I had put the puppets in their box and closed the lid. It seemed now that I had closed the lid on so much more.

Thunder rumbled in the distance. I stepped to the balcony. The sky was a solid mass of grey clouds, black on the horizon, and the wind was tormenting the trees and shrubs in the gardens. The evergreens bent and swayed, dark green, seemingly alive and protesting the wind. It was going to rain. The weather matched my mood of vague depression, and I went downstairs with a slight frown on my brow. I wondered if Corinne had come in yet.

The lower floor seemed deserted. Far back in the kitchen regions I could hear the sound of servants preparing breakfast, but the rooms here were all empty. I wandered through them, feeling sad. Edward Lyon was probably still in bed. Corinne was out riding in the wind. I stepped into the parlour, lingering by the door. A vase of fresh white roses sat on a table, and I touched the petals, veined with gold. I heard a noise across the room and looked up to see a strange woman staring at me. She seemed as startled as I.

'Who are you?' she demanded.

'I—I am Julia Meredith.'

'Oh, Corinne's little guest. I had forgotten you were to come. I frequently forget things. Do you know who I am?'

'You are Agatha Crandall.'

'Right. I suppose they've told you all about me.'

'Why—'

'Come, come, child. There's no need to be coy.'

'They told me you were Mrs Lyon's companion.'

'Right. That I am—or was. You are very young.'

'I am eighteen,' I said, somewhat stiffly.

'Nonsense. No one is that young.'

'I shall not argue with you, Mrs Crandall.'

'Good. Come closer. I want to see you.'

I stepped forward, hesitantly. There was something about the woman that intimidated me. She was old and sharp, standing there sternly with magnificent posture. Her bright blue eyes were intense, and her hair was worn in rather girlish ringlets that fell in a cascade at the back of her head. It must once have been a lustrous black. Now it was streaked with silver. Her face was thin, sharp, with deep hollows beneath the cheekbones. I could see tiny purple veins in the skin that stretched over the sharp bones—the drinker's curse. Her lips were thin and pale, held tightly together now as she stared at me. She wore a robe of violet velvet. The nap of the velvet was shiny, and the lace at the throat and wrists was slightly brownish with age.

'You're pretty,' she said tartly. 'Too pretty. So was the other one.'

'Other one?'

'Don't ask questions! That's the privilege of the very old. I am very old, as you can plainly see. Do I frighten you?'

'Not a bit,' I replied.

'Then stand up straight and stop looking down at the floor. Why have you come here?'

'Mrs Lyon invited me.'

'Tut! I want the real reason.'

'That's the only reason. She was kind enough to ask me.'

'So they've involved you in this little charade, have they? A pity. You look so innocent.'

'I don't know what you mean.'

'Don't you?' Her intense blue eyes looked into mine, searching. I felt uncomfortable under the hard gaze, but I did not look away. After a moment she said, pressing the thin lips tightly together. 'Perhaps you don't, I shall have to keep my eye on you just the same. You behave yourself, hear me? I could be wrong—yes, I could be wrong.'

'About what?'

'Never you mind. Just behave.'

She was talking in riddles. I could not understand what her strange words

125

meant. I remembered that she drank large quantities of liquor, and although she did not appear to be intoxicated at the moment, her brain was probably fuddled by the alcohol. She stood staring at me, her eyes full of something that I could not properly identify. Mischief? Perhaps. The old woman looked very mischievous. She would probably avoid any real trouble, but I thought she probably relished a good scrap. I could not dislike her, just as I could not dislike a troublesome child, and that is what she reminded me of.

The front door slammed loudly, and in a moment Corinne came storming into the room. She was wearing the outfit her nephew had described to me, the tan riding habit, the hat with the billowing moss green veil. The veil half concealed her heavily made up face, and it swept behind her now as she entered the room. She brought an air of electricity with her. The room seemed to be charged with tempestuous vitality. She stopped and stared when she saw me standing there with Agatha Crandall. She did not look at all pleased.

'You're up?' she snapped, addressing Agatha.

126

'Yes, dear,' Agatha said. I noted the acid tone of her voice. She smiled at Corinne, and the smile was malicious.

'That surprises me,' Corinne said, her own voice far from sweet.

'Really?'

'Yes. It surprises me that you were able.' She emphasized the last word.

'Everyone seems to exaggerate my drinking,' Agatha remarked. 'It may be a small vice, but at least it doesn't *hurt* anyone. I could think of a lot worse things a person could do.'

'What do you mean?' Corinne demanded.

'Tut, my dear. Have I scored?'

They stood glaring at each other. I could feel the animosity. It was like being in the room with two cats, both holding back, both arched and ready to let fly with fang and claw. Corinne jerked off her hat and threw it across the room, the veil fluttering wildly. It landed on the sofa. Agatha lifted an eyebrow and smiled her superior smile. It was evident that these two women could not stand each other, and I wondered why Corinne kept Agatha at Lyon House, that being the case.

'What has she been saying to you?' Corinne asked me.

I started to reply, but Agatha Crandall spoke up before I could get the words out.

'Nothing, dear. Nothing at all. Just little pleasantries. Nothing else—yet.'

'If you dare—'

'No, dear, don't fly into one of your rages. You *know* how they upset you.' She spoke in the dulcet tones of the paid companion. 'You would just have to spend the rest of the day in bed and take some of your nasty medicine. Besides, you know they're absolutely meaningless with me. Save them for someone they will impress.'

Corinne was smouldering, her dark eyes full of anger. I thought she was going to hurl something at the other woman, but she manged to control herself. Her mouth twitched and she clenched her hands. She whirled around, her back to Agatha Crandall. Her shoulders trembled.

'There, there,' Agatha said. 'That's better. You know how these rages affect you. At *your* age you simply must avoid them. You work yourself into such a frenzy, such a frenzy, and for no purpose.'

'Why don't you go open another bottle, Agatha,' Corinne said, the words full of rancour.

'Oh, I don't think so, dear. I don't think

so. Now that Julia is here I believe I will abstain for a while. I must keep sharp and alert. You never know—' Her voice faded off, but the smile remained. She had the look of one with a great secret, bursting to tell it yet refraining because of the power it gave her.

Agatha Crandall left the room, very satisfied with herself. Corinne stood at the window, mastering her rage. I was embarrassed. I was completely bewildered by the ugly scene and did not know what to say now that I was alone with Corinne. I was upset; the peace and harmony I had first felt at Lyon House had been rudely disturbed.

'That woman is intolerable!' Corinne cried, turning to face me. 'She is wretched when she's drunk, of course, but when she's sober she's even worse! Wretched, wretched woman!'

'Surely she meant no harm,' I said.

'Meant no harm! The old harridan would love to upset everything!'

'If you feel so strongly about it, why don't you get rid of her?'

'I might,' Corinne said, her eyes snapping. 'I just might! She can't treat me like that—'

Corinne saw my expression, and she calmed herself. She picked up the hat and held it in her arms, the moss green veil sweeping the floor. Corinne enjoyed scenes, and she no doubt derived great satisfaction from her eccentric tantrums and the confusion they caused, but she had not enjoyed the scene with Agatha Crandall, nor had her emotion been simulated. Her shoulders slumped now, and there was a look of concern in her dark eyes.

'What did she really say to you?' she asked. 'You stay away from her,' Corinne said. 'She's a wicked old woman who loves to stir up trouble. She finds life unbearable, so she spends most of her time trying to make it unbearable for everyone else. She resents me because I had been kind to her and tried to help her. That's what always happens when you are good to someone. Why I put up with her I don't know.'

Edward Lyon came sauntering into the room, his hair mussed and his face still showing signs of sleep. He wore a brown velvet smoking jacket with his black trousers and a pair of soft brown leather slippers. When he saw Corinne's expression he stopped and shook his head. Then he made as if to make a hasty retreat.

'Another of those mornings,' he said, grinning.

'Agatha,' Corinne said, as if the one word explained everything.

'I see,' Edward Lyon said. He looked at me and lifted an eyebrow. 'Has Agatha been bothering you?' he asked pleasantly.

'Not at all,' I replied.

'She's been babbling again,' Corinne said, 'telling this child Heaven only knows what kind of nonsense! We are going to have to find a way to stop her. We are simply going to have to do something, Edward. I can't take any more of this!'

'Do you think so?' he asked casually.

'Yes. The woman is impossible!'

'Very well,' he said, 'don't get into a stew about it. We'll work something out. Now I suggest we all have breakfast. I saw Cook going into the dining room with the most marvellous plate of biscuits.'

'Is that all you have to say?' Corinne cried.

'Yes, dear, at least for the moment. I'm hungry.'

'You're as bad as she is!'

'We abound with passion here,' Edward

Lyon said to me. 'You will find it most invigorating.'

Corinne was sulky all during the meal, and Agatha Crandall sat with her peculiar little smile, hardly touching her food. I had no appetite myself, and only Edward Lyon ate heartily. He buttered the biscuits and spread them with strawberry jam. He was obviously quite accustomed to these scenes and clearly did not intend to let them ruffle him. He was immune to his aunt's moods and enjoyed his breakfast as much as he would have had all been peaceful accord.

Shortly after breakfast it began to rain, pouring in great blinding sheets, and making the world outside a whirling mass of grey. The rain splashed against the windows, and the house was so dark that we had to light the lamps. Agatha Crandall went up to her room, and Corinne sat in the parlour, brooding over a deck of cards. She clearly did not want company, so I avoided her. Edward Lyon talked to me for a little while and promised to take me for a canoe ride tomorrow. He went off to work on some accounts, and I found myself alone.

I wandered into the library, searching for a book. I finally took down one of Dickens' novels and curled up on the sofa. The curtains were parted and I could see the rain splashing against the glass. I tried to read, but even Mr Dickens was no comfort now. I could not concentrate. I looked at the walls of beautifully bound volumes, the lamp light glimmering on their gilt titles. There was an enormous grey marble fireplace with tall black andirons and screen, enormous chairs covered with green leather, as was the sofa. A beautifully varnished globe of gold and red and brown stood on a revolving stand. It was a comfortable room, but I felt no comfort. I could not forget the ugly scene this morning. I had the feeling that it concerned something far more important than anything either woman had said.

CHAPTER 8

The gardens were lovely, bathed now in sunlight that fell in glittering white rays from a silver-grey sky. I strolled down the neat flagstone path, stopping to admire a bed of vivid blue gentians, walking on to see a bed of pink and purple geraniums. The path twisted and turned among the beds. I walked under arches of white trellis that held small pink roses. The fragrance was overwhelming, heady. I closed my eyes to savour it better. Even though it was three miles to the sea, I could smell the salty tang in the air. It was a glorious day, and it seemed incredible now that yesterday had been so grim and grey and depressing. The rain had washed everything clean, and the sunlight made everything sharp and bright.

I was waiting for Edward Lyon. He had promised to take me for the canoe ride this morning. I had awakened early after a night of fitful sleep, and I had hurried outside after a solitary breakfast. No one else had been up at that early hour, and I was content to examine the gardens and think my own private thoughts.

They mostly concerned Edward Lyon. He had had a long talk with me last night, finding me still in the library after dinner. Languorous, rather lazy, he had stretched out on the sofa, regarding me with eyes whose lids drooped sleepily. He asked me all about the music hall and the people there and then he asked me about my sister Maureen, and I found myself telling him all that I remembered of that beautiful stranger. He told me in turn about his childhood at Lyon House and how he had been a mischievous, moody little boy who was always getting into trouble. I could not deny the fascination the man had for me. Every detail about his life seemed incredibly important to me. I was a little afraid of him.

Perhaps I was not so much afraid of him as I was afraid of myself. I had had absolutely no experience with men, and I was a little bewildered by my reactions to his presence. I was polite and cool and modest on the surface, the properly bred young woman, but within there was something that I did not think proper at all. I wished I could discuss it with Laverne or Mattie, but as it was I would have to fend for myself. I knew Edward Lyon was dangerous for me, and I knew I was not capable of coping with him if he chose to become attentive.

He was suave, sophisticated, a man of the world, handsome, well bred and formidably intelligent, for all that he had not done well at Oxford. He had the poise and polish of a man much older, while I was as green and inexperienced as it was possible to be. I had never had so much as a school girl crush on anyone, and if I was to be initiated into those mysteries of life that the chorus girls babbled so much about, it was far better that I choose a less adept instructor.

I thought of the mysterious woman Molly had mentioned. I tried to visualize her. She would be beautiful, worldly, a suitable match for the man. With women like that available to him, he would have little use for someone like me. I knew that. I knew that I was courting disaster when I thought about him in this way, but it was exciting. I might think my own thoughts, but I had sense enough not to let anyone else suspect them. I would continue to be polite and friendly with Edward Lyon, content to play the role of the child he must think of me as.

He came out of the house now, blinking a little at the sunlight and running his fingers through his thick auburn hair. He was wearing a suit of some light grey and white striped material and he carried a straw hat, suitable for canoeing. He put the hat on his head and sauntered towards me, his hands jammed in his pockets. His green tie was a little crooked and the hat was perched at a jaunty angle.

'Morning,' he said. 'Been up long?'

'For hours,' I said. 'Long before Corinne went for her ride. I saw her come in a while ago.'

'Incredible,' he cried.

'What?'

'That anyone can get up that early. I would lounge in bed half the morning if I thought Corinne would tolerate it. I'm lazy by nature, you know. The life of leisure—that's for me.'

'Then how do you explain rowing—and soccer at college?'

'Sports. That's play, not work.'

'You don't like work?'

'Does anyone?' he asked.

'I don't mind it,' I replied rather primly. Edward Lyon threw back his head and laughed. It was a rich sound. I blushed a little, feeling that he was mocking me. His dark brown eyes were full of good humour, and he flung his arm casually around my shoulder, walking with me down the path. I was uncomfortable, but I tried to appear unconcerned. I could smell the pungent smell of his shaving lotion and the weight of his arm on my shoulder made me awkward.

'You're a remarkable child,' he said. 'Refreshing. Corinne is going to fight me for your company. This sunlight is a bit much, isn't it? Blinding!'

'It's lovely,' I remarked.

'But not at this hour. Are you sure you don't want to postpone this canoe ride till the afternoon?'

'You promised,' I said, 'but—if you don't think you can manage—'

'Silly child. I can manage all right. I can canoe in a gale. Do you take me for a weakling?'

'Not exactly.'

'I was a champion pugilist in college. Won a couple of prizes. For a while I thought of doing it for a living—but a Lyon in boxing trunks! My ancestors would have turned over in their graves. Besides, it took a bit too much effort. Nevertheless, if anyone ever bothers you, just let me know and I'll flatten the villain with one mighty blow.'

'Wouldn't that take a bit too much effort, too?' I asked sweetly.

He chuckled. 'I suppose you think I'm disgraceful?'

'A little,' I admitted.

'Marvellous,' he said. 'Women always find the caddish type irresistible. Virtue is becoming only in women.'

'Then why are men so apt to seek the company of the unvirtuous women of the world?'

'La,' he said, still chuckling. 'There are things that aren't fit for such young ears.'

We had left the gardens behind and were walking down the flagstone path to the river. Trees grew on either side, their leaves dark green and rustling lightly in the breeze. We passed a little clearing with buttercups making bright yellow spots on the grass. An ancient gazebo stood in the middle of the clearing, the roof sagging, the white paint peeling a little from the sides. It must once have been lovely, but now it was boarded up, the planks nailed haphazardly over all the octagon sides. I asked Edward about it.

'I understand it was the favourite retreat of my grandmother,' he replied. 'There was some sort of accident there long ago. It was boarded up then and hasn't been used since.'

'It's rather isolated,' I remarked. 'It

must once have been a perfect place for a romantic tryst.'

I watched his reaction carefully. I had remembered that Molly said her friend saw Edward Lyon and the mysterious woman walking down to the gazebo, and I was deliberately baiting him. He merely smiled, not at all disturbed by the remark.

'Undoubtedly,' he replied. 'Probably was, too. Those ancestors of mine were a gamy bunch, despite the beards and stern expressions.'

We passed the clearing and the path curved around a group of trees. I could see the river now, the water very blue, sparkling with silver reflections. Willow trees grew thick on either side of the water, their graceful jade green leaves dripping down into it. There was a boathouse and a little pier. The canoe was already on the water, tied to the pier and bouncing on the slight waves. It looked terribly flimsy, and I was a little dubious about getting into it. Edward Lyon saw my apprehension and grinned.

'Nothing to be afraid of,' he said.

He took my hand and led me over the wooden pier. He helped me into the canoe, holding my hand firmly while the boat rocked under my feet. I was afraid I was going to pitch into the water.

'Steady,' he said. 'Careful there. Sit on those pillows. Relax. It looks shaky, but it won't tip over unless you make a sudden move.'

He climbed into the boat, moving rapidly and with assurance. The canoe rocked and the water splashed around us, but Edward Lyon merely laughed and unfastened the rope that held it to the pier. In a moment we were moving down the river. There was a basket of food in the middle of the canoe, with a checked tablecloth folded over it. I could see part of a loaf of bread and the top of a wine bottle sticking out.

'My idea,' he said. 'I thought we would stop somewhere on the way back and have a picnic lunch. We can cool the wine in the water.'

'How thoughtful,' I remarked.

'Oh, I'm thoughtful, too, as well as disgraceful.'

He looked up at me and grinned, and I smiled back at him. It was so peaceful on the river, and I was completely at ease now. The gentle motion of the canoe as it glided down the river and the steady sound of the paddle dipping into the water were relaxing, and all disturbing thoughts were banished. Edward Lyon paddled steadily and skilfully. I could see the muscles working under his suit, and I knew that it was hard work, but he seemed to be using no effort at all. He was completely relaxed, his lips resting in a slight grin, the white straw hat slanted rakishly over his head.

I lay back on the cushions, looking up at the patches of sky visible through the branches of the trees. We drifted under willow trees and the long leaves parted for us and stroked the canoe like strands of soft jade cloth. The bank was shady, frequently covered with dark green moss and slick brown mud. The silver sunbursts in the middle of the river were blindingly bright, and when the canoe passed over them they shattered and caused the water to shimmer with silver shavings. There was no sound but the dip and splash of the paddle, steady and monotonous, and the frequent cry of a bird in a thicket.

'What are you thinking?' he asked.

'How very peaceful this is. Not at all like London.'

'London isn't very peaceful, is it?'

'Not at all, but I love it.'

'Then why did you leave it?' he inquired.

'It wasn't my decision.'

'Oh? It does seem strange. I understand your puppet act was one of the primary attractions at the music hall. It seems odd that your guardian would send you off.'

'Bert and Sarah will fill my spot. They're old favourites.'

'Do you miss them all already?'

'A little, but I'm happy to be here on the river.'

'I'm happy you're here, too. Their loss is my gain. I won't let them have you back for a while. You can consider yourself my captive at Lyon House. Try to get away and you'll have me to reckon with.'

'Then I suppose I must enjoy my captivity,' I said idly.

'That's the attitude, lass. Don't give me a hard time and we'll do fine. I'm mean when crossed.'

'I can't visualize you being mean under any circumstances,' I told him.

'Oh, I can wield a whip with the best of them. Give me a dark cape and waxed moustache and I'd be a proper villain, terrorizing widows and throttling defenceless maidens.'

'You seem to be a man of many facets.'

143

'Keep them guessing. That's my motto.'

He pulled the paddle in and let the canoe drift with the current. We passed under a stone bridge, those in the water stained with moss. A long shadow fell across the water. I dangled my hand over the side of the canoe. The water was icy cold, although the sun was warm. Insects darted across the surface of the water, skimming on gauzy wings. The sun felt good on my cheeks.

'I hope your aunt didn't mind us going off like this,' I said.

'Corinne is jealous, but she'll get over it. She feels mistreated. She loves to sulk almost as much as she loves to rage.'

'Will she really mind?'

'Of course not. She wants you to enjoy yourself.'

'She seemed so upset yesterday,' I said.

'Corinne had one of her bad days yesterday,' Edward said. 'Unfortunate for you, it being your first day at Lyon House, but don't let it bother you. She has them frequently, but they pass, like storms. She is always in such a better mood afterwards. She'll probably be all charm and politeness today.'

'I understand,' I replied. 'I think she's endearing.'

'That's an odd word to apply to my dear aunt.'

'She's different from anyone I've ever met.'

'That she is.'

'I think I am going to like her. She and Mrs Crandall had a really bad scene yesterday, though. I thought they were going to tear each other apart.'

Edward Lyon frowned, his dark brows pressing together and his eyes growing dark. 'Agatha is bad for Corinne,' he said. 'They're very much alike, in some ways, both old, both self-willed. But whereas Corinne is hot tempered and boiling over, Agatha is sly and stealthy. I wouldn't have too much to do with her if I were you, Julia.'

'I felt sorry for her,' I remarked.

'Agatha? Don't fool yourself.' His voice was sombre.

'If they fight so much, why doesn't Corinne send her away?'

He shrugged his shoulders and looked at me with extended palms. 'It puzzles me,' he said, his tone lighter now. He grinned. 'I think Corinne keeps her on just to have a scrapping partner. The others are very expendable, you know, the regular servants. One of her tantrums, and they pack up and leave, but Agatha stays on for another round. They both love a good fight. The eccentricities of the old—' he laughed, and I was relieved to see the good humour coming back.

The canoe drifted on down the river. We passed under another bridge and soon the river grew much wider. The willow trees were scarcer, and I began to see fields. They extended away from the bank in levels, brown and golden-brown and sometimes green. On the horizon there were oxen and men pushing ploughs, and sometimes cows came down to the bank of the river to drink. Soon there was nothing but the sky about us, and the currents were stronger. Edward Lyon took up the paddle again, working strenuously but without apparent effort. Around a bend, far ahead, I could see the village. The trees and spires and rooftops looked very small.

'Does the river pass right through the village?' I asked.

'Yes. It narrows again, then goes right past the church and the inn and the post office, behind them. The inn has a terrace in back so the guests can sit at tables and watch the river traffic. There isn't much of that today, but sometimes there are dozens of boats. The fishermen go out almost every day. The river leads out to the sea.'

We came closer and closer, and the river grew narrower. We began to pass houses and trees, and soon we passed under a great stone bridge. A little boy sat perched on it, dangling a fishing pole into the water. We were in the village now, and there were several other boats. I watched the people moving down the shady riverbank sidewalks. An old man worked on an ancient grey fishing net extended over poles, mending the tears. A woman pushed a vegetable cart heaped with carrots and beets. The houses were backed against the river, and some of them had yards that came down to the concrete bank. I saw rear windows and sometimes lines of wash. It was a curiously intimate view of the village.

There was more traffic on the river now, several fishing boats going downstream. There was a sailboat with a faded blue sail and a large, flat barge loaded with fish. We heard the shouts and cries of vendors.

'I love rivers,' I said, watching the activity. 'When I was a little girl I used to love to sit on the banks of the Thames and watch the barges go past. It was endlessly fascinating.'

'The Thames this isn't,' he replied, smiling at me.

'Look, there's the inn,' I said.

The terrace came right down to the edge of the river, paved in flat red tiles, with a railing at the bank. There was a huge oak tree in the middle, its large limbs spreading shade over the dozen or so tables that set outside. Several people were drinking beer, and a plump waiter in a soiled white apron was removing empty steins from a table. A woman with two small children sat sipping tea while the children nibbled cakes, and an ugly man with enormous shoulders and a broken nose sat sullenly with a companion who was hidden behind a newspaper. One of the children waved at me, and I waved back, smiling.

Edward Lyon looked in that direction. The lines of his mouth suddenly grew very harsh, and his dark eyes looked flat, hard. He steered the canoe quickly to the bank, where the concrete wall would conceal it from the people at the inn. I thought his face was pale now, and I was about to ask him what was wrong when he spoke.

'I think we should go back now,' he said flatly.

'But—whatever for?' I was bewildered by his sudden change.

'Don't ask questions,' he said sharply.

He turned the canoe around and began to paddle in the direction that we had just come. I could see the effort now. He seemed to be straining with the paddle. The muscles bulged beneath his suit, and he paused to take off his jacket. I was frowning, but he took no notice of me. He was intent on getting away from the village.

We were silent. We passed under the bridge where the little boy was fishing. Two small companions had joined him now, and they waved at us. I did not wave back, and Edward Lyon had not even seen the children. I watched the village grow smaller and smaller as we left it behind. We had reached the wide part now, and soon we were around the bend and the village was out of sight. Only then did Edward Lyon relax.

He looked tired. His forehead was moist, and there were perspiration stains on his shirt. He brought the paddle in and let the canoe drift. He took a handkerchief from his pocket and mopped his forehead. He looked at me for a long time, still not speaking. The canoe drifted through a bed of water lilies, pink and white flowers resting on flat green pads. He reached into the water and plucked one of the flowers. He handed it to me with a nod of the head. 'For you,' he said.

'Thank you,' I said, a bit too prim.

'I suppose you wonder what that was all about?'

'I'm sure you had your reasons,' I replied.

'Yes, I had my reasons.'

I stroked the wet blossom, not looking at him.

'You're not going to ask any questions?'

'I think not.'

'Good. You're learning fast. Would you like to pull up here and have our picnic?'

'No, I—I think I'd rather go back,' I said, feeling like a sulky child.

'I'm not in much of a mood for a picnic myself. We'll head for home.'

He paddled steadily, and soon the willow

leaves were touching our arms again. Dragonflies darted around the canoe, and once a fish jumped up right in front of us. We arrived at the boathouse and he helped me up onto the pier. We were walking towards the gardens before he spoke again.

'You are not ever to go to the village alone,' he said. 'Not under any circumstances. Do you understand?'

I looked up at his face. His eyes were very serious and his mouth was grim. I nodded meekly. I did not ask questions. I was learning.

CHAPTER 9

I could not understand his strange conduct. At lunch he was casual, all charm and pleasantness, and he talked about our trip down the river as if nothing had happened to terminate it so abruptly. I tried to find some clue in his conversation. There was none. It was clear that he did not intend to mention the incident again. He began to talk about the forthcoming fair and tried to get Corinne to show some interest in going herself. She merely snorted and peeled her peach, calling him a fool. Edward Lyon teased her a little more and then asked to be excused. He spent the rest of the afternoon in his rooms.

Corinne was in a better mood today. After lunch she insisted on taking me to the gallery and showing me all the family portraits. We walked down a long hall paved in black and white marble, the walls covered alternately with faded red velvet draperies and immense paintings of Lyons. The hall was cool and draughty, and our footsteps sounded noisily on the marble floor. Corinne pointed to each portrait in its heavily ornate gold frame and made some comment about that particular ancestor. Her remarks were wicked and witty, and once or twice she revealed a particularly salty anecdote which brought a blush to my cheeks.

The men were all sober and very stern, usually with heavy beards. I noticed the dark eyes Edward Lyon had inherited, but not one of his ancestors seemed to have his jaunty attitude. The women were tepid, only one with Corinne's blazing red hair. At the end of the gallery there was a blank space, the wall a little yellowed where a portrait had once hung. I asked Corinne about it.

'Can't you guess?' she replied.

'Your portrait hung there?' I said hesitantly.

'Of course. I had it removed! I didn't want that beautiful face on display, haunting me, taunting me. I relegated it to the attic. I wanted to burn it but, after all, it was painted by a master!'

'I would like to see it,' I remarked.

'What! And make comparisons? Not on your life!'

'That's foolish,' I said, rather rudely.

'You can talk. You are young, and quite lovely.'

'Is youth and beauty everything?'

'You'd be surprised,' she snapped, peeved.

'I'd hate to think my life was over just because I lost my youth and whatever beauty I might have possessed,' I told her.

'You think my life is over?' Corinne Lyon cried.

'No,' I replied politely. 'You seem to be the one who thinks that, Mrs Lyon.'

She tapped her foot on the marble and

looked at me with a crooked smile on her heavily painted lips. Her cheeks were chalky with powder, a bright red spot of rouge rubbed into each, her lids coated with blue-grey shadow. Her make up was that of a character actress who is to play a roguish countess or a tipsy old dame, I thought. Corinne wore a robe of shiny grey velvet, trimmed with dyed blue fur. She toyed with a grey fan snapping it open and shut.

'You're a cheeky child,' she said. She seemed to be amused.

'I'm sorry.'

'Don't be. At last I've got someone who can give as well as take in a tussle. I'm tired now,' she said abruptly. 'You may escort me to my room. I'll nap till dinner time.'

We walked slowly upstairs. Corinne ran one gloved finger along the railing of the staircase, and when she found the glove tip covered with dust, she railed at a servant who was coming downstairs with an armload of linen. The poor girl, gauche and raw boned, looked panic stricken. I was slightly embarrassed, but Corinne chuckled wickedly as the girl fled down the stairs.

'Now tell me about your trip,' she said as we walked along the hall to her room. 'Did you enjoy it?'

'Very much. The river was lovely.'

'I suppose Edward was up to form?'

'What do you mean by that?'

'Tosh! A girl your age should know. The man's a scoundrel. He is my nephew, but I know him for what he is. Don't go letting him put ideas in your head.'

'He was a proper gentleman, very polite.'

'That must have been disappointing!'

'Why—' I stammered.

'When I was your age if a man took me on a canoe ride and acted like a proper gentleman I would have been furious!'

'Well, I'm sure Mr Lyon had no intention—'

'He's a man, isn't he?'

'I'm sure he thinks I'm a child.'

'Good! Perhaps Edward has a little sense, after all, but I wouldn't trust any Lyon as far as I could spit. My nephew has all their bad qualities—and then some.'

'Besides,' I continued, 'I'm sure Mr Lyon has someone else he is—is interested in.'

'That's a modest way of putting it,' she said.

'Does he?' I asked, ashamed of the question.

We stopped in front of the door to her room. She opened it and stood in the doorway, regarding me with a curious expression, her head held a little to one side. Her eyes danced with mischief, and I felt uncomfortable. I think she guessed a great deal from my demeanour, and the old lady seemed to be delighted when a blush stole up my cheeks.

'I wouldn't be surprised if he does,' she said waggishly. 'The servants talk, and I'm not exactly deaf. No, I wouldn't be surprised if he does.'

With this enigmatic statement she whirled into her room and shut the door behind her. I stood in the hall for a while, wondering exactly what she meant. Had Corinne heard talk about the mysterious woman who came to Lyon House? I wondered. I shook my head, thoroughly irritated with myself. It could not conceivably matter to me if Edward Lyon had a mistress who stole in to see him under cover of darkness. It wasn't my concern at all and I tried to tell myself that I couldn't care less about the matter.

I felt very much alone. It was late

afternoon, and the house was still. Corinne and Edward and Agatha Crandall were all in their rooms, and the servants were busy with their various tasks. I wandered through the rooms, unable to explain my strange restlessness. I touched cool surfaces of furniture, examined objects, strolled through room after room and tried to banish the feeling that possessed me.

It seemed as though everyone in the house was waiting for something. Even the house itself seemed to be waiting, and the stillness now was the curious stillness before a storm, a stillness heavy with foreboding. Perhaps that explained the strange moods, the outbursts of temper, the display of nerves. Agatha Crandall with her alcohol and her secretive manner, Corinne with her flashing temper and moments of sadness, Edward Lyon and his bewildering conduct this morning: all seemed indicative of something hanging over this place. I felt it, too; it was almost tangible. I hurried outside, hoping the sunshine and fresh air would rid me of this mood.

In back of the house there was a shaded porch and a small drive that tradesmen used when making deliveries. A path led through vegetable gardens down to the smoke house, and beyond that was a wooded area that led down to the gazebo. I walked away from the house, moving quickly as if in flight from the melancholy that had threatened to overcome me. I would not give in to that feeling. I would not be sad. I would not pine for London and Mattie and the music hall and the life I had loved so much. It would only make things worse.

There was a stillness outside, too. The sky was grey now, and the sun slowly sank, leaving a misty trail of violet shadows in its wake. No wind rustled the leaves of the trees. It was as though the whole world was holding its breath. I walked past the vegetable gardens, past the smoke house, was soon in the woods. I could hear the water running along the riverbank and smell the crushed milkweed. The stillness, the silence, unbroken by bird or breeze, was vaguely unnerving. I could hear my own footsteps crushing the dead leaves and acorns underfoot. I wanted to cry out, to shatter the silence.

I stopped and leaned against the trunk of a tree. To my surprise, I was breathing heavily, as though I had indeed been pursued. It was foolish to have worked myself up into such a state, and for no reason, I told myself, and yet I had the curious sensation that there *was* a reason. It was not clear, but it was there. I closed my eyes, trying to relax. I felt the rough bark of the tree against my back. I felt the woods all around me, smelled the soil and the sap, and after a few moments I was ready to laugh at myself and run back to the house and get ready for dinner. Then I heard the woodpecker.

It was coming from somewhere near the gazebo, making quite a lot of noise. I decided to go see if I could spy it. I loved birds. Back in London I had a portfolio filled with coloured pictures of various kinds. I had never seen a woodpecker before, and it would be exciting to see one now. I hurried towards the sound, trying to move quietly so as not to frighten the bird away. Through the branches of the trees ahead I could see the top of the gazebo. The noise was louder, and I suddenly realized that it was no bird at all.

Edward Lyon was standing beside the gazebo, a hammer in his hand. He was nailing a board back in place, and when he finished he flexed his shoulders and stood back. He gave the last nail a final bang and then put the hammer down, sighing. I wondered why he hadn't had a servant attend to the job. He turned around and saw me. He looked startled, then guilty, as though he had been caught in some mischief. He shifted position as I approached him, wiping his forehead with the back of his hand.

'What are you doing here?' he asked. His voice was not friendly.

'Just—strolling. I thought you were a woodpecker.'

He arched a brow.

'I heard the hammering,' I explained. 'I thought it was a woodpecker at work. I see I was mistaken.'

'I noticed this morning that one of the boards was loose,' he said. 'I thought I'd better come down and fix it.'

I thought this quite strange. Edward did not strike me as the kind of man who would be bothered by a loose board on a deserted gazebo. He stood with his legs wide apart, his palms resting loosely on his hips, watching me with rather belligerent eyes. I had the absurd impression that he had actually been inside the gazebo, had come out and was boarding it back up. For some reason he reminded me of a dog who was guarding a bone, and I wanted to laugh.

'Can't depend on the servants to take care of these things,' he continued. His voice was pleasant now, and he seemed to relax. He rubbed his palms against his thighs and smiled at me. He stepped away from the gazebo and came towards me. I watched him with curious eyes.

'I—I thought you were still in your room,' I said. 'I didn't hear you leave the house.'

'Oh, I left around four. Had to go to one of the tenant farms, look at the bull that's going to win the blue ribbon for me at the fair. Then I remembered the loose board—'

'I see.'

'Do you always keep track of people?' he asked quietly.

'I'm afraid I don't know what you mean.'

'You don't? No—I suppose you wouldn't. I must remember that you are eighteen years old and quite unsophisticated.'

'Please do,' I said icily.

He grinned pleasantly, all the charm

returning. I was determined to resist the charm. He seemed to be aware of the resistance, and the grin widened on his lips. He flung an arm casually about my shoulders and led me along the path, away from the gazebo.

'Don't take things so hard,' he said. 'We're a strange lot, all of us around here. Myself included. It takes a little time to get used to us.'

'Really?'

'Indeed, yes. Come now, don't pout.'

'Why should I pout?'

'I'm afraid our picnic this morning wasn't exactly what it started out to be,' he said. 'I'm sorry about that. You must have thought me an absolute ass—acting the way I did. I've been a little on edge today. You must forgive me.'

'There is nothing to forgive,' I replied.

'You must give me a chance to make amends,' he said.

'Please don't give it a second thought.' My voice was very cool.

He laughed softly to himself.

'Temper, temper,' he said. 'Don't turn sarcastic on me. That would be more than I could bear. Come—let's go back to the house. Perhaps we will go on our picnic soon.'

'You needn't try to humour me,' I said stiffly. 'I'm not a child, so please don't treat me like one.'

'I wouldn't dream of it,' Edward said, chuckling. 'Believe me, that's the last thing in the world I'd think of doing.'

I sat before the mirror, nervously twisting a curl around my finger. My eyes were very dark blue now, and they seemed to be the eyes of a stranger. I wondered what was happening to me. What had become of the little girl with the puppets? I was afraid, but it was not a tangible fear, like the fear I had felt when I was followed in the fog. It went much deeper, and I felt it had become a permanent part of me. I was a different person, and I did not like the change.

I tried to compose myself. In a few moments I would have to go down to dinner. I would have to smile and be gracious and play my part well. I applied tiny spots of rouge to my high cheek bones and rubbed the colour in until there was the merest hint of flush. The soft grey shadows surrounded my eyes, making them seem all the larger, more pensive. I began to brush my hair.

Molly came into the room and gave me a jolly curtsey. I was very glad to see her and managed a smile.

'What a lovely dress!' she exclaimed. 'It's the colour of rose petals. Suits you dandy, it does. Makes your skin glow.'

'Thank you, Molly.'

'I came to help you get dressed. See you've already done it. Can I help you with anything else, Miss Julia?'

'Not at the moment. I'm almost ready to go down.'

Molly began to gather up the clothes I had taken off earlier. 'Did you have a nice time with Mr Edward this morning?' she asked.

'It was very nice,' I replied.

'I noticed you didn't eat the picnic lunch. Cook was furious. Mr Edward came into the kitchen early, and gave her instructions on just what to pack, and her in the middle of breakfast preparations. Didn't you feel like eatin'?'

'We decided to come back early,' I replied.

'Oh,' Molly said.

She smiled impudently and folded the clothes. She was determined to have a romance, and any remark I made she would interpret to suit her own fancy. I was irritated. I finished doing my hair and stood up. The rose coloured skirts rustled as I walked across the room.

'Did you hear what happened at the village this morning?' she asked.

'No. I'm in a hurry, Molly, and—'

'Great fuss. A couple of ugly lookin' customers took rooms at the inn and started makin' their presence felt. They're from London and have come down on some kind of business, they say. One of them picked a fight with Anson Ross—he's the lorry driver and strong as an ox. The stranger knocked him downstairs. There was the biggest commotion, and Anson left with a bloody nose and all kinds of bruises. The innkeeer threatened to throw the men out, but they gave him some money and he shut up about it. They seem to have a lot of money. Bertie saw 'em, says they look like thugs, real thugs.'

'What kind of business are the men here for?' I inquired.

'Something to do with land. They're scoutin' around for land, want to buy some for a client in London, they say. Bertie says he's seen land agents before, and he don't believe for a minute these men are what they claim to be.'

I made no comment. I stood with my hand resting on the door frame, suddenly very interested in Molly's chatter.

'Funniest thing—' she said, her voice full of curiosity. 'The men were askin' questions about Mr Edward and the old lady, wanted to know where Lyon House was and how long the old lady had been here, things like that. Strange, isn't it?'

'Not necessarily,' I replied.

I turned my face away, afraid it might betray me. I did not want her to see the effect her words had on me. I tried to appear very casual, as if I found nothing at all disturbing in what she told me.

'If you want to know what I think, I think they're not land agents at all,' Molly continued. 'I think they're lookin' for Mr Edward. Maybe he owes some gamblin' debts in London and they've come to collect 'em. Mr Edward was always gettin' into debt, they say, and the old lady was always scoldin' him about it and refusin' to give him any money.'

'Perhaps you're right,' I said quietly.

'Or maybe it involves that woman—you know, the one I told you about. Maybe one of the men in the village is a jealous lover, come to challenge Mr Edward to a duel or horsewhip him or something. It's ever so excitin'!'

'Now, Molly—' I said.

'Don't you think we should warn Mr Edward?'

'I wouldn't say anything, Molly.'

'But—'

'It probably amounts to nothing. The men are probably what they say. Anyway, even if they're not, Mr Lyon can handle any situation that might occur.'

'Do you really think so?'

'Of course.'

'They might come to Lyon House,' she said, obviously delighted with the idea.

'I doubt it,' I replied, my voice very calm and logical. 'I must go down to dinner now. Don't say anything about this, Molly. It might disturb Mrs Lyon. Let's just keep it to ourselves.'

'Oh, I won't breathe a word, Miss Julia. I promise.'

I left the room and walked down the hall, pausing at the top of the stairs. The house was shadowy now, and I had the feeling that something was closing in on me. It was an absurd feeling, but it was so strong that I glanced over my shoulder at the dim recesses behind me. I was a young woman in a rose coloured gown, going to have dinner with an eccentric old woman and her charming nephew in a lovely old home, and it was nonsense to have this feeling, but I had it just the same. It followed me as I started slowly down the staircase.

It was very late, but I could not sleep. The French windows were open, and a strong breeze billowed the draperies into the room. They made a flapping noise, the stiff material rustling. The moon was full, and clouds drifted across its face, causing my room to be alternately filled with mellow silver light and drifting shadows. I did not even try to sleep. I knew it would be impossible.

Agatha Crandall had joined us for dinner tonight. She had been cheerful and bright consuming great quantities of wine, but there was an edge of malice to her every comment, and she watched Corinne and Edward with amusement that she did not try to conceal. It was almost as though she knew that they were in some kind of trouble and enjoyed watching them squirm. Her talk had gradually begun to slur as she drank more and more, and she finally lapsed into silence, a smile on her thin lips.

Edward tried to be pleasant and gallant, but he was upset about something and his efforts to charm had a hollow quality as though he were performing for my benefit. Corinne stared moodily at her plate, toying with her food. Occasionally she lashed out at Agatha, but that seemed to tire her. I wondered if they had all somehow heard about the men in the village and that was the reason for this conduct. It was more likely that Edward had seen them this morning. That would explain why he had turned the canoe around so abruptly and headed back to Lyon House.

I was trying to remember something now. There was something I had seen or heard that had some connection with all this, but I could not recall what it was. It was there in the back of my mind, taunting me, and I knew that it had a bearing on what had happened. I tormented myself, trying to cast back in my mind and bring it to surface. It was connected with London and the music hall, and I kept seeing Bert Clemmons' face and hearing his slurred voice, but the words were not clear.

I got out of bed and put on my robe. I did not turn on a lamp for I did not want anyone to know of my sleeplessness and possibly guess the reasons for it. I walked over to the French windows and stepped out on the balcony. The marble was cold to my bare feet, but I did not go back in for my slippers. I leaned on the railing, the breeze blowing my hair away from my temples. The air was fresh and clean. I breathed deeply, trying to clear my mind of everything. I could hear the wind in the trees and the noise of the crickets in the garden. I stood there for a long time.

I remembered.

Bert had been drinking at Finnigan's Bar. He had met two men who had bought drinks for him and asked him questions. They had asked about my sister Maureen and wanted to know if I ever saw her. They had asked if Maureen ever sent me any money. Bert had described the men, one with a broken nose and enormous shoulders, the other thin and tall with blond hair and grey eyes. I was sure that those were the two men in the village.

They had been at a table behind the inn

this morning. I remembered the man with the large shoulders and crooked nose. The other man had been reading a newspaper, his face concealed. Edward had seen them, too, had noticed them when I waved to the child. That was when he had turned the canoe about so suddenly. How had he known them? What connection did he have with them? He had warned me never to go to the village alone, and I was sure that was the reason why.

I felt a chill, not caused by the cold marble or the breeze blowing across my cheeks. It was caused by something else, something dark and mysterious and threatening. The two men had been in London. They had asked about me, about my sister. Now they were in Devonshire. They had asked about Corinne and Edward Lyon. They had asked how to get here. They intended to do something, and somehow or other I was involved.

Clouds passed over the moon and there was darkness, and then there was a rift in the clouds and moonlight spilled over the ragged edges, flooding the gardens with misty silver. It picked out the winding white path, stroked the petals of the roses, gilded the tops of the shrubs. The boughs of the trees were very dark, black arms reaching up to touch the silver. The beauty of the night was no comfort to me.

I remembered Mattie's voice that night when I had listened at the door. I remembered her words: 'Lyon House is the only answer,' and then, 'She will be safe there for the time being.' I had been sent away because something had threatened me, and now it seemed that it had followed me here. I did not know what it was. I only knew that I was a pawn in some affair that involved Lyon House and the people who lived here and, perhaps the sister I had not seen for eight years. There was another man involved too, the man who had followed me to the music hall under cover of fog and then, incongruously enough, came in to watch my act every night. Where did he fit in? What was it all about?

The moon was obscured by clouds again.

I could not afford hysterics. I had to be calm. I had to wait, just as the others were waiting. Lyon House was not a haven after all.

CHAPTER 10

Three days passed, and there was no sign that the men in the village had sinister intentions. They had gone out with surveyor's tools and looked at several tracts of land, Molly reported, and yesterday they had gone, paying the innkeeper and leaving the village. However they had not left Devonshire, Molly insisted—they were still in the vicinity. They had been seen going down the road, and one of the farmers reported seeing them crossing a field. Molly claimed that they had moved to a spot where they would attract less attention, and she waited with excitement for the inevitable drama she expected to occur any day now. I was less sure about it. Perhaps I had been wrong about them. Perhaps they were really land surveyors after all. It was easy enough to invent shadows, I thought, particularly when one was upset.

Edward Lyon was quite busy, coming and going. He was inspecting the tenants farms, he claimed, and he smiled half humorously as he told me about the cows and manure and barns and fields, picturing himself among them. It was hardly the proper background for a man of his tastes, but he shrugged his shoulders and mentioned the call to duty and came in all dirty and sweaty, dust on his boots, his hair disarrayed, a wry smile on his lips. He hoped to sell some livestock at the fair, and most of the tenant farmers would have stalls there to sell their produce. He was pleasant and charming, and if he had been sober and serious that morning as we came back in the canoe, there were no signs of it now.

Agatha Crandall kept to her room most of the day. She did not come down for meals with the family. I was walking down the hall to my room one night and she opened her door, peering out at me. Her eyes were frightened, and she seemed tense as she clung to the door and stared at me. Then she put her finger to her lips as though in warning and shook her head. I could smell the fumes of alcohol wafting from her room. As I walked on down the hall I thought I heard her laughing, but I had the strange feeling that the sound

174

was not laughter at all. It could have been sobbing. She was obviously in an alcoholic stupor.

Corinne was tense and irritable, pacing through the rooms, looking out of windows, snapping at everyone who came near her. She did not go out at all, except for her habitual ride, and I had the feeling that her self-imposed confinement was taking its toll on her nerves. Lyon House might have been a prison for her, however luxurious, and she paced like an animal longing for freedom but afraid to step outside. One day a servant girl dropped a tray on the way to the dining room, and Corinne flew into such a rage at the sound of the crash that I feared she would have a stroke. She dismissed the girl on the spot, despite floods of tears and wails of apology, and when the girl left, carrying a battered suitcase, Corinne stared at her as though she actually hated the poor creature. That night she sat in the parlour, sulking silently, and I knew the dismissal of the servant had merely been a way to release tension caused by something else that seemed to preoccupy her mind all day long. She was pleasant to me, but I stayed away from her most of the time.

I spent much of the time in the library. The days were cool and cloudy, and the library was comfortable and warm. I found a stack of battered romances, their bindings limp, their pages thumb marked, and I read for hours on end, curled up on the sofa, an apple in my hand. I escaped into the world of lovely damsels and dashing soldiers of fortune and castles with moats and towers. After I had finished the novels, I found a fascinating book on botany with large coloured engravings. I had always been interested in flowers and leaves, and I jotted down notes on various specimens to be found in this area. The fourth day after our canoe ride to the village was sunny and warm, and I decided to go out and look for plants. I would take my sketchbook and watercolours and perhaps even paint some of the things I found.

Corinne was delighted with the idea. She was impressed by the notebook and nodded with approval as I described what I had learned from the botany book.

'Marvellous!' she cried. 'It seems you have a thirst for knowledge and learning. That's so much better for you than reading all those novels. I want you to learn a lot of things and be very bright. Did you go to school?'

'Occasionally,' I replied. 'Mattie and Bill couldn't always afford it.'

'Bosh! Didn't that sister of yours send you money?'

'Sometimes. Not enough for schooling.'

'Did you like school when you went?'

'I adored it,' I admitted.

'Well, I'm fond of you, child. When you go back to London, I shall see to it that you're enrolled in the best school for young ladies. All that music hall business can't be good for you. You've got breeding. It shows. We want to develop it!'

'That's very kind of you,' I said politely, 'but—'

'No buts! Why must everyone argue with me?'

Her voice was crisp, almost irritable, but she looked up at me with an expression of real concern in her eyes. Why should Corinne Lyon care about me? I wondered. The raging dragon who had sent the servant girl off in haste wanted to pay my expenses at school. Why? I supposed the rich and eccentric had their whims, and this must be a sudden whim. She must have sensed what I was thinking,

177

for she snapped hatefully and told me to go on about my business. Was the dreadful temper and disposition as much a prison as the house, I wondered? Did it imprison a Corinne who was really thoughtful and kind?

There was no room for these thoughts as I raced outside. I was too happy at being out in the sunshine and roaming over the countryside to give much serious thought to anything. I wore a pink and white dress and my hair flew free behind me, catching in brambles. The dress was soon splattered with mud and torn, but I did not care. After being confined in the house for three days, it was glorious to be in the fresh air, to feel young and healthy and so alive to everything about me. I was amazed at the watery blue of the sky, the delicate veins in a green leaf, the lichen that clung to the bark of a tree. I ran through the woods like a young cat, heedless of decorum and propriety. It was as if I had just been released from a prison of my own and was savouring the new freedom I felt.

I sat down on the bank of the river, out of breath. I was rather ashamed of my abandon, but I felt alive with every fibre. I could feel muscle pulling and blood coursing and life charging through me. It was a rare feeling, something I had seldom felt before. Perhaps it was relief after the tedious days inside. Perhaps it was merely youth. I took out my sketchbook and began to draw the fern that grew along the sandy white bank. I leaned back against an old log, my shoes off, my toes in the warm sand. The first drawing was not satisfactory, and I started a new one, peering carefully at the fern and then carefully copying it on the coarse paper. Birds fluttered through the branches of the trees and the water gurgled pleasantly as it flowed over pebbles. Insects buzzed, darting across the rays of sunlight that slanted through the trees.

I looked through my notes, identified the fern and wrote its name beneath the completed drawing. The spot was idyllic and charming, and I was loathe to leave it, but I wanted to find another specimen to sketch. I would show them proudly to Corinne, and I knew they would please her. I smiled as I thought about what she had said this morning. It would be nice to go to school, to really learn about history and math and all the things I was so ignorant of, but it was, after all, probably just a whim of hers, one she would quickly forget. Still, it had been nice of her to even mention it.

I strolled through the woods, calmer now, a little tired from my earlier enthusiasm. I saw a rock in a clearing, a ray of yellow sunlight beaming down directly on it. A tiny green grass snake curled at its base as though warming itself in the heat. I saw aspen trees with tremulous leaves that fluttered in the slight breeze, and elm and maple and oak. I collected leaves from each of them and pressed them in my book. I saw tall sunflowers growing directly behind a fence that enclosed one of the fields, their large brown centres surrounded by vividly gold petals. It was pleasant to see a flower and not know what it was, to look it up in my notes and identify it.

I spent three hours in this manner, wandering around the woods and crossing the fields that were worked by the tenant farmers. I crossed a brook, stepping carefully from one stone to another, the water splashing over my bare feet, my shoes held high in my hand. I climbed over a weathered grey stile and found myself in the middle of the apple orchard that Edward had pointed out the day I arrived in Devonshire. The trees spread heavily laden branches, the fruit green but turning rose coloured. The ground beneath was shady and moist, covered with dead leaves. There was the heady odour of rotting fruit. Bees buzzed around apples fallen the year before and not gathered, brown and sour now. I pulled a green apple from a branch and bit into it. It was tart and sour but I ate it just the same. My fingers were soon stained with the juices, and I ate two more, sitting on the stile with my sketchbook in my lap.

I drew an apple tree, looking up now and then to get the right detail of branch and leaf, munching on the green apples as I drew. I was not pleased with the finished product, so I drew a single leaf, trying to make the veins identical to those in the leaf I held in my hand as an example. I was absorbed in my work and did not hear footsteps approaching. I was not aware of anyone near until a long shadow fell across the paper.

I looked up, startled. I saw the man and recognized him immediately. I identified him from the thin pink scar that ran from cheekbone to chin. He was the man who had followed me in the fog, I was sure, the same man I had seen in the music hall, sitting at one of the front tables. He did not wear a checked cloak now. He wore a loose white shirt and a pair of doeskin breeches that were stuffed into the tops of tall black boots that had turned-back cuffs, the kind of boots I had always fancied pirates would wear. He looked something like a pirate with his sharp nose, the darkly tanned skin stretched tightly over the bony face, the line of pink scar making a severe contrast.

My first impulse was to run. I stared at him, too frightened to even move. He stood with his hands on his hips, looking at me with dark brown eyes that were almost black. They were intense eyes, burning darkly. He was very tall, taller than Edward Lyon, with a thin, lanky body that was nevertheless muscular and strong. He would be lithe and rapid, steely in combat, I thought.

'Who—who are you?' I asked, finally

managing to speak. My voice trembled, and I had to hold my sketchbook tightly in my hands to keep them from shaking.

'I am Philip Ashley,' he replied. His voice was coarse and guttural, a harsh voice that was strangely appealing. A buccaneer's voice, I thought to myself. 'What are you doing in my apple orchard?'

'*Your* apple orchard?'

'I've just rented the Dower House. The apple orchard goes with it. I suppose that makes it mine, as long as I pay my rent.'

'You—you live here?'

'For the time being,' he retorted sharply. 'You haven't answered my question, young woman. Who are you?'

I knew very well that he knew who I was. I started to blurt that out, to accuse him of following me in London, of spying on me, but something held me back. A curious calm came over me. I was no longer afraid. I was merely fascinated, as one might be fascinated by a deadly snake. This man evidently wished to pretend he didn't know me. I could pretend as well. I could be innocent and naive, and perhaps I could learn what this was all about. It might be a dangerous game, but I threw caution aside and looked up at him with large blue eyes.

'I am Julia Meredith,' I replied. 'I am staying at Lyon House. This used to be part of the estate. I didn't know anyone was living here, or I wouldn't have trespassed.'

He scowled, looking at me with fierce eyes. There was nothing soft or pleasant about Philip Ashley. He was not at all handsome—that was not the word one would use to describe him. Tall, rangy, with long legs and arms and thin shoulders that jutted out beneath the loose folds of linen, there was something fascinating about him. I could not visualize him in a parlour; he would not fit. He would look at home on the deck of a pirate ship, cutlass in hand, or in front of an army, leading his men on to slaughter. He looked as if he wanted to slaughter me now, and I drew back on the stile.

'Don't look that way,' he growled.

'What way?'

'As though I were going to throttle you just because you stole some apples.'

I looked down guiltily at the apples cores on the step beside me. He saw the look and laughed. The laughter had the same quality as his voice, harsh, guttural, ugly yet appealing. The man had great force of character; it emanated from him in overpowering waves. No one would ever be unaware of him. I regarded him now. He was no longer a shadowy figure in the fog. He was no longer the mysterious man who came to the music hall each night to see my performance. He was a man of flesh and blood, and as such he was less terrifying, although I felt a tremor as he fixed his eye on me and arched one dark brow.

'What's that you have?' he asked.

'My sketchbook. I've been sketching plants.'

'Hand it to me.' It was a command, and I held the sketchbook out to him. He flipped through the pages, examining my work. His thin lips curled up at one corner, wryly. He arched his brow again and handed the book back to me.

'Abominable!' he said.

'Thank you,' I replied crisply.

'Have you ever drawn before?'

'Not often.'

'It shows. Here—' he took the book away from me again. 'Let me show you how it's done. It's clear you don't know the first thing about sketching. Give me the pencil.'

He rested the pad on the top rail of the fence, flipped over to a new page and stared down at the blank expanse of white for a moment. Gripping the pencil with fingers that looked far too brown and strong for such a slender object, he made a few strokes. He glanced at me, dead serious now. There was a frown on his face, and he seemed to be concentrating on some inner image. He stared at me, not seeing me, and then he turned back to the sketchbook. He made a few more strokes, held the pad out to examine the finished result, then handed it to me. It was a sketch of my face. I was amazed at the likeness. He had achieved in a few moments what I could never have done.

'That's the way,' he said. 'Get the picture focused in your mind and put it down on paper, quickly, before the image fades. Don't fuss. Don't bother with neatness and exactness. Above all, don't study what you're doing, just slap it down.'

'Are you an artist?' I asked.

'Hardly. I dabble a little. That's why I'm here.'

'To sketch?'

'To paint.'

'What do you do for a living?' I asked.

'Nothing much,' he replied. 'I dabble. I buy, I sell. I loaf most of the time, travel a lot.'

'You're from London?' I asked.

'One of the best families,' he replied, making a mock bow.

'It's a wonderful city. I live there, too,' I said.

He did not rise to the bait. He did not intend to discuss the city. He stood there with his hands on his hips, his legs spread wide apart, staring at me rudely while I gathered my things together. I got down from the stile, brushing my skirt. I was suddenly aware of how I must look, my dress dirty and torn, my hair tangled. There was probably dirt on my face as well. I drew myself up with as much dignity as I could muster under the circumstances.

'I must be going now,' I said in a cool voice.

He smiled that diabolical smile. I blushed.

'You look like an urchin and try to speak like a duchess,' he said. 'Don't look so offended and above all, don't blush. I abominate young ladies who blush. They think it coy and appealing, while actually it makes them quite unattractive.'

'You're incredibly rude,' I said.

'I also abominate men who mince and flutter over young ladies because they happen to have a pretty face. Your face is pretty, by the way. I'd like to paint it some time.'

'That's quite out of the question,' I replied coldly.

'Pity. It would make a good canvas.'

'If you will get out of my way, I'll leave now. I promise not to disturb you any more, Mr Ashley.'

He grinned, stepping aside with a flourish of one long arm. 'Any time at all, lass. Disturb me all you like, as long as I'm not working. Then I would probably hurl a paint box at you.'

He walked along beside me taking great long strides. He was so very tall, casting a long shadow on the path. We walked through the orchard and passed Dower House. It showed signs of his occupancy. Smoke rose from the chimney and the front door was open, a beautiful rust-red dog curled in front of it. He lifted his head as we passed. He was an Irish setter and one of the most beautiful dogs I'd ever seen. He leaped off the porch and bounded up to us. Philip Ashley laid his hand on the dog's head, stroking it.

'What a lovely dog,' I remarked.

'I wouldn't go anywhere without Harrigan,' he replied.

'One thing I want to say before you leave, Miss Meredith. You shouldn't roam around like this alone. It isn't safe.'

'It's perfectly safe,' I snapped. 'Whatever could happen to me?'

'Suppose I was a rake with a taste for young ladies with blonde hair? I could sweep you off your feet and carry you away to a fate worse than death. Fortunately, I don't particularly care for blondes.'

'You're being absurd,' I said.

'On the contrary, I'm quite serious.'

I looked up at him. His face was expressionless, the thin pink scar a disconcerting line against the tanned skin. He was serious. I wondered what his game was. It was perplexing, to say the least. He had followed me in the fog, night after night, and then he had come brazenly in to the music hall, sat at one of the front tables, making no effort to conceal himself.

Now he had followed me to Devonshire, and he was warning me not to wander around alone. What was he planning? If he meant to do me harm, he had certainly had the opportunity. Instead, he was showing a serious concern for my welfare. I did not trust him. He was waiting for the right time, the right moment to carry out some scheme, and then he would be as ruthless as his demeanour suggested he could be.

'I seem to be getting all kinds of warnings,' I said.

'Oh?'

'Edward Lyon warned me not to go to the village alone.'

'Then I wouldn't go alone,' Philip Ashley replied.

'This is Devonshire,' I said crisply. 'It isn't London. There are no white slavers lurking around every corner. There are no thieves or pick pockets or thugs waiting to ply their craft. The most dangerous thing I can think of is a bull getting loose, or perhaps catching poison ivy. I am eighteen years old. I am a full grown woman. I believe I can take care of myself, thank you.'

'You look twelve,' he said, 'with that dirt

on your cheek.' I wiped my cheek angrily. He grinned.

'Now tell me about Lyon House,' he said. 'Is your family staying there?'

'I have no family. I am visiting Mrs Lyon.'

'I've heard a lot about her. I must call on her. It's the neighbourly thing to do.'

'I wouldn't advise it,' I said crisply. 'She doesn't like strangers, Mr Ashley.'

'Unsociable?'

'Extremely.'

'So I've heard. I wonder why. Doesn't sound like the Corinne Lyon I used to know.'

'You know Corinne?'

'I met her once when I was a boy. My father knew her well. He sold her several valuable items.'

A woodpecker was pecking on the oak tree in the front yard, its scarlet head vivid on the grey body. The noise was loud and monotonous, and the dog barked at the bird and ran towards the tree. Philip Ashley paused to watch as the woodpecker flew away, scolding the intruder. The dog, sleek rust-red in the sunlight, ran around the yard in circles until the woodpecker had disappeared, then he came bounding up to his master, looking pleased with himself.

'I saw Mrs Lyon riding down the road this morning,' he said. 'Perhaps flying is a better word. She had a long green veil that trailed behind her. Quite an energetic old lady, isn't she?'

'Riding is her outlet,' I said. 'You said that your father sold her several things. Is he a tradesman?'

He ignored the question. He seemed to be thinking about something else. A fence surrounded the lawns of Dower House and we had arrived at the gate. A chain was fastened from the gate to the first slat of the fence, and a rusty lock hung on the chain. I looked around in despair, wondering what I should do. Philip Ashley smiled, touching his lip with the tip of his tongue. He shrugged his shoulders.

'I have no key,' he said. 'It seems to have been lost. I'll have to saw the chain one of these days. Anyway, it keeps peddlers away. I come and go through the back yard. There's a stone fence there, quite easy to leap over.'

He seemed not at all concerned at my dilemma. I felt another blush coming on, and turned my face away, not wishing to appear coy or naive.

'Have you any suggestions?' I asked my voice icy.

'Tea, perhaps? I could brew some up in a few minutes.'

'No, thank you.'

'You could come in and see my paintings,' he suggested casually.

'You're abominable!' I said.

'So it would seem. All my friends tell me that.'

I was furious with him, but I did not intend to let him foil me. I put my foot on the bottom rail of the fence and climbed up, tottering just a little. Philip Ashley made no effort to help me. He stood with his hands in his pockets, his head cocked a little to one side. I climbed over with as little awkwardnesss as possible, anxious to keep my petticoats hidden. I leaped to the ground on the other side of the fence, and as I did so I heard a loud rip. My skirt had caught on a nail and a great tear had parted the material, exposing great quantities of ruffled petticoat. I gasped, whirling around so that he could not see them. Philip Ashley laughed. He was still laughing as I ran down the road to Lyon House.

CHAPTER 11

The presence of Philip Ashley made itself felt very soon in the county. He was the kind of man who could never go unnoticed. He would either dazzle or terrify wherever he went. He seemed to do a combination of both in the village. He went there every day, and at first the villagers had been highly suspicious of the demonic figure who stalked down the streets. His tallness, his lose-limbed gait, the bright pink scar on the darkly tanned face all set him apart from the ordinary, and Molly said that little children had run from him at first. He bought painting supplies from the hardware store, set his easel up down by the river and began to paint. He had gone to the inn several times, and each time he had bought rounds of drinks for all the customers. He was very liberal with his money at all the stores, and this helped win the villagers over. Soon the very children who had run from him were sitting politely for him as he painted their portraits, holding the coins he gave them in their grubby hands.

Molly had seen him herself, and she was ecstatic in her descriptions of him. She claimed that the village girls were bedazzled, each trying to win his favour. Two of them had fought for the privilege of bringing his lunch from the inn to the spot where he had installed his easel. The much discussed Connie Brown, the voluptuous baker's daughter, had offered to sit for him, and Molly suggested that merely sitting was not at all what she had in mind. The arrival of Philip Ashley was causing almost as much excitement as the county fair, which was now being set up outside the village.

His presence was strongly felt at Lyon House. I had not mentioned my encounter with him to anyone, but Corinne soon had the news that the Dower House had been rented out. She was furious, particularly when she discovered that the man who had rented it was an artist—riff-raff, no doubt. She claimed that the old harridan in London hated her and deliberately let Dower House to the most unsuitable tenants, just to spite her. She was even more furious when the man had

195

the audacity to call on her, presenting himself at the front door as though he were a friend of the family.

We were in the parlour at the time. Agatha Crandall was with us, her face just a little flushed from the alcohol she had been consuming. When the maid came in to announce the visitor at the front door, Agatha sat up alertly, watching Corinne with sharp eyes. The maid handed Corinne a small white card with Philip Ashley's name printed on it. She flew into a rage, telling the maid to send him away at once.

'Imagine the nerve of the fellow!' she cried.

'He says he knows you, ma'am,' the maid said timidly.

'Absurd! How could he possibly know me? Tell him to go away and not come back. Presenting his card like a gentleman! Send him away, girl. I have no intention of letting such riff-raff in my parlour!'

'Don't be so hasty, Corinne,' Agatha said, her voice very sweet. 'Some very respectable men paint now. Besides, he says he knows you. It would be interesting to see just how that could be possible.'

'It's none of your business, Agatha!'

'You may be making a mistake,' Agatha purred.

The maid was still standing in the middle of the room, a look of bewilderment on her bland face. Corinne whirled on her, her brown eyes blazing. 'Move, you ninny! Do as I told you!' The girl ran out of the room, her face scarlet. Corinne sank back on the sofa, a deep frown on her face. Agatha Crandall stood up, her violet taffeta skirts rustling. She parted the draperies and looked out the window, watching the man leave. I could see him from where I sat. He walked down the drive with his arms swinging, his dark chestnut brown hair blowing in the breeze. He did not look at all disconcerted by the rude dismissal.

'He's very tall,' Agatha said. 'Stork-like, those long legs. Come look, Corinne. Perhaps you do know him after all.'

'Don't bother me,' Corinne snapped.

Agatha Crandall let the draperies fall back in place. She smiled and patted her girlish curls.

'I think someone from Lyon House should extend a polite welcome,' she said. 'The servants have been saying all kinds of fascinating things about the young man. Perhaps I'll pay him a call.'

Corinne looked up sharply.

'You wouldn't dare!' she said violently.

'But, Corinne, dear, I would. I am not bound to this house like you are. I can come and go as I please. I think it would be quite exciting to pay my respects. Perhaps he would like to paint me.'

She left the room, smiling enigmatically. Corinne sulked, her face set in a disgruntled expression that did not leave it all day. She was in an even uglier mood than she ordinarily was, and I stayed away from her. That night she and Edward closed themselves up in the parlour, supposedly to talk over accounts. I found that odd, as Corinne had never shown any interest in them before. They both wore grim expressions when they came out, and I could not help feeling that they had been talking about the new tenant of Dower House. Edward went over to the sideboard and poured himself a stiff drink. When he had finished it, he poured another, something I had never seen him do before. I wondered what could explain this strange conduct.

I thought about all this that night as I lay in bed. Philip Ashley appeared to be exactly what he said he was, a painter who had come here to paint. That was exactly what he was doing, and there could be no mistake that he was an artist of sorts. His quick sketch of my face had proved he knew at least something about sketching. He was painting down by the river in the village, and Molly reported that some of the canvases were quite good, although she was certainly no judge of art. If I had not known for sure that he was the man who had followed me in London, I would never have questioned his authenticity. He was a painter. He wanted to get away from the uproar of the city for a while so that he could paint in peace. That was understandable. Many artists preferred to work in the country.

The fact remained that he had appeared at the music hall every night, and after I told Mattie about it she sent me away. Now he was here in Devonshire, causing all kinds of comment, making no effort to remain unobtrusive. He had appeared shortly after the arrival of the two men who had inquired about me in London, the two men Bert had described. Edward Lyon had seen these two men, had recognized them and hurried me away from them. They had left the village, but Molly assured me they were still somewhere in the county.

Edward had seemed upset tonight, and Corinne was nervous. Agatha Crandall made mysterious comments and acted like the possessor of an important secret. All of this had something to do with me, some way, somehow. It was like a wheel, going round and round, destination unknown. I was at the centre of that wheel, and the revolutions around me seemed to make no sense. I remembered the moments of fear in London, the darkness and the secret threat. It seemed incredible that it had followed me here. It was incongruous with the sunshine and flowers and apparent serenity of Devonshire, and yet it was here.

I closed my eyes, trying frantically to sleep. My mind was a whirl of questions, faces, images, all of them blurred together. I saw dark shadows closing in, and I heard words that were not clear. Over and over I saw one face, a face that would seem to explain this whole thing, but it was indistinct, the features blurred behind a veil. I felt sure that if I could rip that veil aside everything would be clear. I went to sleep finally, but it was a sleep filled with nightmares.

Agatha Crandall did not appear at lunch the next day, but she came to the parlour later on that afternoon. I was reading a book about trees, and Corinne was playing solitaire, slapping the cards ruthlessly on top of each other, occasionally emitting a sharp cry of irritation when they did not fall to suit her. She looked up when Agatha came in and pushed the tiny card table away from her knees, scattering the cards on the floor. Agatha arched an eyebrow and swept across the room in a very grand manner, holding herself very erect. She smelled of gin.

She wore a suit of plum coloured taffeta, the jacket trimmed with bits of grey velvet. On her head was mounted an enormous hat of plum velvet, a dozen slightly tattered grey plumes curling about the brim. A thin veil of plum gauze half-concealed her face, but I could see her eyes snapping with excitement. She slowly pulled off one long grey velvet glove, tossed it on the sofa and then began to remove the other, deliberately making a small production of it. The room was tense. Only the sound of her taffeta skirts rustling broke the silence.

'Well?' Corinne said finally. 'Where have you been?'

'Can't you guess?'

'Don't make riddles!'

'I've been out.' She spoke each word carefully, as though it took an effort to enunciate each one clearly.

'You've been to the tavern, it would seem! You reek of gin. If the windows weren't open we'd all be asphyxiated from the fumes!'

'Mr Ashley gave me the gin,' Agatha said, tossing her other glove on the floor. 'He was very polite, very polite indeed.'

'So you went to see him after all?'

'Indeed I did, dear,' she replied smugly, sitting down carefully. She slumped a little on the sofa, but she held her hands folded neatly in her lap, and there was a small smile fixed permanently on her lips.

'And he plied you with liquor?'

'Plied? No, dear. He served it in a tea cup, a tiny cup with a blue rim. He didn't have any glasses. The place was really a mess. There were paintings stacked all over the room, and some of the furniture still had sheets covering them. Dust everywhere. The man is a wretched housekeeper. There was a dog in the room, gnawing a bone at my feet. Disconcerting, to say the least.'

Corinne was silent. Her fingers moved restlessly in her lap. She was furious, but, more than that, there was a look in her eyes that I could only describe as fear. She was afraid of something. It showed in the movement of her hands, in the way she sat on the edge of her chair.

'Mr Ashley is quite interesting,' Agatha continued. 'He told me all about his painting and his studies in London. He is a wealthy man, and he does not have to work. So he paints. He talks in a coarse voice, like a thug. The sound of it is enough to startle one. And he looks like Mephistopheles himself, heavy arched eyebrows, a sharp nose and a scar, dear, going right down his face. He explained it to me, the scar. He said he got it duelling.'

She paused dramatically, waiting for questions. She looked at Corinne, then her eyes swept over to me. She was enjoying herself immensely. This seemed to be an important event in her life, and she was determined to suck every drop of pleasure from it.

'Duelling, yes, but not what you think.

He was taking fencing lessons at the academy and somehow or other the protective ball on the tip of his partner's sword came off. The scar was the result of that accident. So he says. It's probably a story. He probably got it in a street fight. He looks like the sort who would participate in tavern brawls, although he was a perfect gentleman to me, you understand. Very attentive, he was. He was most curious about you, my dear.'

Corinne tensed. She started to speak, then she clamped her lips together tightly. Agatha waited a moment, then she continued her monologue. She held her hands out, examining them casually as she spoke.

'Most curious. It seems he met you once when he was a little boy. You made quite an impression on him. His father is an art dealer, and he sold you several nice things.'

'I never knew an art dealer named Ashley,' Corinne said. 'The man is lying.'

'Nevertheless, he described you vividly—at least he described you the way you used to be.' She made this thrust with a cruel jab, looking up to see how Corinne would take it. Corinne did not blink. She stared at Agatha with eyes that were now expressionless.

'He wanted to know about you and about Edward and all about Edward's trips to London. And—' She paused again, this time looking at me. 'He was most curious of all about Miss Meredith. Yes, he wanted to know all about her and why she was here and how long she would stay.'

'What did you tell him?' Corinne said, speaking each word separately. Her voice had the quality of steel.

'I have tact, my dear.'

'What did you tell him, Agatha?'

'Nothing. He kept plying me with gin—your word, plying. I kept on drinking it, and I pretended to be very groggy, and you can see I am not the least bit groggy. I did not tell him anything. You can relax, dear. When I left he did not know anything he didn't need to know, rest assured. He asked me to call again. He seemed quite anxious that I call again. He serves very nice gin. I may call again.'

She burst into a girlish giggle at this last, then she slumped back on the sofa, exhausted. Corinne stood up, very composed, very regal now. She clapped her hands sharply and a servant girl came into the room. Corinne told the girl to

205

summon Clark. Clark was the gardener, a burly, taciturn man who silently appeared in the gardens every morning and spent all his free time in his room, sleeping. He came in now and Corinne pointed to Agatha, not saying a word. Clark scooped her up, supported her on his shoulder and led her out of the room. Agatha staggered, the preposterous hat tipped at a crazy angle on top of her head.

I was in the library later on when Corinne came in, saying that Agatha was safely in her room, sleeping off the effects of the gin. She seemed disgusted with the whole business, all signs of the earlier fear gone. My sketchbook was on the desk and she picked it up, idly flipping through the pages. I had not shown the sketches to her after all. She paused, turning around to face me. She held out the sketch Philip Ashley had done of me. I explained the sketch and told her briefly about my encounter with him, leaving out most of the details. She looked alarmed, far more alarmed than she had been earlier in the day.

'What did he say to you?' she asked carefully.

'Nothing much. He was—polite.'

'You're sure of that?'

'Of course.'

'Why didn't you tell me about this sooner?'

'I—I just didn't think it was important. Was it, Corinne?'

She hesitated, decided not to make an issue of it. 'No—' she said, 'It wasn't—important. I just thought he might have—might have been rude to you.'

'He wasn't,' I replied calmly, puzzled by her attitude.

'Don't go there again, Julia. I suppose I don't have to tell you it would be highly—improper. You are very young—'

'Of course I won't,' I said lightly. 'I wouldn't have in the first place if I had known Dower House had a tenant. Do you like my sketches?' I asked, changing the subject. 'I tried to get all the details right. I like the one of the fern, don't you?'

Corinne was unusually cheerful at dinner that night but I could tell it was a forced cheerfulness. She was nervous, on edge, and her talk had an almost giddy quality. She drank three glasses of wine, which was unusual; she usually didn't take any.

Edward talked about the stalls the farmers were going to set up for the fair day after tomorrow, and he mentioned a steer which he hoped would win a blue ribbon and fetch a good price at the market. Both of them were talking for my benefit and I could sense that they wished to be alone, to discuss something much more urgent than the fair. I went to my room immediately after dinner, hoping to give them the opportunity they so obviously wanted.

It was much later when I came downstairs. I had left my book in the parlour and had come to fetch it; I wanted to read for a while before going to sleep. As I approached the parlour, I noticed that the door was pulled to, although it was not completely closed. I had my hand on the knob when I heard voices. I stood very still. Edward's voice was calm, soothing, while Corinne's sounded strange, as though she was on the verge of hysteria.

'It takes time, you must realize that,' Edward was saying. 'It will work out, just as I told you it would. It just takes time.'

'I'm afraid,' Corinne said. 'Not for

myself. I don't give a damn about myself. I'm afraid for Julia. Why can't we just drop everything and get her out of here? I'm afraid for her. She is so innocent. She has absolutely no idea—'

'Calm down. Everything is all right. It's nerves, just nerves. No harm will come to her. I'll see to that. She's safe here. You really must get hold of yourself. You must. I hate to see you upset like this.'

'Mattie would never forgive me if anything happened to Julia.'

'Nothing is going to happen to her. Just hold on—'

'She'd never forgive me. I'd never forgive myself.'

'Relax,' he said, his voice soothing. 'Just relax—'

'And now this—'

A servant was coming down the stairs. She turned towards the parlour and I hurried away from the door. I slipped through the dining room and down the hall. It was not Julia going down the hall. It was someone else. I had an impulse to laugh. I wanted to laugh and laugh. It could not be Julia going down the hall. It had to be someone else.

CHAPTER 12

It was cool outside. There was a chillness in the air that cooled my burning cheeks and steadied my trembling hands. I took deep breaths, delaying hysteria and finally conquering it. In its place came a frightening kind of calm. The words that I had overheard, the emotions I had felt took their place in that bewildering parade of events that had begun when I had first been aware of someone following me in the fog as I walked to the music hall back in London. There must be a solution to it all; there must be an answer. I knew I could not go on like this for long. If something terrible was going to happen, I wished that it would happen now so that the tension would be over.

I moved away from the house, hardly aware of the cold night air on my arms and shoulders. The heels of my shoes tapped on the tile of the terrace and my skirts made the noise of gently crackling flames. The pounding of my heart had subsided, and I was breathing evenly. I paused, looking up at the ink-black sky frosted with tiny pin points of stars. I no longer wanted to laugh. I wanted to be someone else, in another place. I stood listening to the crickets making their noises between the cracks of the tile, and far off, in the darkness of the trees, I could hear a solitary bird calling hopelessly for its mate.

I strolled among the gardens, feeling that none of this was real. The house, shrouded now in shadows with just a few lights burning in the windows, seemed unsubstantial. It might vanish in the mist. The garden was a maze of dark shapes and shadows, touched here and there by rays of moonlight, and none of it seemed real to me. It might all have been a stage set cleverly arranged, and I felt unreal, too.

I wished that this was a part in the theatre that I could put aside. I wished I could take off make up and costume and become once again the Julia who was secure and happy. For a while, as I strolled among the gardens, I thought about the little girl with the puppets, about Mattie and the boarding house and the noise and music and laughter of that life, and

211

I longed to be a part of it again. Then I realized that this was foolishness. In a little while I would be crying, and tears would do no good.

I came out of my reverie, and for the first time I became aware of the cold air. I folded my arms about me and rubbed them, welcoming the discomfort. At least it was something I could act against. I could go inside any time I wished and find the comforting warmth of my room. But I did not want to go inside just yet. I wanted to stay out here and be uncomfortable and think about what I must do.

There was no clear course of action. I could not take matters into my own hands and bring things to a head, because I did not know what was gong on. I could not go back to London. Mattie had sent me away, and she had asked me to trust her. It would do no good to go to Corinne, or Edward and ask them to help me, for they would give me careful evasions and half truths and pass the matter off lightly. They were trying to protect me from something, and it seemed essential that I know nothing about whatever it was they were protecting me from.

Everything was lovely and peaceful and I

must enjoy myself. I must be a good child. I must not ask too many questions, and I must not go to the village alone. I must not talk to strangers. I must pretend, as everyone else seemed to be doing. I did not know how much longer that would be possible.

I felt that I was trapped in the centre of a silken web, the strands drawing tighter and tighter, the danger drawing nearer and nearer, and I could do nothing about it because I did not know what the danger was. There was nothing to fight. There was nothing to struggle against. All I could do was wait.

A mist had risen from the river. It spread in swirls, moving low over the ground and coming to dance at my feet. Soon it would rise up and veil the rose bushes, and in an hour or so the gardens would be invisible. The mist churned as I passed through it, and I could feel the damp tendrils on the hem of my skirt. I was off the tiled terrace now, my shoes crunching on the damp ground. The gardens were behind me and I was walking down the path towards the river. I wanted to watch the dark waters rushing along in the moonlight.

I passed the small clearing where the

gazebo sat. It looked more dismal than ever in the darkness with its decaying roof and boarded sides. The mist swirled against it, hiding the bottom, and it seemed to be something ugly and evil floating in the grey-white swirls. I walked around the dark clump of trees that hid the river, and I could see the flimsy little pier built out over the water. The moon shed very little light, but my eyes were accustomed to the dark.

I stepped on the pier. A frog croaked and splashed into the water and I could smell damp, rotten wood and moss. The pier seemed to rock and sway as the dark water slapped against its planks. The water moved rapidly, jet black. A ray of moonlight struck it and was drowned, the strands of silver shattered and destroyed. The mist hung above the surface of the water, gradually thickening.

I must have stood there for over ten minutes, lost in thought. I had come outside without thinking. I had strolled in the gardens and come down to the river without giving a second thought to the darkness. No one knew where I was. They must all suppose I was in my room. I was suddenly aware of the darkness, of the black trees, of the fact that I was alone. Lyon House seemed very far away, hidden by the stretch of woods, and the night was suddenly oppressive.

There was nothing definite I could ascribe this feeling to. There was no sound, no movement in the shrubbery, and yet my whole body seemed to be poised, listening, every sense sharply aware of my position. The water slapped against the wooden planks. A frog croaked on the other side of the river. The breeze caused the leaves to rustle slightly overhead. I stood very still. It was cold and damp and there were chill bumps on my arms. I felt someone watching me.

I tried to tell myself that it was my imagination. I had been unnerved by what I had overheard and I had come outside to calm myself down. I had been on the verge of hysterics, and in that condition it would be easy to imagine things. I told myself this, but I did not believe it. If that were the case, I should have felt this earlier, and it had come up on me all at once. There was a reason for it, and the reason was not in my mind.

I turned around, my back to the river. I looked at the path that led back to

Lyon House. There were dark trees on either side, thick shrubbery pressing close. I would have to pass through several hundred yards of wooded area before I reached the gardens. I wondered what folly had ever possessed me to come here, so far away from the house. I felt weak now, too weak to move, certainly too weak to walk up that dark path. I could not rid myself of the feeling that someone was close by, watching every move I made.

My first impulse was to rush headlong through the woods and get to the house as quickly as I could, but I did not think I could make it. I could not force myself to run. I wanted to scream, but I knew that no one at the house would be able to hear me. I stood for several long minutes, listening, trying to convince myself that there was no one there.

I could see nothing but the dark black shrubbery and the thick trees. The moonlight gleamed faintly along the pathway in shiny patches. I heard a noise that sounded like heavy breathing. It took me a moment to realize that it was only the wind sucking through the cracks of the pier. I could not stand here forever, I told myself. I moved off the pier. The heels of my shoes sank into the soggy earth. The mist swirled about my skirts, almost knee high now, as I walked towards the path, moving slowly. Every step I took required great will power. I was almost at the beginning of the path when I saw the light. I stopped, frozen in place.

It was back in the woods, several yards away. It was a tiny glowing orange, the burning butt of a cigar. I put my hand on my breast, sighing deeply.

'Edward,' I called. 'Is that you? You frightened me half to death.'

There was no answer. The silence was frightening.

'Edward! I know you're there.'

There was a violent streak of orange across the darkness as the cigar was tossed away, and then there was nothing but black. There was no sound, no movement. It was not Edward. I felt the flesh at my temples grow cold, and the back of my neck felt as though an icy hand had been clamped against it. I closed my eyes, and I saw clouds of blackness pressing at me, but I did not faint. My breath came in short gasps. I could not move. My knees felt as though they would collapse beneath me.

I peered into the woods. I could not

even tell now where the cigar had been. I felt the eyes watching me, and it was an acute sensation, as real as the cold air stroking my bare arms. I was standing in a small patch of moonlight, and the man in the woods could see me plainly. I stepped quickly towards the trees on the opposite side of the path. He could not see me in the darkness, just as I could not see him.

A thorn caught my skirt. There was a loud rasping noise as the material ripped free. I plunged on. A branch struck my face. I felt the sting across my cheek, sharp and painful. I fell against the trunk of a tree, and gasped. I felt as though my lungs would burst. I must have stayed there for five minutes, the bark rough against my back. There was no sign of pursuit, no noise. I was breathing evenly now, making no sound at all, and all around me the woods were silent.

I knew he was there. I could feel his presence nearby. He was moving quietly, as quietly as a dark shadow would move, black against black. He would stop and listen, alert, and then move on, searching for me. He had seen me come this way and he had heard me, but he could not see me. I was as invisible as he. I had no idea who he was. I did not particularly care. I only knew that he was my enemy, the dark, faceless enemy who had brought me to this point.

I heard the loud flapping of wings as a bird darted out of the underbrush. There was one noisy snap as a foot stepped on a dry twig, and then there was silence again, a silence filled with listening. He was quite near now. Perhaps he was close enough to reach out and touch me. The very air seemed different, laden with another presence, and I imagined that I could smell leather and perspiration, the odour of man. I heard the sharp intake of breath, and it startled me to discover that I had made the noise myself. Had he heard it, too?

I knew that I had to move. I had to get back to Lyon House. I could not stand here and wait for him to find me. I did not know if I was brave enough to move. My body might have been tied to the tree, and my blood might have been ice. I felt numb. I flexed my fingers and was surprised to find that they moved at my command. If I could move my fingers, I could move the rest of my body. It was a discovery like that an infant makes when he learns he can stand on his own two feet and not fall.

I was surrounded by the dark trunks of trees. The brush was thick and there was no path here. I would have to stumble around in the darkness and hope to find my way. I was so frightened and confused that I did not even know which direction the gardens were. I saw a dark form several yards away from me, black outlined against the night, and I was not sure that it was a tree. It wasn't. It moved. It moved cautiously towards me, so slowly that the movement was hardly discernible, like the movement on the hands of a clock. He could not see me. I was certain of that. He was not coming directly towards me, merely in my direction.

I edged away from the tree. I slipped behind it. I held my hands out in front of me, touching branches and trunks. I moved as quietly as I could and as quickly, but it seemed that I was walking underwater. It seemed that every step I took crashed in the night like a small explosion. My skirts rustled with scratchy rhythm. My feet scraped the damp ground. I might as well be blind, so dark it was. The underbrush seemed to reach out with thorny fingers to obscure my way. Somewhere behind me I heard a cough.

He knew that I had eluded him, but it was only a temporary thing. He would find me. He had stopped. He was listening again. I stopped, too. I could break into a run and hope to reach Lyon House before he caught me. It was what he expected me to do. I knew that as long as he could not see me or hear me I was safe. That gave me very little comfort. I felt like an animal, being tracked by a dangerous prey. I tried to avoid panic; my only hope was to remain calm and outwit him.

I could hear the water rushing, and I smelled the lichen and moss on the rocks at the river bank. It confused me even more. I was lost; I had no idea where I was. I had thought I was going away from the river, and it seemed I was getting nearer to it. I began to move in the other direction, holding my skirts tight and stepping lightly on the ground. For a while it seemed I had lost my prey. An owl hooted. The wind caused the leaves to crackle overhead. I heard no footsteps behind me and I stopped for breath, shivering with cold.

A twig cracked; he was coming towards me again. He was not trying to conceal the noise now and was rushing through the woods. I realized with horror that I was standing in a patch of moonlight, plainly visible to him. I darted to one side, seeking the security of shadow. I stepped on a rock and had to grab a tree limb to keep from falling. My ankle throbbed painfully. I must have wrenched a muscle. I ran on, as heedless of noise as he.

I came into the small clearing where the gazebo stood. It was half concealed by mist now, but it gave me the sense of direction I needed. I knew where the path was that led back to the gardens. I slipped through a group of trees and I heard him crash into the clearing behind me. My lungs were bursting and my ankle throbbed, each step an agony. I knew I could not outrun him; I leaned against a tree, waiting, resigned.

I could see him in the moonlight through the branches of the trees. He seemed confused, as if he did not know which way I had gone. He was still in the clearing, beside the gazebo, partially hidden by the mist, but I could see that he was tall. He wore a dark coat. That was all I could tell about him in the darkness; he might have been anyone. He stood beside the gazebo, looking around, and I saw him slam his fist into his palm, disgusted.

A bird squacked in a thicket behind the gazebo. The bird saved me. The man went plunging into the woods towards the sound, away from me. I closed my eyes as the moon disappeared behind some clouds.

Time passed. The woods around me grew silent. I was alone. The wind stirred the branches over my head, and they groaned. The moon came out from behind the bank of clouds that had obscured it and moonlight poured through the leafy canopy, spilling silver at my feet. The night was calm. All this might never have happened. It had the quality of a nightmare come to life, but it was over now. My ankle throbbed and my skirt was torn. My sides hurt from running and I was cold. There was no sign of my pursuer; he must have thought I was back in Lyon House. I was sure that he was no longer in the woods.

I found the path and walked slowly back towards the gardens. I was not afraid any longer. All fear, all emotion had been drained out of me, and I moved as though in a trance. My ankle did not hurt as much as it had before, but I tried to put most of my weight on the other foot.

The path was bright with moonlight. The wind was strong now, tearing the mists to shreds and carrying them away. The sky was mottled grey, huge grey clouds rolling on a surface stained silver. There was Lyon House, sharply outlined.

All the mist had been blown away from the gardens. They were grey and black and silver, strewn with shifting patterns of shadow. Edward Lyon was standing at the edge of the patio, his arms folded on the cold marble of the railing. He wore a black cloak and it billowed away from his shoulders like dark wings. He looked startled when I walked towards him. I could see his face clearly. The wind blew ragged locks of hair across his forehead.

'My God!' he exclaimed. 'What are you doing out here?'

'I went for a walk,' I said flatly.

'Like that? Without a shawl?'

'I wanted some fresh air.'

He shook his head in disgust. He was the bewildered parent incapable of understanding the conduct of a precocious child.

'I thought you were in your room,' he remarked.

'I went down to the river,' I said.

'Oh?'

He studied me. He saw my face, and he saw the condition of my dress. Alarm spread over his face.

'Someone followed me,' I told him. My voice was emotionless.

'You're certain?'

'Quite certain,' I replied. 'A man. He was watching me. I don't know how long he might have been there. He was smoking a cigar and I saw it. I thought it was you.'

'I've been in the library,' he said. 'I just came outside.'

'He threw the cigar away when I called your name. He followed me through the woods.'

'Good Lord—'

'He's gone now,' I said.

'You didn't imagine all this?'

I did not answer. I did not think an answer was necessary. Edward took my arm and led me into the house. We went down a narrow hallway, and he opened the door to a small storage room. It was piled full of old magazines and boxes and rain coats. Several rusty lanterns hung on the wall. I smelled mildew and yellowing paper. There were no curtains at the windows, and moonlight poured through the panes in bright rays.

Edward took down one of the lanterns.

'I'm going to take a look,' he said.

'There's no need,' I replied. 'He's gone.'

'You go on up to your room. I'll be back.'

'I'll wait here,' I said.

'Very well. Keep quiet.'

He left, moving very quietly. He obviously didn't want to disturb anyone else in the house. I stepped to the window. I saw him stop outside to light the lantern. It glowed dim yellow. Edward walked across the gardens and vanished into the first clump of trees. For a moment I could see the yellow globe moving in the darkness, and then it was gone. I still stood at the window, my cheek against the cold glass. This was all as unreal as the woods had been, the passive continuation of a nightmare.

There were cobwebs in the corners of the storage room. When the moonlight touched them they looked like strands of gossamer. I sat down beside the window, completely calm. I wondered vaguely if I shouldn't be having an attack of vapours, reclining on a sofa with a bottle of smelling salts. It seemed the thing to do, but I was no longer in the least upset. My ankle had even stopped throbbing.

Edward must have been gone half an hour. I saw him coming back through the trees. He stopped to blow out the lantern before he came into the gardens, then walked quickly across the terrace and disappeared from view. He opened the side door so quietly that I wouldn't have heard him if I had not been listening for the sound. In a moment he was standing in the doorway of the storage room. He looked irritated, as though he had been sent on a fool's errand, and he hung up the lantern without saying a word.

He told me that he had found no sign of anyone. I had not expected him to find any. I knew that he did not believe me. He did not say so, but he said it was very easy to imagine all sorts of things in the dark woods with trees and shadows and the wind blowing. I did not insist on the matter. It was clear that he considered me a foolish child, ready to dramatize myself at the first opportunity. I let him think so. He stretched and yawned, ready to put an end to it all. As we walked down the hall to the main part of the house, he asked me not to say anything about all this. It would upset Corinne, he said, and I agreed not to mention it.

He walked with me to the foot of the stairs and then made a bow, mock gallant. He grinned, all charm, as though he considered the whole thing rather amusing now. I went on up the stairs without acknowledging the grin. I did not find it amusing at all.

CHAPTER 13

The wagon wheels creaked noisily as the horses trotted over the winding dirt road that led to the fair grounds. The wooden seat was uncomfortable and the odour of damp hay was quite overwhelming, but Edward Lyon, with typical whimsey, had decided that a hay wagon was the best vehicle in which to arrive at the fair. It would set the mood, he claimed. I sat beside him, high up on the wooden seat. A huge mound of hay rose behind us, bits of it spilling over our shoulders when the wagon went over a particularly nasty rut in the road. The wagon creaked, the harness jingled, the horses trotted noisily. Edward Lyon held the reins firmly in his hands, relaxed and apparently at ease.

He seemed to have forgotten all about the incident that had happened two nights before, and evidently he wanted me to forget it too. He had made no allusion to it, and his whole manner had been that of an adult trying to distract a child who has just had a nightmare. He was charming and witty and paid much more attention to me than he did ordinarily. He and Corinne had both insisted that I attend the fair, although I had protested that I had no interest in the event. Edward had practically abducted me this afternoon, and he seemed determined that I enjoy myself.

'I do hope the steer takes the blue ribbon,' he remarked. 'There's a good chance he will. A great brute of an animal, he is. You must come look at him before the judging.'

'I'll do that,' I said, without enthusiasm.

'It's a beautiful day for the fair,' he said.

'Lovely,' I replied.

'You'll get a chance to observe some local customs.'

'Jolly,' I said.

'Sulking?'

'Just bored.'

He grinned. 'You won't be for long.'

I didn't reply. The wagon went over a large rut. We bounced. I had to seize his arm for support. He laughed, clicking the reins. He was in a fine mood, humorous and expansive, evidently looking forward to the event. I wished I could show a little more interest, but seeing livestock and watching wrestling matches held no appeal for me. I was too preoccupied with other things to be concerned with making merry. My dour mood didn't seem to bother Edward at all.

'Have you ever been to a county fair?' he asked.

'No, I haven't.'

'They get rowdy, rather. It's a very festive affair for the country folks, and festivity means beer and bodies and fights. All inhibitions are forgotten, and the sober, hardworking men who toil in the fields all season long are ready to break loose and let off steam. You'll see bodies rolling in the sawdust and bloody noses, but it's all in the spirit of fun.'

'Really?'

'The day really belongs to the young people. Brawny lads take this opportunity to seize a lass they've been eyeing all year and pay rather ardent court. Anything goes. They dance the polka and, later on, wander off down to the river. Many a maid is undone.'

'Charming,' I said.

'Does everyone good to loosen up a little,' he remarked.

'I see,' I said.

'Do you dance the polka?' he asked.

'I'm afraid not.'

'Shame. Maybe I'll teach you.'

'I'm not a country maid,' I replied.

'You look like one in that dress.'

'Do I?'

'You've got hay in your hair,' Edward said. 'That adds just the right touch. You might have just come from the dairy, finished with milking the cows and ready to gather the eggs. I hope some lusty lout doesn't mistake you for a farm girl and whisk you off to the polka.'

'It isn't likely,' I told him primly.

'Never can tell,' he replied, chuckling.

The wagon turned around a bend. I could see the fair grounds ahead, spread out on a stretch of ground that led down to the river. It was like something out of the Arabian nights, I thought—tents of all sizes and colours billowed in the slight breeze. Dozens of stalls were set up, banners and pennants waving from them, and a painted carousel went round and round to the brassy notes of a calliope. It was a vivid patch of colour, furious with activity. Hundreds of people milled about already, and more wagons were arriving every moment. Edward clicked the reins and the horses hurried towards the spot.

Wagons, carts, vehicles of all kinds made a ring around the fair grounds. Edward stopped beside a wagon heaped with cabbage. He helped me down, and I brushed hay from my skirts. Livestock stamped behind a roped-in area nearby, filling the air with the pungent odours of manure and sweat. There was a pen of pigs, the squealing animals rolling in the mud. The noise was deafening.

He took my hand and soon we were in the midst of the fair. It was a spectacle of sight and sound and smell, engulfing us immediately. Wagons heaped with produce stood beside ploughs. Animals bellowed. Children ran through the crowd, laughing and squealing. A man in a soiled white apron sold steaming frankfurters smeared with mustard, and at the stall beside him a stooped old man with grey hair held the strings of a dozen coloured balloons that bobbed in the breeze. Two tall, husky lads were arguing violently beside a barrel of dill pickles, their faces ruddy, their fists clenched. They shouted vile oaths at each other until a girl in a scarlet dress threw herself between them. They all three moved off, arms locked together, to get a pitcher of stout ale at the next stall.

I could not resist the vigour and excitement of the fair. It was a constantly moving kaleidoscope of colour, banners waving, music blaring, the very air charged with the abandon of holiday spirit. I saw girls in vividly coloured dresses flirting outrageously with solemn looking lads in boots and leather jerkins. Everyone seemed determined to have a good time, and there was something rather frightening in their determination. They moved from place to place, pushing and jostling anyone who got in their way, as though desperate to get all possible pleasure from this. I saw faces tense even as they smiled, and bodies seemed to be hurled with explosive energy. I could see how all this could easily get out of hand. I stayed close beside Edward, excited but somewhat intimidated.

Edward seemed amused by it all, yet he was not a part of it. He wore his finest grey suit, his black boots gleaming with polish, a pearl stickpin in his sky-blue ascot. He was rather like an adult indulgently watching the antics of playful children, but when someone jostled against us, he got out a strong arm and shoved the person aside, as roughly as anyone. He was amused by the boisterous atmosphere, but it did not touch him.

He kept glancing over his shoulder, as though he were looking for someone, I noticed. He really paid very little attention to anything we were doing. If he stopped at a stall, he glanced down at the merchandise, made a reply to my comment if it were necessary and then turned to look over the crowd, his eyes searching. Once I asked him if he were expecting someone, but he denied it and took my elbow to lead me to the next stall. He was charming, making witty comments now and then about various sights, but the charm was mechanical. I felt he was not really with me, and as the day wore on I noticed a slight edge of irritation in his voice as though something hadn't turned out as he had expected.

He took me to see the bull that had been raised on one of the tenant farms. It was an enormous beast, fierce looking, with a sleek black coat. It snorted and stamped, tugging at the rope that held it to a stake. As it moved, I could see the muscles rippling under the satiny black. I had never seen such a powerful animal. Edward told me about its line, about the special food that had been given to it. He would make a magnificent stud, Edward claimed.

The livestock auction was held in the middle of the afternoon. A man with garters on his shirt-sleeves banged a gavel and took bids, and a crowd of men examined the animals and bid in loud voices. Edward's bull had won the blue ribbon, and it fetched a good price, but he did not seem to care much. The crowd was thick around the livestock pens, the air heavy with the odours of manure and damp hay and sweat and stale beer. The sun beat down fiercely, and I felt slightly nauseated as I stood in the crowd with Edward, my arm in his. It was after five when the auction was over, and the atmosphere of the fair had changed considerably.

Business was over. The livestock had been sold. Those who had come solely for this purpose were gone now. Most of the children were gone as well, and those who remained were tired and contrary. There was no longer a light, carefree feeling in the air. Men who had been drinking steadily all day had sullen expressions, and some of them staggered. The carousel still went round, the calliope as brassy and loud as before, but there was a blaring, irritating quality about the music now.

'Are you tired?' Edward asked.

'Very. We've been here for hours.'

'What do you want to do next?'

'I'm ready to go,' I said.

'Nonsense. Come, I'll win you a doll.'

We stopped at the shooting gallery. Edward paid his money and took up the rifle, leaning on the stall and aiming at the balloons that were revolving on a platform twenty yards away. He was cool and precise, holding the gun casually yet firmly, his arm crooked at just the right angle. I listened to the rapid explosions, heard the balloons burst. My head was aching a little, and when Edward put the gun aside and handed me the doll he had won, I took it with a petulant smile. He looked triumphant, proud of his achievement. A little girl with a dirty face was standing with her mother at the next stall, trying to sell flowers that were wilting now. She looked at the doll with longing eyes, and I gave it to her. Edward did not seem to appreciate the gesture.

'I'm too old for dolls,' I said crisply. 'I'm not a child.'

'I'm beginning to notice.'

'Then why treat me like one?' I asked.

He narrowed his eyes but did not reply.

'It's been a long day,' I said. 'Shall we leave?'

'Not just yet,' he said. 'There'll be a fireworks display later on. You won't want to miss that.'

'The cattle have been sold,' I said. 'I've had enough festivity for one day. The crowd is getting restless.'

'They're anxious for the wrestling matches to begin. Come, I'll buy you some lemonade. You'll feel better.'

I did not complain anymore. I knew that he did not want to go. He was cool and calm on the surface, a pleasant smile on his lips, but there was something else in his manner. We bought the lemonade and stood under the shade of an oak tree to drink it. Edward Lyon leaned against the oak tree, his face in shadows, watching the activity of the fair. His eyes still seemed to be searching, and I knew that he was waiting for something or someone. I sipped the cool lemonade, feeling a little better, yet I was puzzled by his conduct. Edward was not enjoying himself yet he was determined to stay. I could not understand it.

I was after six when the wrestling matches began. This was a big event for many of the men, the main reason they had come to the fair. A ring had been roped off, heavy mats placed over the ground, and country lads with naked chests and oiled muscles stood flexing their arms, ready to fight. There was a prize of money for the champion, as well as a black leather belt with silver emblems. However, the real reason for the contests seemed to be for gambling purposes. Bookies circulated among the crowd, sly, ferret eyed men who did not belong in the village. Edward explained that they moved from fair to fair all over England, making money from dog races and wrestling matches and the like, swindling the yokels and causing trouble wherever they went. Men studied the various contestants, judging them as one might judge horseflesh before placing their bets. Each seemed to have a favourite, and Edward said that some of the boys who would wrestle had been in training all year long, hoping to win the money.

The sun had begun to sink, a great orange ball in a darkening blue sky. The shadows were long and heavy, spreading over the fair grounds. Two men circled around each other on the mats, fell upon one another in a great tangle of arms and legs. I looked away. I studied the men in the crowd. I saw tensed bodies, glazed eyes, slack mouths, flushed faces. They shouted loudly, crying for blood. In the ring there was a mass of straining, jabbing flesh, and I felt sick. I thought of the Romans who crowded the amphitheatre, urging the gladiators to kill. This seemed as barbaric to me.

Edward Lyon had a slight smile on his lips as he watched the fights, amused by them but clearly above this sort of thing. He had nevertheless placed a bet on one of the men who was going into the ring now. I watched his reaction during the fight. As the bodies crashed on the mat, thrashing about, he seemed to enjoy it as much as the others. His eyes glittered darkly. The smile curled tightly at the corner of his mouth. I wondered if there was a streak of cruelty in him, carefully concealed under the fine gloss of manners. The bell rang and the match was over. His man had won, coming out of the ring bruised but victorious. Two men carried the other man out and dabbed his face with a damp towel.

'Looks like I won,' Edward said.

'I think it's beastly,' I replied. 'I feel ill.'

He grinned. 'Too much for you?'

'Quite.'

'I'll just go and collect my bet. I'll be back shortly.'

He went to collect his money. I felt someone tugging at my arm and turned round to find Molly standing beside me, a vivid smile on her red lips. Her curls fell in a glossy black tangle about her shoulders, and her eyes sparkled. She wore a bright blue dress with pink bows at the bodice, which she filled amply. The dress was soiled with perspiration and the skirt was streaked with something that looked suspiciously like grass stains.

'Isn't it exciting!' she cried. 'I'm havin' the grandest time!'

'I haven't seen you around today, Molly,' I remarked.

'Oh—' she said, stretching the word out, 'Bertie and I've been here most of the day, but we've been down by the river, watchin' all the boats and things.' She smiled coyly.

'Where is your Bertie?' I asked.

'Oh, he's goin' to wrestle! Isn't it wonderful? I do hope he wins! And where is Mr Edward?'

'He's gone to collect the money on a bet he placed,' I replied.

'Look, there's Bertie! I've gotta run and wish him luck.'

Molly rushed over to speak to the boy. He was a giant, over six feet tall, his tanned body rippling with muscle. Waves of dark blond hair fell over his forehead, and his dark grey eyes were full of confidence as he wrapped tape about his wrists. His nose was slightly crooked, his mouth thick lipped and sensual. He grinned when Molly touched his shoulder and made a fierce expression for her. Molly giggled and stood up on tiptoes to whisper something in his ear. He stroked her shoulder and drew back his lips, exposing his teeth. Molly pretended to swoon then skipped back over to me as the bell rang for the match to begin.

'He's just grand!' Molly cried. 'Dumb as can be—and fresh! But what can you expect?'

Molly jumped and squealed during the contest, elated. I looked around for Edward, wondering where on earth he could be. Almost half an hour had passed since he left me. The match ended. Bertie had lost. Molly frowned and said he was too confident and really a dumb creature but she was going to let him dance with her just the same. I paid no attention to her chatter. She noticed this.

'Is something wrong, Miss Julia?'

'I was wondering where Mr Lyon has gone.'

'He should have been back by now,' Molly said.

'I know. I think I'll go look for him.'

'You'd better wait,' Molly said. 'Bertie will be here in a minute, as soon as he's washed up. We'll help you look for Mr Edward. It isn't a good idea for you to be alone—'

'Don't be silly,' I said.

Molly looked a little doubtful, but she was too excited to have much concern about anything. She said she would see me later and stood up on her tiptoes to see if she could spot Bertie. I pushed my way through the crowd.

I searched for Edward but did not see him anywhere. I passed stalls with barren shelves, the merchandise all sold or put away. The carousel had stopped and the painted horses looked tired and bedraggled. A man was spreading sawdust over the emptied livestock pens and steam rose from piles of manure. A dog scratched about in an overturned vegetable cart. Those people not watching the wrestling matches walked aimlessly, waiting for the activity of the night. Men were stringing Japanese lanterns around the dance pavilion. A man sprinkled sand over the wooden floor and a huddle of empty chairs around the pavilion waited for the musicians to arrive. I could hear the shouts of the crowd at the wrestling ring, far away now. The sun had disappeared, leaving dark orange banners on the sky. Shadows were thickening, spreading purple over the ground.

Edward was standing by our hay wagon,

talking intently with a man I had never seen before. He was short and stout, wearing a black and grey checked suit, an apple green tie and a dark brown derby hat. His face was fleshy, the jowls hanging down, and his small brown eyes shifted about as he talked with Edward. The two men stopped talking as I approached. Both seemed to resent the intrusion. Edward frowned. The man in the derby gave me a long appraising look. He had the look and smell of London about him. He was not one of the bookies. I wondered who he was and what Edward had to do with him. Their abruptly concluded conversation seemed to hang in the air, waiting to be continued. I felt uncomfortable.

'Were you looking for me?' Edward asked, casually. 'I thought you would still be watching the fights.'

'I couldn't take any more. You were gone so long—'

'I collected my money and then ran into an old friend.'

'Oh?'

I waited for an introduction. There was none.

'Are you ready to leave?' I asked.

'I have some business to discuss,' Edward

said. 'The dancing will start in a little while. I'll meet you by the pavilion, Julia.'

'Who's the girl?' the stranger asked, his voice heavy.

Edward ignored this, 'I'll see you later, Julia,' he said.

He had not introduced me to the man. He had no intention of doing so. There was a moment of awkward silence, and then I turned away. I headed back for the grounds. The men waited until I was out of hearing range before resuming their conversation. My head was throbbing. I wondererd why Edward had not wanted the man to know who I was, and I wondered if he were the man Edward had been looking for all afternoon.

CHAPTER 14

The wrestling matches were over. The crowd spilled over the grounds once more, talking too loudly. The sky was a very dark blue, turning purple, the air thick with shadow. The musicians were playing at the pavilion. The sound drifted to where

I stood, leaning against a deserted stall. In the distance I could see the Japanese lanterns, bobbing smears of colour against the darkness. I saw a man stumbling towards me, and I hurried away, not wanting to be alone. Molly would be at the pavilion with Bertie. I did not know how long it would be before Edward would be ready to leave.

The pavilion was surrounded by darkness, shadows thick all around it, but it was a jewel box of light and colour. The lanterns swayed in the breeze, spilling splotches of colour on the dancers. Strapping country girls danced with muscular lads. The girls wore vivid dresses, the skirts flashing like butterfly wings as they whirled in the dance. The boys wore boots and dark pants and leather jerkins over white shirts, the sleeves gathered full above the wrists. Faces were flushed. Bodies moved furiously to the music. The noise of boots stomping the wooden floor reminded me of a cattle stampede; it almost drowned out the music. Boys seized girls about the waist, twirling them around. Music blared and bodies whirled. It was a moving frieze of energy and vigour, red blood and muscle.

The music stopped and the dancers

paused, chests heaving, foreheads beaded with sweat. I stood among the shadows, just outside the circle of lights, watching. I noticed a particularly beautiful girl with red-gold hair, wearing a yellow dress that had been fitted with men in mind. She swirled the skirts of her dress, swaying to and fro as a dozen boys surrounded her, each begging for the next dance. I heard one of them call her Connie. She must be the notorious baker's daughter. I watched her as I might have watched a particularly exotic animal in a zoo.

The music began again, and the stomping and whirling started once more. I saw Molly, radiant with her Bertie. I watched the dancing for a long time, and all the time I wondered when Edward would come. Time passed, and he still did not come. The dancers grew tired, and the music changed from rowdy polka to a slower, more sinuous sound. Bodies were closer together and faces were more expressive. Molly danced with her hand caressing the back of Bertie's neck, her lips half-parted. There was intimacy where there had been abandon, meaning in every movement.

I felt isolated standing there in the shadows, watching something I was not part of. I felt like an orphan standing outside a grand house, watching a festive party through the opened windows. It was absurd, of course, but that was the feeling I had. I was very lonely, and I realized it without shame. My life had always been full of people, full of activity. The rich, crowded life in London was behind me now. I had been cast out, for reasons I could not understand. I was in a strange, alien part of the country, and I did not belong here. I had no one to turn to and I felt that lack very strongly now.

Everything was in shadow now, only the dance pavilion brightly lit. Couples began to steal away, hand in hand. Shrubbery rustled. A cold night breeze sprang up. My arms and shoulders were cold. I was exhausted by all the activity and excitement of the day. I wanted to go back to Lyon House. I did not belong there, either, but at least I had a room of my own where I could brood in comfort.

I felt rebuffed by Edward's treatment of me. I was seeing facets of his character I had never suspected. He was charming and easy-going on the surface, but there was much more there than met the eye. He seemed to be bothered by something.

Perhaps it was a gambling debt, I thought. That would explain his nervous restlessness today. Perhaps the strange man had come to collect money from Edward, money he didn't have. Molly had mentioned something about Edward's gambling. She said Corinne had scolded him about it and refused to pay his debts.

I was thinking about this when I heard footsteps approaching. At first I thought it was Edward coming to fetch me and then I saw the two boys. They had both been drinking. I could smell the fumes. They were both large and blond, country boys who spent most of their time behind the plough and were unaccustomed to the spirit of revelry. Seeing me in the shadows, they stopped, grinning at one another. Evidently they had not been able to find a compliant wench, or they would have been moving about on the dancefloor with the others.

I backed away a little, sensing trouble. As they came nearer, I had a feeling of unreality. Edward had jokingly predicted something like this. The boys came closer.

'Hey, Rodd,' one of them said, 'look here what I found. All ready 'n waitin' for a good lookin' fellow like me to come along. All by 'erself, too.'

His voice was coarse and rather slurred. His shoulders strained against the material of his shirt, and his large brown hands hung down at his sides. He looked stupid and dangerous.

'Ain't fair,' the other said. 'I saw 'er first, Clem.'

'Find one for yourself. This un's mine.'

They glared at each other, fists clenched, neither looking at me. They were young and raw and ugly, and I might have been a pretty toy they had discovered. The one called Rodd pushed the other away, and he seized my arm before I could move. I was terrified.

'Wanna dance, sweetheart?' he said.

'No, thank you,' I said crisply, but my voice trembled.

'Aw—come on. Be friendly.'

'Let go of me.'

He ignored the remark. He began to chuckle with delight, proud of his toy.

'Shove off, laddies!'

I recognized the voice immediately. He stepped out of the shadows and came towards us slowly, casually. The lad holding my arm looked completely bewildered.

'Hey, who do ya think you are? This here's—'

'I said shove off!'

The voice was harsh and menacing. Philip Ashley stood in a patch of moonlight, looming there like a demon. The boy saw the man's face, and he released me immediately. Both of the boys stumbled away, reeling off into the darkness. Philip Ashley watched them leave. He arched a brow and turned to me.

'Are you all right?' he asked.

'I'm a little shaken up, but—I'm all right.'

'It seems I've done my good deed for the day,' he said.

'Thank you,' I replied.

'Very foolish of you to stand about like this, alone. You should be in bed—with a glass of warm milk.'

'I'm quite capable of taking care of myself,' I said icily.

'So I've just observed,' he said, grinning.

I blushed. This seemed to delight him.

'Where is your Mr Lyon?' he asked.

'He's—he's talking with a friend.'

'Conspiring would be a better word. That would be Mr Herron.'

'Herron?' I said.

'I saw him earlier. Wondered what he was doing in these parts. He is a friend of your Mr Lyon?'

'I've never seen him before today.'

Philip Ashley nodded his head. I could see his face very clearly, the moonlight sculpturing it in silver and shadow. It was sharp, all angles. The jagged line of the scar was like a black mark in the light. The dark eyes studied me.

'Fortunate that you came along when you did,' I said.

'Indeed,' he replied.

'Or had you been there all along?'

'All along?'

'Watching me.'

'Let's say—watching over you.'

'You admit it?'

'I admit standing in the shadows, watching over you to see that nothing happened, to prevent any such episode as the one that I did indeed prevent.'

'Why?' I asked.

'I saw you wandering around the grounds alone. I saw it could lead to trouble. Does that satisfy you, lass, or do you have other questions?'

'Why did you follow me in London?' I asked bluntly.

'So you know about that?'

'Yes, I know.'

'I tried to stay concealed. I didn't want to frighten you.'

'And you came to the music hall afterwards to see me.'

'I came to the music hall, yes, but not necessarily to see you.'

'You left as soon as my act was through.'

'Indeed I did.'

'Explain that,' I demanded.

'When the time comes,' he said.

'I want to know now!'

'Steady, lass. You're losing control of yourself.'

'Tell me,' I insisted.

He laughed softly. I turned to leave.

'Where do you think you're going?' he asked sharply.

'I'm going to find Edward—Mr Lyon.'

'His job will be to find you,' Philip Ashley replied. 'The damn fool must be out of his mind, letting you wander around like this. It would serve him right if something happened to you.'

'I don't need a chaperone,' I said angrily.

'But you have one,' he said. He gripped my arm firmly.

'You're insufferable,' I said.

'Then you'll have to suffer.'

'Will you let go of me, Mr Ashley?'

'No, I won't. You're coming with me.'

'I most certainly shall not,' I replied.

'You have no choice in the matter. I'm bigger than you are and far stronger.'

'You're making fun of me!'

'I'm stating a fact. Come along.'

'Where are we going?'

'Down by the river.'

'If you think—'

'Don't flatter yourself. It's quiet there, and we can see the fireworks. Your gallant Mr Lyon should be ready to leave by the time they are over, and perhaps he'll remember that he is responsible for you.'

'What do you know about Edward Lyon?'

'Enough, lass,' he said.

I did not say anything more. I walked quietly beside Philip Ashley. It seemed all the energy had been drained out of me. I was still weak from the encounter with the two country roughs. We walked past the dark, deserted stalls, stepping over the litter of the day. Now I could hear the river rushing along the banks. The lights and music of the dance pavilion were far behind us now. The music was like a faint, tinny echo, the lights mere coloured shadows in the distance. I felt the cold night air on my shoulders, and I shivered. The ground was damp, marshy, and all around us the shrubbery rustled. Philip Ashley led me to a bench beneath an immense oak tree, by the river's edge. He motioned for me to sit down, and I obeyed.

'What do you propose to do now?' I asked tartly.

'Wait,' he said.

'I want to go home.'

'That's too bad. You'll wait.'

'You are the most abominable—'

'Shut up,' he said harshly. 'I've had enough out of you for the time being. I'm not enjoying this a bit more than you are, lass. If I didn't think you'd be carried off by ruffians, I'd turn you loose.'

'Why should you care what happened to me?' I snapped.

'I said shut up,' he replied, his voice husky.

It was calm and serene. The water rippled with silver shavings of moonlight. A frog leaped from a log and plopped into the water. The smell of the milkweed blended with that of damp earth and dead leaves. The sky was very black, softly gilded with moonlight. I was consumed with anger, my cheeks hot, my mouth pursed tightly. I wanted to throw something at this boorish creature who kept me captive, and yet I was curiously flattered at the same time. At least he showed some concern for me, which was more than Edward had done. I knew that I should have been afraid of him, but I wasn't.

'What do you want of me?' I asked.

'From you? Nothing, my dear.'

'Why did you follow me the other night?' I asked.

'Pardon?'

'The night before last, in the woods.'

'What are you talking about?'

'You were watching me. You followed me.'

'No,' he said, 'I didn't.'

'You followed me in London. You were watching me tonight—'

"But I did not follow you in the woods.'

'Then—who did?'

'Tell me about it,' he said. His voice was strangely heavy. He stood with his head cocked to one side, listening very intently while I told him what had happened. In the moonlight, his face was grim. He looked angry, and I could see him tense.

'Damn fool!' he said. 'Who?'

'You should be kept locked up, you know. If you're not a part of all this—'

'A part of what?'

He ignored the question. 'You're certain of this? You're absolutely sure you didn't imagine it?'

'That's what Edward thought. No one will believe me.'

'I believe you,' he said.

'I don't understand,' I said. 'I don't understand any of it.'

'You will,' he replied, 'in time.'

Philip Ashley knew something, but he did not intend to tell me. I looked down at my hands in my lap. I wanted to cry with frustration. They all seemed to be in a conspiracy of silence, even this man. There was something behind all that silence, and it threatened me. Why did they refuse to let me know what was going on?

'Why should I believe you?' I asked. 'Why should I? I know you followed me in London. I know you followed me tonight. Why should I believe you when you say it wasn't you in the woods?'

'You have a nice point there.'

'I—I don't know if I believe you or not.'

'No. Then you should be terrified. I could easily toss you into the river, here and now.'

'You could—'

'And I might just do that if you don't be quiet. I'm thinking. I want you to be still.'

'Be still yourself!' I said irritably. Philip Ashley laughed harshly. The sound was diabolical there in the darkness. He scooped up a handful of pebbles and tossed them into the water. Each one made a loud splash as it hit the surface. A frog croaked angrily. Crickets chirped near the base of the tree, and the buzzing of insects filled the air. When he had thrown all the pebbles, he folded his arms across his chest and leaned against the trunk of the tree. His face was silhouetted by the moonlight, the sharp nose prominent, the jaw thrust out. He seemed to be oblivious to my presence. I found that more intolerable than his insults.

'You made quite an impression on Mrs Crandall,' I remarked after a while.

'A most unusual lady,' he said. 'Most unusual.'

'She was greatly impressed with your gin.'

'Guzzled down near a whole bottle of it,' he said. 'I've never seen the likes of it.'

'That's rather unfair, don't you think?' I said.

'Unfair?'

'Getting her drunk in order to pump her for information.'

'Is that what I was doing?'

'Isn't it?'

'Perhaps. She had some interesting things to say.'

'Corinne was furious. She claims she's never laid eyes on you before in her life.'

'Perhaps she hasn't.'

'Why are you so interested in us?' I asked bluntly.

'Let's just say I have a great curiosity about my neighbours,' he replied glibly.

'I wish I knew who you were.'

'Philip Ashley, painter and scoundrel, at your service.'

'Why are you here? What are you after? I know you didn't come to Devonshire just to paint.'

'Very perceptive of you.'

'I'm going to tell Edward all about

this. I'm going to tell him everything you've said.'

'I wouldn't,' Philip Ashley replied quietly.

'Are you threatening me?'

'Perhaps.'

'Who are you? What do you intend to do?'

He chuckled. 'A very sinister character,' he said. 'Perhaps I am planning some heinous crime. Don't get in my way. It suits me to spare you at the moment, but later on I may have no such qualms. Stay out of my way and behave yourself.'

'I almost believe you,' I said. 'I wouldn't be surprised at any thing you might do. Anyone who would get a poor befuddled woman drunk and then laugh at her is capable of anything foul.'

'Quite capable,' he remarked casually.

We lapsed into silence. I wondered about this man with his cynical poise and his mocking tongue. He bewildered me and irritated me, and I was unable to resist his fascination. I told myself that I hated him, and I should have been afraid, yet I felt strangely secure here with him, and I was glad he had brought me. My headache was gone. I seemed to be vibrantly alive with every fibre of my being. Philip Ashley had caused this. I did not know how or why, but I secretly revelled in the feeling.

'Will you at least tell me who Mr Herron is?' I asked.

'A chap from London.'

'I wonder what he could be seeing Edward about.'

'I wonder that myself.'

'Is Mr Herron a friend of yours?' I asked.

'I had dealings with him once.'

'Do you know him well?'

'Not well, but well enough not to like him.'

'What does he do?'

'Nothing you would be interested in, my lass. You're asking far too many questions. I shall lose patience any moment now, and you'll surely regret it.'

'No one tells me anything,' I said, frustrated.

'Then you are most fortunate,' he remarked.

'Everyone treats me like a child!'

'You're acting like one now, my dear.'

We were silent as the first flare of the fireworks display lit up the sky. A rocket shot across the darkness, exploding into particles of silvery-blue fire that drifted slowly down and faded. There was another, powdering the sky with green flakes, then red, then gold. It was incredibly beautiful. Each time a rocket was shot there was a loud explosion of noise, then the silent explosion of beauty in the sky. I saw sparklers, glittering, spinning in silver wheels. I could hear the voices of spectators in the distance exclaiming their delight. The display lasted for fifteen minutes, dazzling, overwhelming, and when it was over the sky seemed darker than before and the wind was cold.

'We'll go now,' Philip Ashley said. 'Your escort may have remembered he brought you. He'll be looking for you. I'll take you back to the wagon.'

'Thank you,' I said.

I felt depleted. The day had taken its toll of my emotions. Now I wanted only to be alone. I walked beside Philip Ashley, almost running to keep pace with him. We saw the wagons ahead. The great mound of hay stood out. I saw Edward standing beside our wagon, apparently at ease. Philip Ashley stopped.

'I'll leave you here,' he said. 'Your Mr Lyon is waiting.'

'I—I suppose I should thank you,' I said awkwardly.

'Not at all. The pleasure was all mine.'

'I will see you again,' I said.

'I imagine you will,' he replied.

He disappeared into the shadows. I stood there a moment thinking about him. He was so peculiar, so bewildering. I wondered why I had not been frightened of him. I had every reason to be. I walked to the wagon slowly.

'There you are,' Edward said. 'I've been looking for you.'

'I met a friend,' I said.

'Oh? Jolly. Shall we go?'

'Yes,' I replied.

I was puzzled. Edward did not seem to be at all alarmed by my disappearance. He seemed, strangely enough, jovial. He helped me up on the wagon and swung himself up beside me with boyish enthusiasm. He was grinning to himself, and he clicked the reins merrily as he pulled away from the fair grounds.

'Did everything go well—with your friend?' I asked.

'What? Oh, you mean the chap I was talking with. Yes, everything is dandy in that department, just dandy.'

'I just—wondered.'

'Lovely night, isn't it?' Edward said.

The road was a silvery ribbon in the moonlight enclosed by the inky black borders of trees and shrubs. The horses trotted briskly over the road, eager to be home. The wagon bounced over the ruts, the hay falling on our shoulders. I could feel Edward's elation. He seemed to be on the verge of whistling. I was a little offended that he had taken my disappearance so casually. He had asked no questions. I did not intend to say anything about Philip Ashley. Everyone else had secrets. The encounter with Mr Ashley would be mine.

CHAPTER 15

I was up early the next morning. I had just come downstairs when Corinne threw open the front door and came striding into the house in her riding outfit. The moss green veil of her hat was wrapped around her shoulders. She disentangled it and tossed the hat aside, greeting me as she did so.

Neither of us had had breakfast, and we went into the breakfast room together. It was a small room near the kitchen, papered in vivid yellow. Sunlight poured through the window, making dazzling pools on the white linen table cloth. There was a bowl of blue flowers on the table and it was set for three, blue linen napkins folded beside the plates. Corinne sat down abruptly and rang for the servant.

'Is Edward going to breakfast with us?' I asked.

'It would seem so,' she retorted. 'He's been up for hours, making the damndest noise! Whistling, knocking about in his room, packing up a suitcase.'

'Oh?'

'He's taking a short trip to London, he informed me. Good riddance, I say.'

'Did I hear my name mentioned?' Edward said.

He stood in the door way, smiling at us. He wore dark trousers and leather slippers and a beautifully tailored dressing gown of maroon and black striped satin. His hair was mussed, rich auburn waves falling over his forehead. Edward managed to look elegant even at this hour. He took his chair, his dark brown eyes full of mischief.

'What dreadful things have you been saying about me?' he asked Corinne.

'Just that I'd be glad to be rid of you for a few days.'

'Only three, as a matter of fact,' he replied.

'I wonder if I could go to London with you?' I asked.

'Out of the question!' Corinne snapped.

I turned to her. She was aware of how abruptly she had spoken, and she tried to pass it off with a laugh.

'It'll give us a chance to really visit,' she said, 'with Edward out of the way. Besides, I don't care to be alone.'

'There is Mrs Crandall,' I said.

Corinne snorted, thus dismissing Agatha Crandall.

'Why this sudden urge to go to London?' Corinne asked Edward.

'Business,' he replied, smiling.

'Some wench, most likely,' Corinne said.

'Not this time,' her nephew replied, 'although I might find time to look up some old friends.'

'You'll find the time,' she said grumpily.

The servant came in with the breakfast tray. There was a plate of crisp, lean bacon and a heap of golden scrambled eggs, slices

266

of ham and a rack of toast. Edward spread strawberry jam over his toast. The servant poured coffee, and Corinne scolded when some of it splashed out into the saucer. She demanded that a new cup and saucer be brought, and she watched the servant with angry eyes while this was being done. When the servant left, Edward burst into laughter.

'Really!' Corinne cried.

'The poor girl had nervous spasms,' Edward said. 'Don't you think you're overdoing the dragon bit this morning?'

'No more so than you,' she snapped.

'What do you mean?'

'This good humour! It's disgusting at this hour.'

'I've a reason for it,' he said. 'You should be happy, too. You will be, in a few days.'

'I doubt that,' Corinne said.

Her voice was serious, flat. She looked at Edward sharply, and for a moment their eyes were locked. It was as though they were challenging one another across the table. Corinne's hands rested tensely on the edge of the table. There was a dark look in Edward's eyes that was anything but good natured. For a long moment they were like that, and then Edward shrugged his shoulders and grinned and began to eat his eggs and bacon. There was no more conversation during the meal.

I was in the front hall an hour later. The carriage was waiting in the drive, Edward's luggage already resting on the rack, the driver on the seat, ready to drive to the station. Edward came down the stairs, pulling on a pair of yellow kid gloves. He wore a brown suit, a yellow silk scarf at his throat. He looked as merry as a boy leaving school for the holidays.

'I'm off,' he cried.

'So I see,' I replied.

'Don't look so glum,' he told me. 'I'll be back before you know it. I'll bring you a present.'

I merely frowned at him.

Edward walked jauntily out to the carriage. Corinne stepped out of the parlour and followed him outside. They stood beside the carriage for several minutes, talking. Corinne seemed to be vehement about something, and Edward appeared to protest. I could barely hear their voices, and I could not catch the words. The carriage drove off. Corinne came tearing back into the house, her eyes blazing with anger.

'Is something wrong?' I asked.

'What? Wrong! Wrong—'

She seemed about to burst into a tirade of vehemence but she caught herself. She flicked her skirts behind her and went into the parlour. I heard a loud crash. I stepped to the parlour door to see Corinne standing at the fireplace, glaring at a Dresden figurine that was shattered on the hearth. Destroying the lovely piece had given her enough outlet, apparently, for she seemed to be calmer.

'Forgive me,' she said. 'That boy will be the ruination of me! Why I haven't sent him packing long ago, I'll never know. It's that damned charm of his, I suppose. An old woman like me is a fool for charm. Beware of it, Julia. When you fall in love, fall in love with an oaf, if you will, but beware of the charmer.'

'I have no intention of falling in love with anyone,' I said.

'La, la,' she cried, her good humour restored. 'You will, child. Yes, you certainly will.'

She smiled and flung herself on the sofa, in a much better mood after her outburst. For the rest of the morning, she kept me entertained with stories of her youth, recalling gay, delightful adventures and recounting them with wit and considerable relish. She seemed to have forgotten her argument with Edward.

That afternoon we were in the morning room. It was a tiny room off the parlour, papered in green and white, a cream sofa, a white desk and an overstuffed rose chair the only furniture. Silver inkwell and plume rested on the desk. Through the opened windows we could see the rose bushes and part of the drive. Corinne was curled up on the sofa, paying only scant attention to a novel I was reading aloud to her. The reading had been her suggestion. She seemed intent on keeping me occupied while Edward was gone.

I turned a page and hesitated.

'Are you really interested in this?' I asked. 'I find it tedious.'

'Any fool would know the girl is going to run off with the sailor,' Corinne said. 'I really shall have to order some new books from London. All these things are so pale—' She halted abruptly, listening.

I heard the carriage wheels crunching on the drive outside, and I looked up to see a trim black Victoria turning in front of the house. A small bald-headed man was driving it. Corinne sat up, her face pale. I was startled as I saw the fear in her eyes. She held the material of her skirt bunched up in her hand. Her lips were parted.

We heard footsteps on the porch and then the sound of the knocker hitting against the door. The sound rang loudly in the silent house. A maid pattered down the hall and opened the door. We heard voices. All the servants had been given instructions to turn away anyone who came, but the maid seemed to be having a hard time of it in this case. The man spoke in a firm, insistent voice.

The maid came to the door of the morning room to tell Corinne that a Dr Redmund was calling and would not leave until he saw her. Corinne stared at the maid for a moment, her eyes wide, then she told the girl to show him into the parlour. Her voice trembled slightly.

'I won't see that man,' she whispered. 'I won't! He has a nerve, calling here. If I want to see him, I'll summon him! Julia, you go see him—talk to him. Tell him that I'm resting. Yes, I'm resting and can't see anyone. Get rid of him!'

'Don't you think you should see him,

Corinne? If he's come all the way to Lyon House, it might be something important.'

'I refuse,' she said 'I refuse—absolutely.'

Dr Redmund was standing by the hearth when I went into the parlour. I introduced myself, and he nodded expectantly. He was shorter than I, a dapper little man dressed in a tight-fitting black suit and a plum coloured vest, a chunky gold watch chain draped across its shiny surface. His pinkish face was lined, and his light grey eyes were intelligent. He had a thin moustache over his small mouth, and the top of his bald head glistened like polished glass. A black bag set at his feet.

'Mrs Lyon is resting,' I said. 'She cannot see you just now.'

'I'll wait,' he said, very firm.

'I'm afraid that is out of the question,' I replied, as firmly as he. 'She gave me instructions to send you away.'

'I see,' he said, pursing his lips defiantly.

'I'm sorry you've come all this way,' I said, ill at ease.

'I was making my rounds, thought I'd check up on Corinne. You need not look so pained, young woman. I'm used to her whims and tantrums. I must say it was cowardly of her to send you to oust me. In the old days she would have come storming in here herself, insulted me up one side and down the other and then prattle charmingly while I made my examination. I really do want to see her,' he insisted.

'Perhaps some other day,' I said.

'An examination is long past due,' he continued. 'She was quite ill a few weeks ago, you know, quite ill. There was some doubt—' he hesitated. 'She always has been a remarkable woman,' he began again. 'Her recovery astounded me. When I left her, I was expecting a summons from Lyon House at any hour. When I heard she was up and about again, I was dumbfounded! Dumbfounded,' he repeated.

'She is feeling fine,' I assured him.

'I should be the judge of that.'

'She hasn't been at all ill.'

'Riding again, I hear, I forbid her to continue it, of course, but with Corinne to forbid is to encourage. It'll be the death of her. She might keel over, any morning. Foolish woman, damn foolish.'

I did not know what to say. The doctor did not seem to be ready to leave. He folded his hands behind his back and paced the room, stopping to examine various objects. He reminded me of a perky little robin with his black suit and plum vest.

'I've been meaning to call for the past three weeks,' he said. 'I have been rather busy, of course, what with babies being born and careless farmers chopping their fingers off and frustrated spinsters having imaginary pains. Very busy, indeed. I expected a summons from Lyon House to come any day. I must insist on an examination,' he continued. 'As a doctor, it is my duty to see to it—'

'Corinne will send for you if she needs you,' I said, interrupting him. 'She was quite firm in her refusal to see you.'

He shrugged his shoulders and made a grimace. He opened his bag and took out a small brown bottle. He placed it on a table and looked at it with his head held to one side.

'I've been Corinne's doctor for twenty years,' he said, 'going on twenty-one. Know her inside and out. This farce, this temperament—it really is damn foolishness, you know. Being difficult for the sake of being difficult—she's too much a lady for that. Isn't necessary.'

274

He shook his head. His grey eyes were full of exasperation.

'She didn't used to be that way. A lovelier, more charming creature you couldn't imagine. Such beauty—that was a tragedy, losing it that way. I suppose it marked her.'

'Perhaps it did,' I said, irritated with him.

'It's only natural for her to be afraid.'

'Afraid?'

'Of death. That's why she won't see me. She's afraid to.'

I waited patiently for him to finish. He made a few more remarks, and then he held his hands out in front of him. He examined them for a moment, then rubbed them together briskly, as if to wash his hands of the matter.

'Corinne is a very old woman,' he said, 'and not a healthy one, I'm afraid. It's hard to believe she actually is so old—the way she rants and raves and flings herself about. She refuses to believe it herself, which is why she rides like a hellion and pretends to be such a terror. But she is an old woman. Marvellous, but old.'

I stood very quietly, sobered by his words.

'You still will not let me see her?' he asked.

'No, Doctor.'

'Very well,' he said. 'If anything happens, I will not be held responsible. I shall make a note of the fact that I called and was refused consultation. For my own protection, you understand.'

'I understand perfectly, Doctor,' I replied.

Dr Redmund picked up his bag and started out of the room. I went with him to the porch. He stood on the top step, looking out at the Victoria. The sun glittered on the crushed shell drive. The horse stood patiently in the shafts, a lovely animal with a red-brown coat. Dr Redmund turned to me and spoke in a grave voice.

'Eccentricity, you know, is all very well,' he said, 'but Corinne carries it a bit far. See that she takes the medicine I left. She knows the dosage. Talk to her, young woman, and get her to stop riding every morning. If you don't, the horse is going to come back one morning with an empty saddle.'

He climbed into the Victoria and drove away. I hurried back to the morning room.

Corinne was sitting on the sofa, her back straight against the cushions. Her face was pale and drawn, and it looked like a horribly painted mask. She was like a grotesque doll, discarded by some demon child. She had been listening to the conversation in the parlour; I could tell that. In her hands she clasped a Japanese fan, and was tearing it to shreds. Strips of bamboo snapped, shreds of delicately painted paper tore, the bits and pieces fell into her lap. She did not seem to be aware of what she was doing.

'I heard,' she said. 'I heard what that man said.'

'I'm sorry,' I said. 'I should have closed the parlour door. I did not intend for you to hear.'

'It's not true,' she said.

'Come,' I pleaded. 'You're upset—'

'That's quite all right,' Corinne said. She stood up. The pieces of fan fluttered to the floor. For a moment she looked very old, very frail, and I knew that the doctor had been right. Then she drew herself up, tilting her chin back. She looked regal then, indomitable.

'The doddering old fool!' She snapped.

'Corinne—'

She swept into the parlour, the skirts of her orange and ivory dressing gown flaring. She flew over to the table where the brown bottle sat and seized the medicine. She hurled it across the room.

'There!' she cried. 'So much for Dr Richard Redmund!'

I stood in the doorway, overwhelmed by the angry gesture. I was frightened, too. Corinne moved about the room like a wild animal, her eyes glittering with rage. Her auburn wig was tilted, and the horribly painted face contorted. It was like something out of a chilling melodrama, not real at all—a flamboyant, majestic actress hurling herself into an impossible role.

'He's such a *little* man,' she cried. 'Such a small, petty person! He has no scope, no colour—no guts! He thinks everyone should conduct themselves like—like snivelling spinsters! I won't. I refuse! I will not be intimidated. I will not be frightened by some petty fool's diagnosis! He can't scare me. He'd like to—oh, yes. But he can't! I refuse to be frightened and spend the rest of my life cowering in bed with smelling salts and medicines and a pink lace bed jacket!'

She paused in her flight. She stood in

the centre of the room and glared at me. Her voice was low now, and hoarse.

'He thought I was dying,' she said. 'The fool. The vulture! I was a little poorly, yes—quite ill, in fact—and that fool tried to make everyone believe—it's preposterous! Do you hear?'

She seemed to be waiting for a reply. I merely stared, fascinated and horrified at the same time.

'He was in love with me,' she continued. 'Everyone was then. Such a snivelling little man, so depressing with his bouquet of flowers, his mournful eyes. I scorned him, of course. And this is his revenge, trying to frighten me. I've got more life in me now that he and all his kind will ever have!'

She paused for breath and then seemed to lapse like a mechanical toy that has suddenly run down. She lifted her hand to the side of her face and laid her fingers on her cheek. For a moment, I thought she was going to cry. All the vivacity had gone out of her eyes and they stared at me flatly, as though they could not see.

'You're tired,' I said. 'I will take you to your room.'

To my surprise, she did not protest.

She came with me meekly when I took her arm. The house was very silent, the silence emphasized after her noisy tirade. We walked up the stairs, Corinne moving with the halting, creaking steps of a very old person. I felt she would crumple up and fall apart at any moment. The stairwell was dim, strewn with long shadows. I could hear the clock ticking monotonously in the hall below. As we stepped onto the landing, Agatha Crandall opened the door of her bedroom.

She peered out at us and then stepped into the doorway, a smile on her lips—a curious smile. I could smell the fumes of alcohol, but Agatha Crandall seemed to be sober. Her face was flushed pink and her eyes sparkled with malice.

'I saw the doctor come,' she said in a girlish voice. 'He stayed for quite a long time. Did you see him, Corinne?'

'*I* spoke to the doctor,' I said sharply.

'Oh?'

'Corinne did not want to see him.'

'Don't you think that odd?' Agatha Crandall said. 'Really, Corinne, you should have seen him. Rather, you should have let him see *you*. Why didn't you dear? Were you afraid? Didn't you want the doctor to take a good look at you?'

She began to laugh quietly. Her laughter followed us as we walked slowly down the hall to Corinne's room.

CHAPTER 16

It rained the next day, and the next. The skies turned leaden and grey, and the rain came continuously. It did not fall heavily, just constantly, pattering on the roofs, splashing on the terrace, wet and nasty. The gardens were a sodden mass, all black and grey and muddy brown. The wind tore at the shrubbery, stripping away leaves that pasted themselves on the wet pavement. Lyon House seemed to be isolated from the rest of the world, and it was a grim, depressing place. The grey skies seemed to have cloaked everything below, draining away all colour, and the house was bleak and chilly.

Corinne had stayed closed up in her room ever since the doctor's call, even having her meals sent up. Edward was in London and Agatha, too, remained in her room. Molly had had a quarrel with Bertie after the fair. Even her merry spirits seemed to have been dampened by the rain, and her vivacious chatter had ceased. I felt trapped, cut off, and the house was completely silent, only the monotonous patter of rain making its music as it fell.

I tried to read. I curled up in the library before a yellow-white fire that failed to warm the room. I held a copy of Sir Horace Walpole's *Castle of Otranto* in my lap, but the tale was too sinister and unnerving to read in my present state of mind. I put the book aside and looked out at the dripping grey world. Raindrops slivered down the panes of the French windows, making intricate wet designs, and it was as though I was looking out through a glittering, moving web. I wanted to scream, to hurl something across the room and shatter the silence that was like the silence of a tomb.

I sat for a long time, staring out. I seemed to be hypnotized by the rain. It had a terrible fascination for me; it was ugly and moving, concealing the beautiful gardens, obliterating the sunshine, and light. It had erased all the colour and elegance from Lyon House, leaving only a chill, shrouded prison. The rain seemed symbolic to me—it was like my life, I thought. All the colour, joy and vivacity had gone from it, and since I had left London that life had been obliterated by something as ugly as the rain. I wondered if the rain would ever stop falling. I wondered if the sun would ever shine again and bring back beauty and brightness. I wondered if things would ever again be normal.

I stepped over to the French windows, opened them, and stood in the doorway looking out. There were ugly brown puddles in the garden, and the terrace tiles were smeared with rivulets of brown water and black and green leaves glued to the tile. The rain blew in on me. I felt it on my cheeks and saw stains widen on my blue skirts. Damp tendrils of hair stuck to my temples. I do not know how long I stood there before I slammed the windows shut and stared at myself in the mirror.

There was a look of horror on my face. My eyes were violet-blue, dark and terrified, and greyish shadows surrounded them. My face was pale, the hollows below each cheekbone pronounced. Was I going mad, I asked myself? Was that the purpose of all this, to drive me mad? Was I even now losing touch with sanity? I brushed the damp blonde curls away from my temples and stared at the reflection in the foggy glass. I couldn't afford to let myself get into this kind of state. I had to pull myself together. The rain would stop. Things would be as they had been before. I had to believe that.

I could not wander around this house any longer. I could not drift through the dim, empty rooms like a ghost among shadows. I had to do something to keep myself occupied. There was no one to talk to, and I could not concentrate on reading. I would have to do something else. I decided to paint. I brought my sketchbook and pencils and water colours into the library and placed them on the hearth. Then I sat down on the floor before the weakly burning fire and began to sketch.

I sketched the gardens as seen through the French windows, resting on one elbow and looking up now and then to catch a detail. I tore out the large white page and looked at it with satisfaction. It would make a fine water colour, I decided. I dipped my sable-tipped brush into the cup of water and mixed the colours, losing track of time as I worked. I was vaguely aware of the crackling of the fire as it devoured the log and of the muffled ticking of the clock over the mantle.

I held the finished painting up to catch the light from the fire. I was pleased with it. It was a lovely thing of blues and greys and browns all merged together, the paper still gleaming wetly. I thought it was quite the best thing I had ever done. When it was dry I would add a few strokes of black ink to sharpen the outlines, and then I would show it to Corinne. She would be proud of it.

I moved to close the box of water colours, and as I did so I knocked the cup of water over. The murky water slithered over the hearth in rapid streams and began to seep into the carpet at the edge of the brick. It would leave stains unless I cleaned it immediately. I jumped up and hurried out of the room to find something to clean it with. The servants were all occupied with their tasks, and I did not want to bother them; preparing trays and indulging the whims of two semi-invalid women kept them busy enough.

I asked the downstairs maid where I

could find some rags, and she mumbled something about the cleaning materials and hurried on. I tried to think where some might be, and I vaguely remembered the little closet under the staircase. It seemed I had seen the maid leaving a mop there. I hurried down the dim hall and found the door of the tiny room under the stairs. It was very dark here, as there were no windows about. The old brass door knob felt cold to my touch. I turned it only to find that the door was locked.

I was irritated and in a terrible hurry. In my mind I could see the blue-black water seeping into the carpet and leaving dark stains. I did not have time to hunt down the maid and ask her for the key to the door. I took a hairpin out of my hair and jammed it into the keyhole. The lock was old and flimsy, and I was sure I could spring it in half the time it would take me to locate the key. The hairpin bent, jammed, and then I head a click. I opened the door.

It was dark and musty in the tiny room, and the smell was overpowering. I groped along the shelf that ran along one wall and felt the cold waxy shape of candles. There was also a box of matches. I took them down and lit a candle. In the flickering yellow-orange light I could see mops and a pail and cans of furniture polish, but there were no rags. Piles of tattered old books were heaped in one corner and there was an old dressmaker's dummy tilting on its wire platform. There were heaps of junk all about the room, and cobwebs stretched from corner to corner. I looked around quickly for rags but could find none. I was about to leave the room when I saw the suitcase.

It was an elegant thing of gleaming leather the colour of oxblood. The brass fasteners gleamed too, untarnished. It was a beautiful piece of luggage that might just have come from the showcase, and it captured my attention. What was it doing here among all this junk and rubbish, I wondered? I jammed the candle in an old brass candle holder that hung on the wall and knelt down to examine the suitcase. I had completely forgotten about the spilled water and the library carpet.

The suitcase was not locked. The fasteners snapped open at a touch of the fingertips. I spread it open and examined the contents. It belonged to some woman, that much was evident, and a woman with a rather flamboyant taste in clothes. There was a black feather boa, fluffy and new, and a red satin dress adorned with jet black beads. I took out a dressing robe of yellow silk, petticoats of cream coloured lace, a suit of purple linen with blue cord scallops on the skirt and jacket. There were cambric handkerchiefs and a pair of long black gloves, a brush and comb set of tortoise shell and a flat box of make-up. I examined all the things and then put them back. I closed the suitcase, mystified.

Who did it belong to, and what was it doing here? The door to the room had been locked, and surely there was no reason for this. It held all the cleaning materials, and it should have been left open so all the maids would have easy access to it. The suitcase had been hidden. I had not noticed it at first because it had been crammed in behind a stack of old magazines and some cans of lemon oil. If the candle light hadn't shone on the gleaming leather, I wouldn't have noticed it at all. Someone had hidden it. But who?

I closed the door to the closet and stood there in the hall, holding a candle, a puzzled frown on my face. The suitcase and clothes did not belong to anyone at Lyon House; that was obvious. They belonged to some woman of eccentric taste, clearly not a lady—no well-bred woman would wear such clothes. They were the kind of things one of the chorus girls would have worn, I thought, or a girl whose profession was even more dubious.

Immediately I thought of Molly's 'mysterious woman', the woman who had come secretly to Lyon House to meet Edward by the gazebo. I had paid little attention to Molly's prattle at the time, thinking it merely below-stairs gossip, but now I was not so sure. I tried to remember what Molly had said.

At that moment, Molly herself stepped into the hall. Her face was a bit pale, and there was a dejected look in her ordinarily bright eyes. I assumed she and Bertie were still quarrelling.

'So there you are,' she said. 'I've been lookin' for you.'

'I wanted to find some rags—' I said.

'I can imagine why!' Molly cried. 'I stepped into the library and saw that mess. The old lady would have convulsions! I cleaned it up. I don't think there'll be any signs.'

'Thank you, Molly. I intended to do it myself.'

'No need for you to do such things while all of us are about,' Molly said. 'I was lookin' for you, like I said. Cook wanted to know if you wanted a tray in the library. The old lady and the other one're havin' trays sent up to their rooms.

'That would be fine, Molly,' I said.

'And, uh, Miss Julia—'

'Yes?'

'Would it be all right if I went out for a while tonight?'

'Bertie?' I asked.

'He wants to make up. I'm goin' out with Teddie Rawlson to make him jealous. When he sees me with Teddie, he'll know for sure he's gonna have to mind his manners.'

The sparkle came back into her eyes as she contemplated this scheme of hers, and I noticed spots of colour flush her cheeks. I told her I wouldn't need her tonight, and as she started to go back to the kitchen I stopped her.

'Molly—' I began hesitantly, 'do you remember telling me about a mysterious woman when I first came here?'

'Of course,' she replied. 'I told you, I

saw her myself. Why did you want to know, Miss Julia?'

'Just—curious,' I said. 'Tell me about her again, Molly.'

Molly pursed her lips and cocked her head, evidently relishing the task. Ordinarily scolded for gossiping, she did not often have an opportunity to give herself free reign.

'Millie, my friend, first told me about her. Millie used to work here before the old lady took so sick. Millie said she saw the woman sneakin' around in the garden, 'n she said Mr Edward would come out to meet her and they'd walk down to the gazebo. I didn't believe her, of course. I know Millie has *such* a long tongue—but then I saw her myself. She was walkin' around the drive, and she had a suitcase, as if she meant to stay a long time—'

'A suitcase?' I interrupted.

'That's what it looked like. It was so dark 'n all, I couldn't say for sure.'

'Mrs Lyon was no longer ill?'

'No. She'd popped out of bed and fired all the servants. I was one of the new batch after she recovered.'

'You—have you any idea who this woman was?'

'We all assumed it was the girl friend he had in London, come down here to see him.'

'He had a girl friend in London?'

'Oh, everybody knew that. A real flashy thing she was, too, if what they say is true.'

'You haven't seen her again?'

'No. That was the last time—a few days before you got here.'

'She had come before, though?'

'Yeah, while the old lady was so sick. Mr Edward had to stay here while she was so ill. He couldn't go runnin' off to meet some woman, so she came here instead—he probably sent for her. I wondered if that's why he's gone to London this time?'

I didn't answer the question. I dismissed Molly and went back into the library. In a few minutes, another maid came in with a dinner tray and put it down on the coffee table before the sofa. I didn't have much appetite, and I merely picked at the food. I was too busy thinking about this new development to have any desire to eat.

Edward Lyon had a girl friend in London, a 'flashy thing,' and he frequently went there to see her. There was nothing so unusual about any of that, I thought. I had been around the music hall too long to have many illusions about 'gentlemen.' He had visited her regularly until his aunt became ill, and then it had been impossible for him to go to London for a while, and so the woman had come here—she had been seen by one of the servant girls. Corinne made a remarkable recovery, and in a typical spurt of rage had fired all the servants, had resumed her morning rides and carried on in the old manner. Edward was no longer tied down by her illness, and yet the woman had come again, carrying a suitcase. It was the same suitcase I had discovered hidden in the cleaning closet—I was certain of that.

Why had the woman come back with a suitcase, and what had happened to her? Edward might have been able to deceive Corinne while she was on her sick bed, might have been able to make love to his mistress in comparative safety, but he would never have been able to carry it off while Corinne was up and about. That much I knew. Corinne was sharp and perceptive, and she would have known immediately. There would have been no bounds to her rage. What had the woman come for, and where was she now? Why was her suitcase hidden away in the closet? For that matter, I thought, why had Edward Lyon gone to London so suddenly? Did it have something to do with this mysterious woman, or did it concern the man he had been talking to at the fair? Mr Herron, Philip Ashley had called him. Who was Mr Herron? Who was the woman to whom the suitcase belonged? I pondered over these things, sitting there on the sofa with the dinner tray before me.

I looked up, startled. The rain had stopped, and it was the sudden cessation of noise that had startled me. There was a heavy stillness in its place, and the library seemed suddenly unbearable. The fire had died in the fireplace, a mere heap of ashes now, and the air in the closed room was stuffy. I stepped over to the French windows and drew them open to let in some of the breeze.

It was a wet, stained world I looked out on. Everything was in hues of brown and grey, mud-stained and damp, and the sky was a curious green tint, darkening. The invisible sun was going down, and long black shadows began to reach across the garden like skeletal fingers. The air had a greenish hue, borrowed from the sky. Drops of rain still dripped from the eaves, but the monotonous falling had ceased. The fresh air blew into the library, laden with the odours of damp soil and molding leaves. I left the French windows open and went back to the sofa.

I had not realized how tired I was. I sat back on the cushions, my mind still pondering over this new mystery, and my eyelids grew heavy. I do not know how long I slept, for when I awoke the room was in darkness. A single ray of moonlight poured in through the opened windows. It wavered with milky radiance, the motes dancing and stirring, as though they had just been disturbed.

I woke up all at once, abruptly, sharply alert. I felt a chill all over my body. The room was icy cold, but there was another reason for the chill. I had the acute sensation that someone had just passed through the room, moving stealthily, and I stared at the beam of moonlight where the motes still stirred violently. I tried to tell myself that I had just had a nightmare, but I knew that was not so. The sensation was real. It was as though the air I breathed had just been shared with someone else.

I was tense, and my hands were clutching a cushion. I could hear the clock ticking over the mantle and the soft rustle of the curtains as the wind disturbed them. The rest of the house was in silence, but it was a heavy silence, laden with secrets. I was too frightened to move for a while.

My eyes grew accustomed to the darkness. There was enough moonlight to see that the room was just as it had been before. Nothing had been disturbed. The box of water colours and the empty cup still set on the hearth beside the painting I had done earlier. The corners of the paper had curled up. The dinner tray was still on the coffee table. Walpole's novel still resting on the arm of the sofa. Despite this, I knew someone had walked through the room, coming through the opened windows.

I went over to the windows to close them. I stared down at the wet tiles of the terrace. Were those dark stains footsteps? The whole surface was streaked with mud, and I could not be certain. I closed the windows, fastened them, and drew the curtains, closing off the milky light. I paused, listening. I thought I heard a shuffling noise somewhere in the front part of the house.

There was a lamp and matches on the little table in the hall just outside the library. I stepped quickly across the room and through the door. It took me only a moment to locate the lamp and start it glowing. I wondered what I should do. I knew that Clark, the gardener, would be in his room in the servants' quarters, but I was apprehensive about waking up the servants. There would be a general alarm, and I would feel extremely foolish if it turned out to be my imagination after all. There might be a perfectly innocent explanation. Perhaps one of the maids had gone out to meet her boy friend, like Molly, and had chosen to come in unobserved.

I walked down the hall, holding the lantern high. It cast flickering shadows that moved on the wall like agile black dancers. I went into the parlour. It was empty, and there were no signs that anyone had been there. The dining room was empty, too, the wavering light gleaming on the varnished mahogany wainscotting. As I stood there examining the room I heard a distinct noise in another part of the house. It sounded as if someone had stumbled against a piece of furniture.

I stepped quickly into the hall and called out. There was no answer. Instead there was a listening silence. I moved into the great front hall. I could see the crystals of the chandelier dripping down, catching the light and throwing it back. I saw the front door, the potted plants that stood on either side of it. Behind me the staircase climbed up into a nest of shadows. I turned. Something brushed against me. The lamp went out.

I caught my breath. It had happened so quickly that I did not really know exactly *what* had happened. I stood there, holding the dead lamp in a trembling hand. Had a sudden gust of wind blown against me and at the same time blown out the lamp? No, no, I told myself, whatever had brushed against me had been far more tangible than a gust of wind. Now I was surrounded by impenetrable darkness, and I knew I was not alone.

I waited, unable to move. I could feel someone else in the hall. I could hear the soft sound of breathing. Someone was moving, slowly, very, very slowly, but I could sense the movement. I was cold all over and my hand was trembling so violently it seemed the lamp would shatter to the floor. I waited, and nothing happened.

Gradually forms began to distinguish themselves in the blackness, darker. I saw the outlines of furniture. I saw the tiny threads of moonlight seeping in through the closed draperies. There was a sliding noise, very faint, and it was going away from me. It was going up the stairs. Into that nest of shadows moved another shadow. It was just a shade darker than the rest, but it moved, and I knew it was human. I acted quickly.

I ran silently through the darkness to the table. I groped for the box of matches I knew were there and knocked over a vase. It crashed to the floor with an ear-splitting explosion of sound, but my trembling fingers found the flat box. It was a moment before I was steady enough to strike one of the matches. I had to strike three before I could get the wick to burn properly.

I hurried back to the front hall. The lamp wick waved wildly, and the shadows did a demon dance on the walls. I stood at the bottom of the staircase and called. There was no reply, but the shadows at the top of the stairs seemed to stir. I saw something move. Then I heard a strange noise. I did not know if it was laughter or hysterical sobbing.

Agatha Crandall stepped out of the shadows. She wore a shabby rose coloured dressing robe, tattered lace at throat and wrists. Her hair was wildly disarrayed and her cheeks were flushed. She stared down at where I stood, but she did not seem to see me. In one hand she held a bottle of gin, and with the other she seemed to be pushing at the shadows that surrounded her.

Her body swayed back and forth, into the shadows and out. I could see the rose coloured blur of her robe and the white shape of her face. I watched with horror as she tottered on a pair of high heeled slippers. I saw her step down the first step and then jerk back. She threw her arms out wildly, still holding onto the bottle of gin. There seemed to be a great thrashing of shadows and then she fell. She tumbled down, her body bumping over the steps.

I stood with my back flattened against the wall at the bottom of the staircase, one hand holding the lamp high. I tried to scream, but no sound came. I stared at the body at my feet.

Agatha Crandall looked up at me. Her eyes were wells of sadness. I saw her lift her hand limply, and at the same time I saw the gin spilling out of the bottle and soaking into the carpet. It made a gurgling sound. Her mouth moved, and I heard a faint whisper. I leaned over her and held my face close to her lips.

'Man,' she said. 'Ashley. Go see Beau, Julia. Go see Beau. He is—hurry, before—before. Cheated. Tricked. You, too. Never meant to—' Her eyes grew wide, and her body twitched. 'Man—' she cried in a hoarse voice. Her body twitched again, convulsively.

Then she was silent. I knew she would never speak again.

CHAPTER 17

Corinne's face was ashen as she sat in the parlour. Her hands were covered with black gloves, and they moved in her lap like fluttering birds. She wore a dress of black broadcloth, and the veil she had covered her face with earlier this morning was now draped back over the auburn hair. She had conducted herself beautifully, regally this morning when the men came to ask questions. She had been every inch the grand lady, not once exposing the fierce temper or malicious tongue. She was not stricken with grief over Agatha Crandall's death. She was, in truth, rather relieved, but the doctor and the other men who had come had no idea of this. They asked their questions in gentle voices, shaking their heads solemnly, and Corinne had even raised her handkerchief to her eyes. Once her voice cracked, and they all waited politely for her to regain composure.

The verdict on Agatha Crandall's death was a simple one. She had a drop too much to drink, had lost her balance and fallen down the stairs. One of the high heels had broken off her slipper, and this was taken as the major cause of the accident. The bottle of gin she had clutched even in death was added evidence, if evidence was needed. The body was removed to the mortician's, and the men had gently taken their leave, expressing deepest sympathy.

Corinne had carried it off wonderfully. She had even apologized to Dr Redmund and agreed to let him examine her in the forthcoming week. The doctor generously agreed to handle all the funeral arrangements for her. When all the men had gone, Corinne went into the parlour, threw back the veil and poured a stiff glass of brandy.

'I wish Edward were here,' she said now, moving her hands nervously in her lap.

'He will be back tonight, won't he?'

'He said he would. You never know with him, though. It may be another week.'

'I'm sure he'll return on schedule,' I said quietly. 'Shouldn't you go up and rest, Corinne? This has been quite an ordeal for you.'

'It was,' she said simply.

I had seen Agatha Crandall lose her balance and fall down the staircase, and that is what I had told them. Immediately after the accident the house was full of lights, swarming with servants, and there had been no sign of any mysterious intruder. What had happened before might never have happened at all, I told myself. The wind had blown the French windows back, causing them to slam against the wall and wake me up. I had been alarmed to wake up so suddenly, and all that followed was the product of an over-active imagination.

This is what I told myself, but I was not sure I believed it.

Agatha's cryptic words before her death might have been the gibberish of a drunken old woman. I could not figure them out. I felt they contained some imperative message for me, and I intended to discover it for myself. I knew that it concerned Philip Ashley in some way. She had mentioned his name.

I believed she had given me the name of her murderer. I tried not to think that. If Philip Ashley had crept into the house and gone up the stairs, if he had been the dark form I had imagined sliding along the wall, then where had he vanished to after the 'accident'? Lights burned in every room moments later, and all the windows and doors had been securely locked. I had examined them myself.

I was confused and bewildered. I tried to think clearly with a logical mind. It was impossible. There was no evidence whatsoever of any crime, and yet I kept remembering that nest of shadows at the top of the staircase. I remembered Agatha swirling and weaving, as though fighting someone behind her. Had I seen a dark arm dart out and shove her, right before she fell? I could not be certain.

'You saw it all?' Corinne said.

'Yes.'

'How—treacherous. Tell me again, Julia.'

'She was at the top of the stairs. It was very dark. She was surrounded by shadows, and I just had a single lamp. She wove in and out of the shadows. Then she fell.'

'Dreadful,' Corinne said. 'Dreadful. I always knew that Agatha would have an accident of that kind. She couldn't hold her liquor. The wonder is that it hadn't happened sooner.'

I stared at Corinne. Her voice was cold. I was amazed that she could be so callous. She seemed to sense my thoughts. A curious smile played at the corners of her lips.

'Don't expect me to be a hypocrite, Julia,' she snapped. 'I'm much too old for that. I'm sorry she's dead, of course. But I feel no grief for her. She was a nuisance, a gin-ridden old nuisance. I have no idea why I put up with her for as long as I did.'

'I understand,' I replied.

'I hope you do,' she said briskly. 'You're very young. The young are inclined to be ruled by their sentiment. Later on you'll learn that sentiment should be preserved for something worthy of it. Agatha certainly wasn't.'

She stood up, brushing the stiff black skirts of her dress. She had a look of sadness in her eyes that belied her words. I knew she was far more upset than she pretended to be. She reached up to brush an auburn curl from her temple and then told me that she was going back up to her room. She said she would not be down for dinner but asked to be informed of Edward's arrival, regardless of the hour. She left the room, moving slowly and stiffly.

I was left alone with my thoughts, and they were not pleasant ones. I decided to go up to my room, and met Molly in the hall.

'Did you have a nice time last night?' I asked, knowing how innocuous the question must sound under the circumstances.

'Oh, yes,' Molly replied. 'Teddie took me to the Inn. Bertie came in and saw us together. He was furious! There was almost a fight, but Teddie edged away—left me with Bertie. It was ever so grand! You look a little pale, Miss Julia—'

'I'm all right,' I said.

'You're still upset, and no wonder! That poor old lady—'

'I don't want to talk about it, Molly,' I told her.

'I saw her last night, Bertie 'n I did,' she continued as though I had not spoken. 'I remarked to Bertie how odd it was, the old lady out like that—'

I had not really been listening to anything Molly was saying, but now I paid close attention to her words. Molly knew that she had an important bit of information, and she played it for all it was worth, going into detail and adding her own embellishments.

'Bertie 'n I were comin' back from the Inn. It was late, and the moon was splendid—everything was all lit up. The ground was still wet and drops dripped from the leaves, though it had stopped rainin' hours before. We were comin' back, like I said, and I saw this woman crossin' the road, leavin' Dower House—'

'It was Agatha?' I prompted.

'She was wearin' a long, dark cloak. At first I thought it was the mysterious lady—Mr Edward's friend—'cause we'd just been talkin' about her, remember?

Then I saw it was Mrs Crandall. Her face was all worried-like, and she kept lookin' around as though she expected to see someone jump out of the woods. She didn't see us, though. We were dawdlin' along—'

'She was leaving Dower House?'

'Where that mad Mr Ashley is stayin'. I wondered why she had gone to see him. I said to Bertie how odd it was, her goin' to Dower House. Can't think of why. But she was wastin' her time last night. That's for sure. He wasn't home.'

'How do you know?' I asked.

'He's been gone for two days,' Molly replied. 'Didn't you know? He left with a suitcase and took the train day before yesterday. He left that rusty red dog of his with one of the farmers, asked him to keep it for a couple of days while he was gone.'

'Why did he leave?' I inquired.

'To buy some special kind of paintin' supplies, he said.'

I did not find it at all unusual that Molly knew all this. There was very little that happened in and around the village that was not general knowledge within an hour or so after it occurred. A man as striking and unusual as Philip Ashley could hardly buy a cigar without the whole village commenting on it.

'He hasn't come back yet?' I asked.

'No. Dower House was all dark and closed up last night. Mrs Crandall looked very upset, like I said.'

'What time was this, Molly?'

'Oh, late. After midnight, I would say.'

'Have you—mentioned this to anyone?'

'You're the first one I've told. There's been so much excitement I haven't had time to talk to anyone.'

'I wish you would keep it to yourself, Molly,' I said.

'Is it important?'

'Not really,' I replied glibly. 'I would just prefer you didn't say anything about it for a while. Not to anyone.' I hesitated for a moment and then asked if she was certain Mr Ashley hadn't come back yet.

'Not yet,' she said. 'Bertie delivered some groceries this afternoon, and he said the house was still closed up.'

'Thank you, Molly,' I said, dismissal in my voice.

'Oh, by the way,' she said as I started to walk on down the hall, 'do you remember those two men I told you about—the ones who said they were surveyors? The ones I was so suspicious about—'

'Of course. What about them?'

'Well, they're still around. Everyone thought they'd gone off, but they are still here. Bertie saw 'em prowling around a field near here, one night as he was leavin' me after we'd met in the gardens. He followed 'em. They're stayin' in an old deserted cottage down the river a way—'

'Perhaps they have legitimate reasons,' I replied.

'Them askin' all those questions about Mr Edward and the old lady, actin' so suspicious. Of course, they *could* really be surveyors, but I know criminal types when I see 'em. They're up to no good, no good at all—'

Molly was obviously eager to discuss the whole matter at length. I discouraged her with a sharp look. I was curious about the two men, and I was even more suspicious than Molly, but I had things to do now.

Half an hour later I left the house. It was cool, and I was wearing a dark blue cloak over my light blue dress. I hurried across the gardens, through a patch of trees and was on the road that led to Dower House. It was late afternoon now, and the sky was a faint green shade, growing darker. The trees cast black shadows across the road. There was a brisk wind that caused my cloak to flutter away from my shoulders. My heart was pounding a little at the enormity of what I was about to do, but nothing could have stopped me at that point.

Something was going on, something that had started in London. Philip Ashley had been in it from the first. He had followed me in the fog, and when I had come to Lyon House, he had followed me again. He turned up every time something happened, or his name did. Agatha Crandall had paid him a visit, had come home drunk and muttering enigmatic statements that had infuriated Corinne.

Last night she had gone to see him again, and last night she had died. I was certain that the two things were connected. Agatha's death was the result of her visit to Dower House. Molly said he had not been at home, but perhaps he had returned early, without anyone knowing about it. Perhaps he had followed Agatha to Lyon House, slipping in through the opened French windows and sliding against the wall as he went up the staircase. Agatha had been pushed down the stairs. What I had seen had not been merely the awkward stumbling of a drunken old woman. It had been the struggle of a woman fighting for her life against an assailant invisible to me in the shadows. I was convinced of that now.

I believed Philip Ashley was that assailant.

Dower House looked serene in the fading light. The last rays of the sun washed the cream coloured brick with soft shadow. The brown shutters were closed and fastened. The wind rustled the strands of dark green ivy that clung to the brick. Behind it the apple orchard made a muted background of rose and gold, fading as the shadows spread. It was a lovely place, so calm and innocent to the eye, but I wondered what ugly secrets it would hold.

I had to climb over the front fence, remembering as I did the last time I had climbed it. I had ripped my skirt then, and Philip Ashley had laughed so rudely. In my mind I could still hear that laughter, and it was a demonic sound, endowed with evil. The house looked empty. I went to the front door and knocked loudly, nevertheless, and I could hear the sound echoing in the empty rooms beyond the door.

I have no idea what I would have done had Philip Ashley opened the door. I don't know how I would have explained my rash conduct. But no one was in the house. I could sense its emptiness as I knocked again. I turned the door knob. The door was locked securely. I intended to get inside somehow.

I left the porch and walked around the house, trying each shutter. They all seemed to be secured from within, and I would have had to tear them off to get in. For that I would have needed tools. I had almost given up when I discovered loose shutters on a window in the back of the house. They were latched, but the latch was old and rusty. I pulled at the shutters with all my might. They flew open, tearing the latch off. It dangled there, where he would find it, and he would know that someone had broken in, but I did not care.

The windows the shutters had protected were closed but not locked. I found a stick in the yard and wedged it between the sill and the lower part of the window frame. I edged the window up enough to get my hands under it. The frame was tight, the wood swollen with age, and it took me a long time to push the window open enough to allow me to climb in. I finally managed to do this, falling into the room on my hands and knees. I had a moment of sheer wicked triumph as I stood up and looked around the room.

It was a bedroom, everything tidy and neat. I peered into the closet. His clothes hung there, and his shoes were arranged in neat rows on the floor. I went through each drawer of the bureau, examining all the clothes, looking under piles of handkerchiefs. I did not know exactly what I was looking for, but I knew that when I found it I would recognize it. I put everything back in place and left the bedroom.

I walked cautiously down the hall to the front part of the house. I knew no one was around, yet I had an uneasy feeling. My nerves were on edge, and the strangeness of the house and the boldness of my invasion combined made me wary. My footsteps echoed in the empty hallway. The floor creaked and groaned under my weight, and I felt that someone would jump out from behind every door I passed.

The whole front part of the house was one enormous room, as littered and messy as the bedroom had been neat. A large table was cluttered with rags, papers, pots of paint, a palette crusted with blobs of dried colour. Canvases leaned against the wall in tilted heaps, wads of paper filled the fireplace, books and magazines were stacked on every chair. The huge sofa drawn up before the hearth had broken springs. The nap of the carpet was shiny. A plate with scraps of food and an empty bottle of gin were on the floor beside the sofa. The odours of paint and turpentine and male body were overwhelming.

The presence of Philip Ashley filled the room, even though he was not physically present. His shaving mug and lather brush sat on a desk, a chipped mirror propped up in front of them. A pair of his boots stood awkwardly in front of a chair. One of his shirts was draped across the back of another chair. It was as though he had just stepped out for a moment and would return at any instant. I stood in the doorway, almost afraid to enter a room so redolent of the man I suspected of murder.

I moved over to the desk. Surely any

important papers would be in one of the drawers. I pulled open the top drawer. It contained pencils and paper and stamps and various unimportant objects. The next drawer yielded nothing, nor the next, but when I tried to open the bottom drawer I discovered that it was locked. I did not hesitate. Again I took a hairpin from my hair and proceeded to spring the lock. I was beginning to feel very proficient at the task.

The locked clicked. The drawer tilted open. I took out a dark green folder and spread its contents over the top of the desk. I studied them for a long time. At first I was disappointed thinking this merely a collection of odds and ends, sentimental keepsakes. There were several newspaper clippings, a cheap photo gravure, a bill announcing the opening of an exhibit, a letter. Then I saw that the letter was from Scotland Yard, addressed to a Philip Mann.

Dear Mann,

I will again assure you that our men are doing everything possible to clear this matter up. Your suggestions and efforts are appreciated as sincere, but they have begun to be somewhat a nuisance. You will be a far greater help if you leave the matter to us. Any further interference will be looked upon gravely. Nay, if you turn up here again I shall take it upon myself to see that you are restrained. Is that clear enough?

Yours,
Inspector A.D Clark

I read the letter over again. It did not make sense. Who was Philip Mann? I studied the gravure. It was poorly printed on a piece of heavy cardboard, the colours running together. It was a woman's face. The cheeks were maroon, the eyes brown, the complexion, a yellow-brown due to the poor printing. The elaborately coiled and curled hair was black. I could tell very little about the features because of the terrible colour tones. Who was she? Some woman Ashley kept in London? What was he doing with her picture?

The bill announcing the exhibit was printed in copper ink on expensive cream coloured paper. The letterhead read MANN GALLERIES, with an impressive London address beneath. It described a collection of art objects and uncut precious stones that would be on display during the dates listed below. As I studied it, something began to click in my mind. I remembered something, some overheard conversation. I could not recall exactly what it had been about.

The newspaper clippings clarified that. They gave a complete coverage of the Mann case that had been the talk of London a few weeks ago. I remembered hearing Bert and the girls discussing it one morning at the breakfast table, and I had read an account of it myself one night in my dressing room. I studied the clippings carefully.

Clinton Mann, owner of the Mann Galleries, had given the exhibit described in the announcement, and that night thieves had broken into the galleries and stolen the precious stones. Mr Mann, who lived in an apartment over the galleries, had tried to stop the thieves and they had murdered him. He had been horribly, brutally beaten to death. Scotland Yard had few clues, but they were looking for a beautiful brunette who had been seen in Mann's company in the week prior to the robbery. They believed that the woman was a member of the gang and had set up the robbery. The newspapers made no mention of Mann's family.

I put the clippings down and picked up a book lying on the desk. On the fly leaf, beautifully embossed, was the name Philip A Mann. I was not surprised. I had already guessed that Philip Ashley was Clinton Mann's son. Not content with what Scotland Yard was doing, he was conducting his own private investigation of the crime. I began to remember little things he had said and done. They all fit in place.

I was puzzled. Why had be been following *me?* I certainly had nothing to do with any crime. The police said there was a woman involved, but she was a brunette. She was the woman in the photo gravure, of that I was certain. I had never seen the woman before, or had I? There must be some reason why Philip Mann was so interested in me. When I had accused him of watching me, he had said he was watching 'over me,' as if I was in some danger that he knew about.

Everyone seemed to have been watching over me: Mattie and Bill, Edward Lyon and Corinne, Philip Ashley Mann. Each had expressed concern for my safety in some way or other, each had given me warning. *Don't go to the village alone, don't wander around in the woods at night, don't talk to strangers.* Mattie had sent me away from London because it wasn't safe for me to stay there. Now Devonshire was no longer safe.

It had something to do with the Mann case—I knew that now. Somehow or other I was involved. Had I accidentally seen something, something I could not recall? Was the mysterious brunette one of the girls at the music hall, and had I observed something that would be incriminating to her, something I had since forgotten? These questions revolved in my brain, tormenting me, and I put my hands to my temples, trying to stop the throbbing. My cloak slipped from my shoulders and fell to the floor in a dark blue heap.

The newspaper clippings had given a particularly gory description of the murder. They described the fatal beating with relish, leaving nothing to the imagination. It had been called one of the most brutal slayings of the century. *And now those killers were looking for me.* That was the reason for all the secrecy, all the caution. The men who had murdered Clinton Mann intended to murder me. I did not know why, but it was a certainty that froze my blood.

They had already murdered Agatha Crandall. They could not be far. Perhaps they were moving in at this very moment.

I do not know how long I sat there, paralyzed with fear. The room had grown dim, heavy shadows filling the corners and blurring the edges of furniture and canvas. Only a few weak orange rays of fading sunlight seeped in through the tightly closed shutters. In a few moments, there would be total darkness. The house seemed to close in around me. It was dark and isolated. The wind was banging the shutters I had broken open; they slapped loudly against the house.

The floor creaked in one of the back rooms.

I flew to the front door, my heart pounding violently. The door was locked from the inside. I fumbled with the catch with awkward fingers. The floor creaked again and a soft, shuffling sound followed. *I was not alone in Dower House.* Someone was moving stealthily down the hall. The brass bolt flew back with a loud click as I flung the door open. I didn't pause once; I ran across the lawn and hurled myself over the fence and raced down the road. I ran until I could run no longer.

I stopped—feeling as though my lungs would burst.

I looked back at Dower House, far away now. It looked peaceful. A blur of orange light washed over the walls, and long brown shadows crept across the yard. The door stood open, as I had left it, but no one came out. I shivered, standing there in the middle of the road. I had left my cloak, and the wind was cold on my bare arms. No one had pursued me. I had given in to a moment of hysteria, and my imagination had been over active.

I stood there panting, trying to calm myself.

I walked slowly down the road towards Lyon House. My sides ached from running. My head still throbbed, and there was a voice inside. It was a scratchy whisper, and it repeated the same words over and over. I shook my head, but the voice kept whispering. 'Man,' it said, 'Ashley. Go see Beau. Go see Beau.' I had not been able to make sense of Agatha's drunken gibberish before, but now I understood it. She was telling me about Philip Mann, and what had sounded like 'Go see Beau' in that broken whisper came clear now.

There was something in the gazebo.

I knew what I *should* do. I should go to Corinne and tell her what I had discovered, or I should wait until Edward came back from London and tell him. I was involved in something extremely dangerous, and it was sheer folly to act on impulse, but I could not wait any longer. I had been surrounded by clouds of mystery for so long that I did not feel I could possibly endure any more. I had to act now. I had to see for myself what Agatha's cryptic message had meant.

I skirted the gardens of Lyon House, moving quickly and silently among the thickening shadows. All light had faded from the sky now, and it was a dark blue, streaked with black. The air was hazy, and the tree limbs were like inky black fingers reaching out of the haze. I heard the river. I stepped to the edge of the clearing where the gazebo stood.

The boards had been ripped off the front and I could see inside. Someone had been here recently. I stepped across the clearing and stood before the gazebo, staring inside. There were no floorboards; a mound of earth reared up inside. It was a grave.

I did not hear the woman come up behind me. When I turned, she was only a few feet away. She was wearing the red satin dress adorned with jet beads. The black feather boa was wrapped about her arms. Her dark eyes stared into mine, and then they peered at the mound of earth.

'Corinne Lyon,' the woman said. 'She never recovered.'

CHAPTER 18

It was a beautiful face with fine structure and rich colouring impossible to capture in a photo gravure. The dark eyes glowed, the lids delicately shadowed, fine brows curving in natural arches above. The lips were soft and pleasantly rounded, and below each high cheekbone there was a fragile hollow. It was a face I had seen thousands of times as I stared into the mirror. The colouring was entirely different, but the features were almost identical. The hair fell in natural waves, so rich in colour that the black had dark blue sheens.

'I had to do it,' she said.

'I never suspected,' I replied.

'I am an actress,' my sister Maureen said. 'A fine one, too, even if I do say so myself. Portraying Corinne Lyon was an easy task. She was quite a flamboyant old dame. The part required no subtle shadings, no real art at all. I just had to rant and rave and throw my weight about. The make up was rather difficult, but I got used to it after a while.'

'Why?' I asked. 'Why did you do it?'

'Julia'—she whispered. 'Don't ask me. Please—just go back to the house. I never wanted to involve you in this. I don't want to involve you now. We'll be gone in a little while, and you can go back to London and it will all be over. Will you do that?'

'You are the woman in the Mann case,' I said.

'You know?'

'Just a little. Enough—' I said. My voice was cold.

'You—you think I'm a criminal, don't you?'

'Aren't you?' I asked crisply.

'No!' she said passionately. 'I never wanted any of this! I never wanted any of it to happen—'

For a moment I thought she was going to break down. Her voice was strained and her eyes were full of urgent pleading. Then she gained control of herself. She drew her shoulders back and tossed one end of the boa over them. The gesture was regal. When she spoke again there was an intrinsic dignity in her voice.

'I have never been perfect,' she said. 'I have lived in—in my own style, and it's not the style in fashion today. I have done things that would not be considered proper, but they were proper for me, for my way of life. I will not apologize for them, Julia, not even to you. I have lived my way because I've had to. It's never been easy.'

'I know that, Maureen.'

'No,' she said. 'You don't know, and I wouldn't have you know. I have always wanted you to be—everything I could never be. That's one of the reasons I never tried to see you. I sent what money I could and left the rest up to Mattie and Bill. I knew they'd do the best for you, and I was not able to do anything more.'

We were still standing by the gazebo. It was dark now. The air was thick with hazy blue shadow. A few bright points

326

of starlight were beginning to frost the sky, and the moon was struggling to rise above a bank of clouds. I could see my sister clearly. Her face was suffused with emotion, and it was lovely with a poignant loveliness that made me want to cry.

'I see that I must tell you everything,' she said. 'If I don't, you will think much worse—'

'Tell me, Maureen. I have to know.'

'Yes, I see that now. I must hurry. He'll be coming soon, and we will have to leave. I don't know where to begin—'

'Begin with Clinton Mann,' I said.

She hesitated for a moment, her eyes searching mine, and then she began to speak in that beautifully modulated voice.

'I met Clinton Mann at an art gallery,' she said. 'I go to those places frequently. I love to see beautiful things, perhaps because there have been so few of them in my life. We started a conversation, and he asked me to tea. I—I was very impressed with him, and I could see he liked me. He was much older, of course, but very distinguished, very kind. There was something—magnetic, and I hoped that at last I might be able to have something stable in my life, even if the stability was just being the mistress of a man like him. Does that shock you?'

'No, Maureen,' I replied quietly.

'Three days after we met, he gave me the key to his apartment. He lived over the galleries, you know, and the key opened the main door downstairs. He had mentioned the exhibit, but I had paid little attention to it. Then—how shall I say this—Bart and Jerry found out about my friendship with Clinton Mann. They were staying at the same hotel I was in at the time, a sordid place, so ugly. Earlier, when I was really down—desperate, no food, no money, no hope—I had had a—friendship—with Bart. He was a brute, a monster, but he kept me from starving. I hate to think of those days.'

I said nothing. I was trembling slightly.

'They stole my key. They went to the galleries. They stole the stones and murdered Clinton Mann. I got there just after they'd gone. I had thought I had misplaced my key, but when I saw what had happened, I knew they had taken it. I knew they had done this. I—I saw Clinton on the floor. I saw the blood—'

'Maureen,' I pleaded. 'Don't. You don't

have to tell me any more. I'm sorry. I don't want you to—'

'I must,' she said, and her voice was calm. 'I must tell you all so that you won't think—terrible things about me. Bart and Jerry went back to the hotel, very casual about the whole thing. They went out to dinner, as though nothing had happened, and I broke into their room. I found the jewels and I took them. I was—so frightened.'

She paused for a moment. In the silence we could hear the crickets under the stones and the sound of the river as it washed along the bank. It was cold. I folded my arms about my body, shivering. Maureen did not seem to notice the chill. She was oblivious to it. Nothing was real to her now but the horror of the story she was relating.

'I wanted to go to the police, but I knew I couldn't do that. They do not have much respect for people like me. I knew they would think I was involved—and I was, however indirectly. I knew I had to leave immediately, before Bart and Jerry got back to their room. I went to the music hall and told Mattie what had happened. I had no money. She gave me enough to come here to Lyon House—'

'Why Lyon House?' I asked. 'Were you and Edward—'

'We had been,' she said, before I could finish my question. 'We had been keeping company for a long time, every time he came to London. I never loved him—he's selfish and vain and quite cruel in his way—but there is a physical thing between us. I'm not proud of it. It is something I cannot help. It's there, and I—I am its slave. I tried to break away from Edward, but it was impossible. I had hoped that the friendship with Clinton Mann would give me the strength I needed. But it did not work out that way. I came to Lyon House. I came at night, secretly, bringing the jewels with me. I met Edward in the garden.'

'The mysterious woman,' I said to myself.

'Corinne Lyon was still alive then, but she was dying. There was no question of that. She was so old and she had lived so outrageously, riding every morning, working herself into a fury over the least little thing. Edward took me in, and I stayed in a room upstairs, hiding all day long. At night we would meet in the gardens and talk, plan. He said he would help me. Then Corinne Lyon died—'

'And you took her place,' I said.

'Yes. No one knew she had died besides Agatha Crandall. Edward made a deal with her. He told her what had happened and promised to give her part of the money the jewels would bring. He did not intend to give them back. He never intended to do that, but I didn't know it then. His plan was—fantastic, so fantastic that I believed it would work. I had to hide. I knew the police would be looking for me, and so would Bart and Jerry. No one knew about my liaison with Edward. There would be nothing at all to connect me with Lyon House.'

'So Corinne Lyon "recovered" ' I said.

'Edward buried her here in the gazebo. He'd hidden the jewels here earlier. The next morning I got up, making a remarkable recovery. The first thing I did was dismiss all the servants in a fit of temper. Corinne had hired and fired servants at a shocking rate, so there was nothing unusual about it. The new servants would be less likely to discover the hoax, as they had not been around the old woman before. I took down the portrait of Corinne Lyon that hung in the gallery, and I simply became her. I wore her clothes, her wig. I went riding every morning as she had done. I fooled everyone. Sometimes it seemed I really *was* Corinne Lyon, even to myself.

'Edward made a quick trip to London, leaving early in the morning and coming back that night. I thought he was going to return the jewels, but he wasn't. He was making arrangements to sell them through a fence, a man named Herron. He'd had dealings with Herron before when he'd sold trinkets and various art objects that belonged to his aunt. When he came back that night, he told me what his real plans were. He was going to sell the jewels, and with the money from them we would leave the country altogether. I—I was in too deep by then, Julia. I had to go along with him. You must see that.'

'Of course,' I replied, my voice very low.

'My disguise was working beautifully. No one dreamed I wasn't Corinne Lyon. Agatha knew, of course, but Agatha was being paid to keep quiet. We were afraid she might get drunk and tell everything. She was unpredictable when she'd been drinking—'

Maureen paused. We both knew what had happened at the top of the stairs last night. We both knew it had not been an accident. Agatha was pushed. I thought I knew who had done it, and I knew Maureen knew. I expected her to tell me about it, but that would come later on.

'Why was it necessary for me to come to Lyon House?' I asked.

'Bart and Jerry knew about you. They knew I had a sister, and they knew you worked in the music hall. I—I was afraid they would harm you in some way. I went back to London secretly—on one of Corinne's "bad" days, when she was supposedly resting in her room. I went to the boarding house. You were asleep in your room. I opened the door and looked in on you. I had to see you. I had to see that you were safe.'

'You whispered my name,' I said.

'You were awake?'

'I thought I was dreaming,' I said. 'You went down to the parlour, too. I overheard Mattie and Bill talking. I had the feeling that there was a third person in the room with them.'

'Yes,' she continued. 'Mattie told me

333

that Bart and Jerry were in the neighbour-hood, asking questions about you and your connections with me. They evidently hoped to trace me through you. Mattie told me that a strange man with a scar had been following you and coming to the music hall to see your act. I knew at once that it was Clinton's son. I had met him only once, briefly, but I knew it had to be him. He must have found out about my relationship to you, too, and he, too, hoped to find me through you. None of them knew anything about me except that I had a sister. That was all they had to go on. You can see why it was necessary for you to leave.'

I nodded. 'Did you stay in London and hide upstairs in the dressing rooms the night of the farewell party?' I asked.

'I left the next afternoon, before the party.'

'Someone was upstairs,' I said. 'The dressing rooms were dark. I left the party to go see the puppets. As I left, someone came out from one of the vacant rooms—'

'Bart,' Maureen whispered, 'or Jerry.'

I remembered the sense of danger I had felt that night as I saw the dark figure creeping down the hall towards me. I shuddered to think what might have happened had Laverne not come to fetch me at that moment.

'I came back to Lyon House in a private carriage,' Maureen said. 'I left the carriage and walked along the drive, carrying my suitcase. For a moment I thought all was discovered. One of the maids was in the gardens with her boy friend. I thought she might have seen me.'

'She did,' I replied. 'She thought it was Edward's mistress slipping in to see him.'

'When you arrived at Lyon House, I thought everything would work out as Edward had planned. He was making arrangements with Herron, but it would take time before the jewels could be exchanged for money. You were safe, and everything was going smoothly. Then you went on the canoe ride and Edward saw Bart and Jerry sitting at a table at the Inn. I had described them to him, and he knew at once who they were. They had discovered your whereabouts—someone at the music hall must have let it slip out—and as you were the only link with me, they came here. Philip Mann came, too.'

'Why haven't they done anything?' I asked.

'They watched—and they waited. They asked questions about Lyon House, about Corinne. They were satisfied I was not here, but they all believed I would come here to fetch you. Mann rented Dower House, and Bart and Jerry—pretending to be surveyors—holed up in an old deserted cottage down the river. They've been watching the house, waiting.'

'One of them chased me in the woods,' I said calmly.

'When?' she asked, her voice harsh.

'Two nights before the fair,' I replied.

'My God,' she whispered. 'I didn't know.'

'Edward asked me not to tell you.'

'He knew it would have terrified me. Those animals! They probably meant to make you tell them when I would be coming to fetch you. Edward knew I would have given the whole thing up if I had known. I was already on edge because of Agatha's visit to Mann—'

She cut herself short. She did not want to discuss Agatha. I knew the reason why. I would wait.

She laughed, and it was not a pleasant laugh. 'I saw Bart and Jerry one morning as I was out riding. They were walking down the road with their surveyor tools, in sight of Lyon House. I galloped past them. I even tipped my hat to them. It was the proper, ironic gesture—'

'If they're still around,' I said, 'why are you dressed like this? Why aren't you still in disguise?'

'It's over,' she said. 'Edward met Herron at the fair. They made the final arrangements. Edward took the jewels to London so they could be examined. Herron is going to meet us tonight at the station, and the final exchange will be made. Edward purchased two tickets for France. We are going directly to Marseille, and from there we will board a vessel bound for South America.'

'Did Edward return today?' I asked casually.

'No, last night—' she said, and she knew at once that she had made an error. She stared at me with those dark, lovely eyes, and they pleaded with me to say no more. The wind blew a thick ebony wave across her temple. She reached up to brush it aside, her hand moving like a fragile white bird.

'I see,' I said simply, and those two

words clearly stated everything I knew and felt.

'He had to do it, Julia,' she whispered. 'Agatha had gone to see Mann again last night. She was afraid, and she intended to tell him everything. Edward was coming back to Lyon House when he saw her leaving Dower House. He intended to do it then, but your maid and her boy friend were walking down the road ahead. He—he waited, and then he slipped in through the French windows. You know the rest.'

'Yes,' I said. 'I know the rest.'

'We pretended he hadn't returned from London. He's been in his room all day. No one knew, not even the servants. Julia, don't look at me like that—like you despise me. I—I have to go with him.'

'You said you were not a criminal,' I replied. 'What are you, Maureen? You helped him cover up a murder, and now you are leaving the country with him. That makes you as guilty as he.'

'I had to,' she protested. 'I had to.'

'Why?' I demanded. 'There can be no excuse—'

'I had to,' she said, her voice calmer now. 'I wanted to back out. I wanted to

338

go to the police with everything, but he wouldn't let me. He told me that if I didn't go along with it he would—kill you.'

These two words seemed to hang in the air in the silence that followed. The moon broke from behind a bank of clouds and its radiance flooded the scene, sharpening outlines, deepening shadows. I saw the gazebo with the weathered boards torn off its front, the gaping doorway and the mound of earth beyond, and I saw Maureen, so still and calm that she might have been a statue. The moonlight poured over her face, revealing the finely chiselled features and the dark, tragic eyes. She was a stranger to me, and her tragedy was one I could not completely comprehend.

'He meant it,' she said quietly.

'Indeed I did, and do,' Edward Lyon said.

He stepped out of the shadows. He wore a dark suit and a black cape lined with white satin. The cape fluttered from his shoulders in the wind, the silky whiteness of its lining shining in the darkness. He had been standing just beyond the clearing for a long time, listening. Now he moved towards us in long, casual strides, as though this was a garden party. His casual, debonair manner, the shifting shadows, the moonlight pouring over the haunted face of the gazebo all gave a touch of sheer horror to the scene.

'It's a shame you could not have waited to tell your tale,' he told Maureen. He might have been making polite conversation from the tone of his voice. This tone made the words he spoke all the more terrifying. 'Now I will have to kill her anyway, merely as a precaution. You've made it absolutely necessary. You can see that, of course?'

'No,' she whispered.

'But I must, my dear. Everything is arranged. The plan has worked beautifully. Corinne Lyon and her nephew will disappear, and no one will ever connect them with the Mann case. Everything is clean and neat. We can't afford to be untidy now. Leaving Julia to talk would be untidy, to say the least.'

'I won't let you do this,' Maureen said.

'I'm afraid you have no voice in the matter,' he replied in that soft, dulcet tone that chilled the air about us.

Maureen stared at him for a moment, a look of horror on her face, and then she flew towards him, claws unsheathed, with all the fury and violence of a magnificent lioness. The claws raked across his face only once before he managed to push her aside. She stumbled back against the gazebo and he stood hovering over her, the wind flapping his cape. He doubled up his fist and stared at it a second before hitting her across the jaw. It was a powerful blow. I heard its impact, and I winced as Maureen sank unconscious to the ground.

Edward Lyon turned to face me, very calm, still casual. His face was sculptured by moonlight, each line sharply defined. It was a face of strong virile beauty, even more handsome now that menace gave each feature a strength it had not possessed before. A thick lock of auburn hair had fallen across his forehead, and his lips were gently curled in a vague smile. He was enjoying himself. He was enjoying the power he played with as he terrorized women.

'How shall we do this?' he asked politely, as though genuinely consulting me. 'Shall we be neat? That would be preferable, you must admit. We can be tidy and get it all over with as quickly as possible, or you can scream and fight and make the whole thing unpleasant. I can assure you that you will die in either case, Julia, so why not be sensible about the whole thing?'

'You're insane,' I whispered hoarsely.

'Insane? Perhaps, if to have a dream is insanity. I had a dream, Julia, and I carried it out, calmly and logically, and if that is insanity, I must plead guilty.'

'You don't really think you can get away with this?' I said, trying to still the trembling in my voice.

'Why not?' he asked, and he chuckled quietly. 'Agatha had an accident—one you witnessed yourself—and my aunt died peacefully in her bed from old age.'

'You murdered Corinne Lyon, too?'

'She was a despicable old woman, and she never intended to turn me loose. She kept me here like a pet, her tame nephew, and it would have always been that way. I changed that. A few extra drops of laudanum in her milk—even if they had examined her body it would have looked as if she had taken an overdose through error. So you see, I do intend to get away with it, to use your words.'

'You've done all this—for money.'

'Not money, dear Julia, but the freedom and the power it will give me. As soon as Maureen showed me the jewels, I knew what I would do. She intended to turn them over to the authorities, foolish woman. I had other plans. Those plans are about to be fulfilled, but first I must attend to you. We've wasted enough time in idle conversation—'

He seized my arm, his strong fingers closing about the flesh with an iron-like grip. It was useless for me to try and pull away. He merely tightened the grip with a forcefulness that caused me to grow faint. He led me away from the gazebo, forcing me to move ahead of him out of the clearing.

'Where are you taking me?' I asked.

'To the river. That would be an appropriate way, I should think graceful and Ophelia-like. And when, eventually, your body is recovered it will look like suicide—or a rather unfortunate accident. Yes, the river will suffice nicely.'

We were deep in the woods now moving towards the now menacing noise of the river as it washed along the bank. Trees and shrubs were thick on either side, only a few thin rays of moonlight sifting through the heavy canopy of limbs above. I could smell moist earth and damp bark and lichen. An owl hooted from a thicket, and the sound was sinister. Once I stumbled on a rock, and he jerked me up savagely.

There had been a vague, nightmare quality of unreality about everything that had happened in the clearing. It had all the dim, subdued nature of dream, images and movement divorced from real life. Now, as I felt the pain that shot through my arm, I awoke to the full terror of my situation. This man had murdered twice before, and he intended to murder me. My breath came in short gasps as he shoved me along the rock strewn path that led down to the boathouse and pier.

'I'm sorry it has to be this way,' Edward said. He bent his head close to my shoulder and his lips seemed to brush my ear. His voice was tender, almost apologetic.

'You've been meddlesome from the first,' he continued. 'I didn't want you brought here, but your sister insisted, and at that stage I had to indulge her. There will be no more of that. From now on she will do as I command. It will be a nice relationship. Women want to be mastered by their men, and Maureen is no exception.'

'She'll never go with you now,' I said.

'Oh, yes—she will. Most assuredly. This

will make her want me all the more, for she will believe I've done it all for her. Women are foolish that way.'

'She'll hate you.'

'She hates me now, always has, and that hate drove her to me much more forcefully than love would have done. Love is a weak emotion, for the weak.'

I closed my eyes. I tried to close off the sound of his voice. He seemed to be amused, full of satisfaction. I sensed that he wanted me to beg and plead, to struggle and fight. It would have given him more opportunity to exercise his perverted sense of mastery. I had to remain calm. I had to conserve all my energy. When the moment came, I had to be ready to fight him with all the strength I possessed.

We came out of the trees. A small slope led down to the river. The deserted old boathouse set on the edge of the water. The wood was rotten and the roof sagged. Barnacles clung to the slats in the water. A heavy coil of rope dangled from a nail near a window with broken panes. The pier reached out into the water, and it looked flimsy and dangerous. The river itself was a tumultuous black force, swollen by recent rains. It roared away in the night, shattering the silence.

'The water is quite deep at the end of the pier,' Edward said, his lips still close to my ear. 'With those heavy skirts, you'll sink, almost at once. You couldn't possibly swim in that torrent.'

What he said was true. It would have been impossible for anyone to swim in that dark, angry flood. To torment me, Edward broke a small branch from a tree and hurled it into the water. The branch twirled for a moment on the surface before the water engulfed it and carried it cascading downstream. Edward laughed softly and prodded me forward.

'You—you really mean to do this?' I whispered.

'Of course. I must admit that it would give me more pleasure to do it with my bare hands, but I must not be selfish. I will let the water do the work for me. I have to be careful, you see. When they find you, it must look as though you fell—or jumped. There can be no marks.'

'You have it all worked out, don't you?'

'Come along,' he said. His voice was no longer the polite voice of the social dilettante. It was throaty and harsh, the voice of a man ready to kill.

We were at the pier now. The wooden planks of the platform reached out to a point almost halfway across the river. There were large cracks between each plank, and one of the planks had rotted in two, leaving a large gap. The odour of milkweed and moss was strong here on the river. A frog croaked angrily from its perch on a rock and plopped into the swirling waters with a soft splash. The pier gleamed, wet and evil. I could feel my heart pounding.

It was a long walk to the end of the pier, and a dangerous one. He would have to make it with me. He would have to be right behind me. He would have to keep his own balance, and he would not be able to hold my arm so tightly. Perhaps I could break free. Perhaps I could fall against him and make him lose his balance. There must be some way I could save myself. I closed my eyes and took the first step onto the rickety wooden platform.

The planks were not set close together. There was a gap half a foot wide between each plank, and this required careful footing. Edward held my arm and forced me to move in front of him. The water rushed and roared directly beneath us, knocking against the moorings. The pier seemed to sway. I dared not look down. The swirling, crashing waves inches beneath us made me dizzy and I knew I would lose my balance if I dared look at them. I put my feet forward tentatively, feeling for the next plank. Edward followed, his fingers awkwardly gripping my arm. The pier was too narrow for him to move beside me.

The wet, rotten wood creaked and groaned beneath our weight. I was terrified, yet my mind was clear and sharp. The fingers were not biting into the flesh of my arm now; they gripped it loosely. The pier swayed and groaned, and the waters lashed at it violently, splashing the hem of my skirt. It took five minutes to reach the halfway point, and I looked at the end of the pier with horrified fascination. I could not go any further. My body seemed to freeze.

Edward gave me a shove, but instead of going ahead, I fell back against him. He cried out, and the wind seized the sound and shattered it. I then hurled myself forward. I fell on my hands and knees, gripping the planks in front of me. I turned around, and I saw him precariously trying to maintain his balance. He threw his arms out and seemed to embrace the air, and then he managed to stand erect. He did not move for a while. His chest was heaving, and the wind lashed his cape, making it whip about his shoulders like a pair of demonic wings.

I got to my feet. I stood on the pier, facing him. He was several yards away. His face was a mask of rage, his lips pressed down tightly and one brow arched high. He took a step forward. I braced myself, ready to fight to the death. I was trembling violently as I watched him coming nearer and nearer. He was laughing quietly, and it was the ugliest sound I have ever heard.

He reached out for me. I screamed, and then I saw the streak of orange fire. I heard the explosion. Edward threw up his arms, his eyes wide with disbelief. He staggered backwards. The scream he attempted died in his throat. For a second he balanced on one foot, and then he fell into the surging black waters.

Philip Mann stood at the edge of the pier. One hand gripped a still smoking revolver, and draped across the other arm was the cloak I had left in his front room.

He jammed the revolver into his belt and stepped over the planks towards me. It seemed an eternity before I felt his arms folding the cloak about my shoulders.

CHAPTER 19

Now, in late May, London was aglow with a soft beauty that made me think of a water colour done with delicate strokes. The sky was like a pearl and gleaming like watered silk. The sun gilded even the grubbiest old building with golden light. Even the sooty chimney pots looked new and respectable. The trees that grew along the sidewalks were tall and slender with tan and white bark, their branches bejewelled with tiny green buds that would soon burst into leaf. Children played in the park across the way, coaches and cart rumbled over the cobblestones, hawkers cried their wares. The confusion and noise was overwhelming as I walked down the street, and I welcomed it with open arms.

It was wonderful to know it was all over. It was wonderful to know that all shadows were gone, all threats vanished, to know that I could hurry down the street without a care in the world, smile at strangers and speak to shopkeepers without apprehension. For a while, after that horrible night on the river, I had doubted that I could ever recover. I thought my heart would never be young, my step never light again, but time is a wonderful healer, and now I could almost believe that none of it had ever happened.

Philip Mann had suspected Edward all along. He had seen Edward once in London with Maureen, weeks before Maureen met Clinton Mann, and when I went to Devonshire he was certain the heart of the mystery was at Lyon House. He had met Corinne Lyon years before, and when he saw her racing down the road on horseback, he had been suspicious. He had found out about her recent grave illness. The illness and the horseback rides did not seem to fit, nor did the fact that Corinne refused to see him. When Agatha Crandall visited him and dropped hints of the masquerade, he began to piece things together in his mind. He knew Maureen was an experienced actress, and he knew she and Edward could not leave England until the stones were turned into pounds. He bided his time, keeping a sharp watch over Lyon House and all activity around it.

Scotland Yard had refused to listen to his absurd theories, had not wanted to be bothered by the bunglings of an amateur detective, so Philip had been determined to get proof. He waited until Edward went to London to make negotiations with Herron, then stormed the offices of Scotland Yard and demanded they call on Herron. Reluctantly, they visited his quarters and, terrified, he had told them the whole story. There remained nothing left but to return to Devonshire, arrest all the culprits and recover the jewels which Edward still had in his possession.

While police officials were arresting Bart and Jerry, Philip Mann returned to Dower House. He knew something was wrong when he discovered the shutters loose in back, and he climbed in as I retreated through the front door. Finding my cloak in the front room, he hurried to Lyon House where a nervous maid informed him that no one was at home. He explored the grounds and found Maureen by the gazebo. Barely conscious, she pointed to the river. He rushed to the pier.

The nightmare ended. The fog lifted. With his strong arms around me I knew peace for the first time in weeks.

I returned to London. Mattie and Bill tried to make things pleasant at the boarding house. Laverne and the girls chattered brightly, bringing bits of gossip and trying to cheer me up, but I remained desolate. I was sick with worry about Maureen, and it was only when she came to see me that I began to feel better.

She had given evidence, signed statements and, after a long and unpleasant process of law, had been released. Philip Mann had furnished legal aid and had done everything possible himself to see that charges against her were dropped. Maureen came to tell me that she was leaving the country; she was going to France. An old friend of hers was manager of a small theatrical troupe that played the provinces, and she was going to join them.

I went to see her off.

She was standing on the deck of the boat the last time I saw her. A brisk breeze touselled her raven locks and they blew like soft black feathers across her face. It was a tragic face, the lines stamped with sadness, the enormous brown eyes turned inward on scenes of despair. She leaned on the railing. Her lips were turned up at the corners in a gentle smile. The smile faded as the boat began to pull away and she raised her hand in a last gesture of farewell. I felt that I would never see her again. She would go on to pursue her destiny. There would be a few postcards over the years but something more than space would always separate me from my sister.

Maureen had left three weeks ago. Now it was May. I was walking down the London street, feeling curiously light and gay. I would always carry some sadness in my heart after the experience at Lyon House, but now a world that had seemed forbidding and bleak suddenly seemed full of promise again. I hurried along in the dazzling sunlight as if I expected to behold a miracle at every corner.

I passed a flower cart heaped high with orange marigolds and yellow and white daisies. A little girl in a dark blue dress rolled a hoop down the sidewalk, her long brown pigtails bouncing on her shoulders. I was smiling, and there seemed to be no reason for it. It was the first time I had smiled like this in months.

I stopped to peer through the window of a bookseller's establishment. Through the dusty glass pane I could see stacks of leather bound volumes with gilt edges. Then the door of the shop opened and the bell above it jangled merrily. Philip Mann stepped out on the sidewalk. I stepped away from the window, startled.

He stared at me, frowning. Slowly he arched one dark brow, and a wicked grin spread on his face.

'This *is* a coincidence,' he said.

'I had no idea—' I began.

'Sure you weren't following me?' he taunted.

'I can assure you—'

'You're blushing,' he said wickedly. 'That's a sign of guilt.'

I tossed my head, giving him a haughty look. I started to walk on down the street, but his fingers gripped my elbow tightly.

'Don't run away,' he said. 'We've got a lot to talk about.'

'Really?' I inquired icily.

'A great deal,' he said.

'You haven't seemed to be in any great hurry to speak to me before now,' I said. 'In fact, this is the first time I've seen you since I returned to London.'

355

'You've missed me?' he asked.

'Of course not,' I snapped. 'I merely wondered—'

The grin widened. He could read my thoughts. He knew that I had been pining to see him. He knew that I had rushed downstairs every time anyone knocked on the door. He knew I had secretly hoped to run into him today—every day. The possibility of just such an encounter as this had given each day an added sparkle, had urged me on with light step. Philip Mann sensed this, and it infuriated me.

'As a matter of fact,' he said, 'I had a long talk with your Bill and Mattie last night. Charming people. They tell me you don't want to go back to the music hall to work. They tell me you're restless and undecided about the future—'

'What could that possibly matter to you?' I asked.

'My own future is pretty undecided, too,' he said. 'I've just sold my father's business. I'm a wealthy man now. I'm thinking of buying a little place in the country—a place to go back to. I'm going to do a bit of travelling, knocking about this country and that with paint box, canvas and shabby old jacket. I've been in the book shop to buy maps. I'm leaving London next week.'

'Oh?' I said, trying to keep the disappointment out of my voice.

'Yes. I've been worrying about your sketching—'

'My sketching?' I replied, puzzled.

'You still need quite a lot of instruction. Years and years of it, to be honest about it. To be even more honest, I need someone to keep my paint brushes clean and cheer me up when I'm in one of my rages. You would be hollered at quite a bit, perhaps even knocked about now and then.'

'Mr Mann, are you asking me to *go* with you?' I said stiffly.

He nodded, his dark eyes never leaving mine.

'I've never been so insulted in my life,' I replied.

'Oh, my intentions are quite honourable,' he said quickly. 'Your guardians were quite enthusiastic. I quite shamelessly set out to charm them, and a nice job I did of it, too. Mattie cried, and Bill, fine fellow that he is, slapped me on the back and offered me a cigar. They gave me their blessings and said it was all up to you.'

'Mr Mann,' I replied in a cool voice, 'if this is a joke—'

'Not at all,' he interrupted.

'You're quite insane,' I said.

'Quite,' he agreed.

I stared at him in amazement. His head was lowered, his eyes raised to taunt me with their dark, mischievous stare. He looked more demonic than ever with the bright pink scar and the curling mouth. I turned away. All around me London clattered and clanged with life, but I was oblivious to it.

I was filled with an ecstatic emotion, and I knew that it was joy such as I had never felt before. It was several moments before I could compose myself.

Philip Mann grew impatient.

'Well?' he demanded, scowling.

'I *would* like to improve my sketching,' I said.